CANDIDATE

a love story

TRACY EWENS

CANDIDATE

a love story

For My Maggie,
whose tender romantic heart and
awesome playlist suggestions make
sharing my stories a joy.
Grady is all yours, Mags.

Chapter One

*K*ate Galloway didn't remember buying apple Toaster Strudel. She could have sworn all the boxes were cherry, but biting into the fresh out-of-the-toaster goodness, she definitely tasted apple.

It didn't matter though, because she was going to be late if she didn't find her other black pump in the sea of partially unpacked boxes that littered her apartment.

It was to the point now that she was using the boxes as furniture and storage, moving them around to create spaces. So, her shoe was probably thrown back into a "closet" box, somewhere. She was trying to get her earring clipped, while wobbling on one heel, when she noticed the time. If she left within five minutes, there would still be time for coffee. Her boss had called at 5:30 this morning, something important, could she be in by seven? So yeah, coffee was essential.

Finding the errant shoe behind her bedroom door, Kate took another bite of her strudel and walked to the bathroom to tackle her hair. Grateful that messy buns were still in, she wrapped an elastic around the mass of damp curls, grabbed a yogurt from the kitchen, and her keys, phone, purse, and a folder off her bed. By the time she finished shoving the folder into her briefcase, she was at the front door. Twirling around one last time, she surveyed the chaos of her apartment and told herself, as she had almost every morning for the past two years, that she would start unpacking when she got home. Kate licked a last bit of frosting from the corner of her mouth and left for her morning pilgrimage.

"Kate, we've retained a new client as of last night, and I'm assigning a large part of the project to you. While I'm sure your colleagues here would love this one, you're the best person for the job—we all agreed, right guys?" Her boss Mark turned to the rest of their staff at Bracknell and Stevens, his fear well masked behind a smile, and they all nodded in turn.

Kate had a feeling she wasn't going to like what Mark was about to say next.

He continued, "So just let me finish before you judge or say anything. I really need you to not judge, okay?" he pleaded as he sipped his coffee.

Kate took a seat, looking puzzled, and waited for him to go on.

"Senator Malendar's—"

"I voted for him. He's great, why—" The caffeine had kicked in and she interrupted anyway.

"Kate, please." Mark took a breath and gave her a pointed look, as if he needed her to focus. "Senator Malendar is running for re-election, as you know. He has hired us to bring a fresh perspective to his campaign. Truth be told, his opponent Jeff Driggs is giving him a run for his money. This guy's a Republican, mid-thirties, and from what I was told last night, he's drawing a lot of votes from the younger demographic. The senator's office would like us to help him with his PR and outreach to these same young voters."

Kate was still listening, but still not sure where he was going. Mark took another deep breath. Javier and Max both reached for another doughnut across the conference table, and when Kate looked to them for a clue, they just smiled. Big Cheshire smiles. This was not going to be good.

"There are several components to this, the most challenging being revamping the senator's son's image."

"Mark—" Kate's eyes narrowed.

"Grady Malendar is a direct link to the demographic the campaign is looking for, but he needs reining in. There have been a few situations lately, but he seems to appeal to—"

Kate couldn't hold back any longer. "Situations? Are you joking, that man's a walking situation. Which underage debutante did they find him with now?" she said, setting her pencil down as warmth crept up her face. *This was a joke, right? Was it April first?*

"Kate, this isn't funny. From what I hear he's an asset, has a good relationship with the community, but needs—"

"To grow up?" Kate said, leaning back in her chair and biting her thumb. It was a nervous habit. She caught herself and put her hand in her lap.

"Probably, but he's willing to campaign. We just need to work on his image, play up . . . "

Kate raised an eyebrow.

"Play up whatever we can, and help turn that into something for the campaign." Mark said, and then looked to the rest of the table, hoping someone would chime in, throw him a lifeline, as Kate grew more and more disillusioned.

"I . . . I will be working on the social media components, younger voters, you . . . we'll get to work together," Javier added, chomping into his second doughnut.

Kate tried to meet his eyes, but they averted, and she looked to Max, who cleared his throat.

"Right, this is a really exciting project. I mean, a United States senator's campaign and the youth vote." Max looked back at Javier for words. "That's, um, cool and Grady Malendar is important."

Christ, this was ridiculous. What is going on, and who turned their staff into puppets? Kate thought.

"And let me guess, the son, Grady. That's my all-important, call me at zero-dark-hundred this morning part of the job? Why me?" Kate tried to remain calm.

"Because you can do this and you'll do it well. Grady Malendar is extremely popular and charismatic. You can channel this into a winning re-election bid for his father, I know you can. Remember Randy Nelson, coach at UCLA who was caught selling pot to his players?"

Everyone nodded at the table and Kate could feel Mark winding up for his You Can Do It speech. "You got him a medical marijuana license, convinced the entire university board that he was helping them, for medicinal purposes. Remember that, Kate."

Kate nodded. It was a great save.

"He agreed to cut it out, close up his shop once the dust settled. The man retired last year with full benefits. That was brilliant work. Tough assignment, but those are your specialty. Listen, I know this is going to be a challenge. I'll admit that from the media coverage, Grady is tough, but you're good at this. You know you are. So, that's that." Mark picked up his notes and Kate could see him trying to finish strong, and hand down the order. "Kate, you will head up the Grady Malendar part of the campaign. You will work with Javier and Max, be with Mr. Malendar for the next six months. The senator has specifically asked for someone dedicated to Grady's relationship with the community and voters. You will help him prepare speeches, manage his media exposure, clean up any messes, and accompany him to campaign events to ensure the public sees him in the best light. Congratulations, Kate. This is a big assignment."

The other people sitting at the conference room, her colleagues, as Mark put it, snickered and clapped.

"This is just great. Thank you so much for your confidence in me." Kate stood up and bowed as the clapping now evolved into cheers and whistling. "All of you, I can't wait to work on this very important project. Where is the spoiled little—"

"Kate!"

The room grew quiet and all gazes were now fixed on the door behind her. Javier and Max stood. Without turning around she sensed something, someone was there.

Mark looked panicked. "Kate, I believe you already know Senator Malendar."

She put on her very best PR smile and turned around. Standing just outside the conference room and taking up most of the doorway was a good-looking man in a perfectly cut navy-blue suit. He wore a red tie that complemented his salt and pepper hair. Kate recognized him immediately as Senator Patrick Malendar of California. Through the glass encasing of the door, she could see a group of other suits, not as expensive, standing behind the senator with various electronic devices.

"Yes, of course. So good to see you, sir, and a pleasure to be working with you," Kate said, extending her hand.

The senator, who had either not heard the beginnings of her jabs at his son, or chose to ignore them, smiled, stepped further into the room, and took Kate's hand in a warm and firm handshake.

"Great to see you too, Kate. You guys seemed like you were having fun. Did I interrupt? Are we early?" The senator asked, and Kate turned to Mark hoping he had an answer.

"Not at all, senator. We will be going just down the hall to the larger conference room. It should be all set for our meeting. Your staff can head in there, and we'll meet you in a moment," Mark explained.

"Sounds good." The senator hesitated and turned to the . . . what was the right word? Dashing, yes, that was it, the dashing younger man standing just outside the doorway. Kate had seen photographs of Grady Malendar, often of him doing something completely asinine, but they didn't do him justice. He was tall, broad shoulders, short honey-brown hair, and he had—hands down—the most stunning, ice-blue eyes she'd ever seen. Kate had sworn off men for the rest of her life, but this man was at least fun to look at. His father gestured, and Grady walked into the conference room. Grady nodded to Mark, whom he'd obviously already met, shook Javier's hand, and then turned to Kate.

"Kate, I'd like you to meet Grady Malendar," Mark introduced, and Mr. Blue Eyes smiled a sort of runway model smoldering, but professional smile.

You've got to be kidding? Does that work? Of course it does. Kate, look at the smile for crying out loud. She started to roll her own blue eyes, but Mark gave her a pleading look for best behavior, and she obeyed.

"Mr. Malendar, it is a pleasure. I'm—"

"You're Katherine Galloway." He shook her hand. Firm hand-shake, and it served its purpose. Kate was thrown off for a beat. He came out of the gate collected, almost mature. The strength in his voice, his whole demeanor was unexpected and the public relations part of her was thrilled that there appeared to be something to work with. It was as if there might be something of substance behind the lady-killer smile. She saw it for just a moment.

"Kate, please call me Kate." She took her hand back.

"Kate it is. Thank you for meeting with us. Shall we?" He gestured, and everyone began filing toward the large conference room. Kate stayed behind to collect her notes.

Grady popped his head back into the smaller conference room. "Hey, Kate. You coming?"

"I . . . I just need to get my things. I'll be right there."

"Okay, because you surely don't want to miss a moment of how we're going to contain the spoiled-son strategy." Sarcasm? No, maybe that was anger mixed with his smooth silky voice. Either way, he was still standing there. *Say something clever, Kate.*

"I'm sure our strategy encompasses much more than just following you around, Mr. Malendar."

"Grady, please call me Grady, and from what I hear you've been assigned to keep me in line. Am I mistaken? Kind of like a babysitter?"

So much for clever, it was time to break out the credentials. "Mr. Mal . . . Grady, I graduated top of my class at Columbia. I've been with Bracknell and Stevens for over five years. Now clearly someone thinks you need an image makeover, but I can assure you that I am not a babysitter."

He stood there with his hands in the pockets of his light tan suit, leaning against the door and smiling.

She had just met him five minutes ago and already she was un-nerved and a little pissed. *Babysitter? Just who the hell does this guy think he is?* Grady moved off the door jamb to let Kate pass, and to spite him she gestured that he should go first. She could tell it up-set his prep school sense of propriety, and she saw first-hand what she already suspected, that Grady knew all about maneuvering. His father clearly liked being in control, but Grady was like an ice skater. He glided, smiled, and moved with efficiency. As he walked past Mandy and Sabrina, normally very astute office assistants, both women strained for one last glimpse. Kate rolled her eyes at both of them, shaking her head. Christ, she should have gone for the double latte.

Grady seemed to have a way of walking that assumed people were following him. He did glance over his shoulder to check on her, so that was something at least. He walked with purpose, made quick and fleeting eye contact with those he passed, and carried an air of importance. His laid-back demeanor was not present in his walk, and Kate found that interesting. She wasn't sure if this was his "being made to do something" walk, or if he always carried himself this way. They both entered the conference room, and Kate moved toward the empty leather chair on the far side of the dark-lacquered conference table. Everyone had taken their seats as the senator stood by the window with Mark. He looked as if he was telling a story that required a bird's-eye view of the city. Kate stepped over wires and found Grady, pulling out a chair for her.

"Let's start over, Kate. After all, I didn't realize you graduated from Columbia." Grady spoke close to her ear. "Impressive, in-deed. Allow me."

Kate eyed him suspiciously and tried for a smile. She failed. "That's not necessary, but thank you," she said as she sat.

Grady smiled a full dazzling smile for the audience of onlookers around the table, and then Kate fell a bit forward as he pushed her chair harder than was necessary.

She couldn't see his face, but she was sure the smile was now a smirk.

Chapter Two

*G*rady couldn't remember ever feeling more ridiculous, paraded around like a show pony. He understood the game, he grew up amongst the bullshit, but if he was going to be treated like an idiot he was going to have some fun. He used to love messing with his various nannies and babysitters. Except for Bonnie with the smelly feet. No one messed with Bonnie; she was infamous in his tight-knit Pasadena neighborhood. Her dad was some sort of celebrity cage fighter so all of the kids, and the parents for that matter, smiled at Bonnie and ignored the fact that she could eat a whole pizza by herself, and she wore Converse without socks, hence the epic foot odor.

This babysitter, the one hired by his father and sitting next to Grady like a good girl scout, was no Bonnie. He had never been much for uptight women, but throwing this one off was a distraction from being treated like a child. The more her ears pinked, the closer he moved into a reasonable mood. Katherine Galloway was something. Something all buttoned up and put together, but when he'd pulled out her chair he noticed three things. Her hair was red, still wet in a bun at the nape of her long porcelain neck, but real red, not dyed. He'd been with enough fakes to know the difference. She smelled like soap and pastry. Odd combination, but the absence of perfume was noted. He twirled his pen and wondered if she forgot to spritz before she sauntered to what he imagined was her sensible economical car, or if she chose not to wear perfume. Maybe it was on purpose, too much fun. At first glance, Grady had figured Kate beautifully refined, but not much of a good time. That was until he noticed number three; she was only wearing one earring. Interesting.

"Grady?" He wasn't sure how many times his father had said his name, but it was probably time to answer.

"Yes, Dad. Sorry, I was . . . just jotting down some notes here." He looked over at Kate, whose gaze was glued to either his father, or her absurd color-coded notes. Grady let out a breath and smiled.

"Right, so does all of that sound good to you?" his father asked, holding his cup out to one of his staffers for more coffee. Grady's mind raced for a moment while he recalled the bits and pieces he had heard.

"Sure. Yes, I'm committing to six months of campaigning, leading up to and ending with election night. I am to make public appearances that will be scheduled at least one week in advance, with the exception of the last two weeks of the campaign when I will be needed 24/7." Grady put his pen down, crossed his hands in front of him, and smiled a sarcastic smile that only a father would recognize. "It sounds downright delightful."

Senator Malendar sent a warning glance over his coffee. "Grady, I appreciate your help and I know this is not what you want to be doing, but you'll survive. And the campaign will be better for it."

"Happy to serve, sir." Grady saluted. His father's eyes narrowed, and the room grew awkwardly silent.

"Okay, well, Mark, if you could please review your team's part and what we can expect from Bracknell." Stanley, the senator's campaign manager, patted Grady's father on the shoulder as his words cut through the silence.

Mark stood and proceeded to present a comprehensive campaign strategy complete with social media and video components. Mark was clearly wearing a fresh white shirt, but Grady was pretty sure that was yesterday's blue pinstriped suit. Christ, this poor guy had probably been up all night jumping through hoops for the larger-than-life senator from California. Grady felt the walls closing in. He had agreed to campaign for his father. His mother had asked him to during a teary-eyed lunch, where she seemed so fragile he hadn't seen that he had a choice, but he had forgotten about all the tedium. How did these people ever get anything done?

"So, that should cover everything for now. Of course this plan isn't static, we will adjust staffing and resources as the campaign progresses or your needs change. Do you have any questions, or is there anything we are missing?" Mark finished up.

"I don't. Sounds like you've laid out everything." Senator Malendar looked to Stanley for confirmation and then stood to shake Mark's hand. "I appreciate your putting all of this together on such short notice. Will Ms. Galloway be a dedicated . . . " The senator paused, searching for the right word.

Grady had a headache now, so he pounced. "Babysitter?"

Every face in the conference room was now on Grady, and he wasn't the only one who had had it. Kate glared at him and then he felt a kick under the table. No one else saw, but Grady sure felt it. She'd kicked him! Unbelievable. He looked at her to make some snide comment, and noticed her note pad was facing him with the word *apologize* written in big letters. Holy hell, this woman jumped right in.

He didn't know why he did it, something in her eyes, fire maybe. Clearly she was going to be a handful. "My apologies, that was uncalled for, Dad, please continue."

"Resource, will Ms. Galloway be a dedicated resource for Grady? You mentioned your understanding that we are in need of the youth vote, but I want to make sure Ms. Galloway has the time to dedicate to this . . . project." The senator looked right at Grady. *A project . . . nice return, Dad!*

Grady looked at Kate, who was now nodding at his father, acknowledging her commitment to his "project." She was clearly "on," putting her best professional tight-ass forward. *She kicked me.*

I've known her less than an hour and she kicked me. Christ! It's my turn, Ms. Galloway. Grady listened intently as Kate finished. Her eyes cut to him briefly; he smiled, and then pulled on his ear. Kate looked confused as she took her seat. Grady flipped his yellow pad over and wrote, "Nice earrings!" He waited for it to register, she touched her ears, and then . . . *Bingo!* She blushed.

For most people, a missing earring was probably not a big deal, but Grady guessed it was tantamount to a small crisis for someone like her. It meant she was rushing, or forgetful after a phone call. It meant, the worst thing for her type, it meant she was human, flawed. Grady had dealt with overeducated suits like Katherine Galloway his whole life. They had everything figured out and reeked of superiority. He loved meeting condescension with humor; it was less abrasive than anger and a hell of a lot more fun.

The meeting was over, everyone stood, shook hands. Kate was talking with the senator, her boss, and some other guy sporting what Grady thought was a dragon tattoo that kept peeking out from his short-sleeve polo shirt. Kate had removed her lone earring. Grady smiled. Balance was restored in the Galloway universe, he thought. He joined the group as they began to look down at a laptop.

"This is fantastic. Grady, look, our campaign just sent its first tweet," the senator said with a big grin. For an instant Grady saw his father's vulnerability. Venturing into new territory seemed to unnerve the senator, hence the army of PR and the babysitter. He couldn't imagine his father as anything other than a powerful senator, and Grady was pretty sure his father couldn't imagine any other scenario either.

"That's great, Dad. A little scary for the Twitter population, but great. Hopefully you won't be in charge of your own tweets."

His father laughed and everyone else followed. "Nope, that's Javier here's job. He is in charge of our . . . What's it called again, Kate?"

"Social media presence, sir."

"Right, social media. Anyway, I'll leave you folks to it. Thank you, Mark." The two men shook hands.

"You are certainly welcome, senator. We look forward to working with you and your team. Thank you for the opportunity."

"Kate," the senator turned and took her hand. "Thank you. Be kind to my boy here. He's one of my favorite people when he's not being . . . well, one of my least favorite people." Senator Malendar took Grady's shoulder. His eyes softened and warned at the same time. His father needed him and Grady, despite not always liking him, loved his father.

"We will do our best, senator. Talk with you soon." Kate smiled, looked at Grady, and her face fell. Niceties over, she turned to gather her paperwork.

Grady walked his father to the elevator, but made an excuse to return. He couldn't help it, maybe it was the kick under the table, but he wanted just a little more Katherine Galloway.

"So, I'm curious," he whispered just behind her as she closed her laptop.

Kate jumped a little and turned. "Can I help you, Mr. Malendar?"

"Right, so I'm curious, the earring. Forgotten on your desk after a phone call, or left at home?"

"Excuse me?" Kate moved toward the door with that "I'm very busy and I don't have time for you" purpose.

"Which is it? Did you leave the other earring on your desk, or was it forgotten altogether?"

"Why does it matter?" she asked, as Grady held his ground at the door.

"Just curious, which is it?"

Kate pushed past him, clearly annoyed. "Not that it's any of your business, but the other earring was left at home."

He followed her back toward her office, telling himself he was heading to the elevator anyway. "Interesting," he said under his breath.

Kate turned. "What does that mean?"

Grady put his hands in his pockets. Pink ears again, Kate was uncomfortable, and for some reason he had yet to explore, Grady was happy to fluster her even more.

"Nothing. It just says something about you. If you left the earring behind, you must have been rushing. Do women like you rush, Kate?"

Something flashed in her eyes, warning, but he continued. "Anyway, I noticed the chink in your armor and I found myself wondering."

She wrinkled her brow and dismissed him, moved behind her desk. A classic run to the power position, Grady thought.

"Oh, please. It's an earring, I've forgotten about it already." She shrugged and tried for indifferent.

Grady waited.

"Wondering what . . . exactly?" she asked, taking a seat in her high-backed leather chair.

He walked toward her desk and leaned in, close. "I'm just wondering what or who ruffles someone as tightly knit as yourself enough to leave an earring behind, Ms. Galloway."

Kate let out a slow breath. "I, I simply . . . forgot." She stumbled for words. Grady smiled and then saw the heat return to her eyes. "Mr. Malendar, are we done here, because I . . . "

Grady took Kate's hand to shake and received that same jolt he'd felt when they had been introduced earlier. It threw him, but he polished it over. "Not by a long shot, Kate. We're just getting started. According to the color-coded schedule you gave me in triplicate, we have a meeting at the end of the week. Looking forward to it."

Kate pulled her hand away and Grady laughed as he walked to the elevator.

He was still smiling when the elevator doors opened to the parking garage. He liked her. This whole "handling" business his father had put together was insulting and made him feel even less of a man than he normally did around his dad, but he could have fun with it—with her. She was beautiful, and either didn't know it, or didn't rely on it. The way his body responded to her was something to think about, but not right now. Well, maybe just a little, as he climbed into his Porsche 911. That flushed skin, those gorgeous legs, the same legs she used to haul off and kick him. Grady put his sunglasses on after handing his ticket to the attendant. By the time he shifted into gear and the sunlight hit his face, he was laughing. She'd kicked him. *Unreal.*

Chapter Three

The following evening, after an exhausting day of meetings and scheduling for the campaign, as well as finishing up a media package for Neviant, a new tech company, Kate drove up Sixth Street. She was on her way to a much-needed dinner with her best friend Reagan. Her usual route, the one that avoided Sixth and the Los Angeles Central Police Station, was chaos, bumper to bumper, so in spite of her memories, Kate turned down Sixth Street. As the traffic light changed, she found herself stopped next to the station. *Figures*, she thought, and clicked the little plastic door in the roof of her car, took out her sunglasses, and put them on even though the sun was nearly setting. People used sunglasses for more than just the sun. They masked tears at funerals, helped people hide from photographers. Sunglasses, although they always pinched Kate's nose in a weird spot, created distance. She needed distance, as she told herself not to look over at the station, not to check and see if Nick's bike was parked out front. The light finally changed, but Kate was already trapped in the memory.

"He doesn't love her, Kate. He's really sorry. You should see him." Her brother Neil's, voice sneaked behind the sunglasses, as she remembered him pathetically pleading her cheating husband's case two Thanksgivings ago.

"Is that supposed to make me feel better?" she had asked.

"Come on, you know the pressures of the job, Katie." That was the pearl of wisdom from her father. Her father, the man who raised her, walked her down the aisle. It was all right that Nick had cheated on her because after all, the pressures of the job . . . ? Ethan, Kate's other brother, had punched Nick and broken his nose the morning after Kate found out. A few months later though, a punch and a few cold shoulders was deemed enough punishment for Nick, and she was supposed to forgive. Again. Loyalty to the boys in blue at all cost. That had been her life; she'd never intended to marry a cop. Her father was the Chief of Police for the city of Los Angeles. Both of her brothers were cops. They never said it, but Kate was the traitor, she divorced a cop.

As she turned on Alameda, Kate glanced in her rearview mirror and saw the station fade. She remembered how excited Nick had been, when they'd first moved back to LA, that their offices were close. She even allowed the memory of him calling her down to the lobby one afternoon just to kiss her. It hurt, but not as much. She supposed the author of the completely obnoxious book her mother bought her after the divorce was right . . . time did heal.

Getting out of the car, Kate felt the warm evening breeze push her memories back where they belonged. She was all about moving forward these days, she'd read that damn book cover to cover, and nowhere did she learn how to get back to the strong, funny, curious woman she used to be. Nowhere in all of those pages did she discover when she would stop eating Toaster Strudel for breakfast and dinner, or unpack her boxes. None of that was in there, so now she just had mantras, Pinterest, and a Winston Churchill bookmark reminding her, "When you're going through hell, keep going."

Kate would keep going, but as she walked toward the restaurant, her latest project popped into her already-crowded mind. That last handshake, his eyes, the smug entertained look on his face. Kate felt something she hadn't felt in a very long time, restless. She let out a deep breath she hadn't realized she was holding.

He had no idea who he was dealing with. She wasn't a babysitter, and she sure as hell wasn't his hired entertainment. Kate would need to deal with Grady Malendar. Carefully.

Reagan was already in the booth at Hana's, their favorite Japanese eatery. *Eatery*, Hana's words, not Kate's. Every time someone walked into the small, sparsely-decorated restaurant, the lovely Japanese men behind the sushi bar nod and say something in Japanese. Then the slender hostess looks up through her lashes and says, "Welcome to Hana's Japanese Eatery." So, if Lashes says it's an eatery, who were they to argue? Reagan and Kate did giggle a little every time she said it, which was not particularly mature, but they were seldom mature when they were together.

Kate had met Reagan their freshman year in high school. Reagan cried when Kate left for Columbia. She was her maid of honor when Kate married Nick, and when Kate moved back home, it was as if she had never left. Reagan had picked Kate up off the floor, literally, at least once over the past couple of years. She was the one person in the world Kate knew for certain would love her forever, and Kate adored her right back. They were "bookends," as her father liked to say. Kate in high heels, Reagan wearing clogs. Reagan was artistic and Kate did Reagan's taxes every year. They complemented each other, and at this point in their lives they were truly on opposite ends. Reagan was getting married in five months, and Kate had been divorced for just over two years. It made for interesting late-night conversations. Kate always pointed out how fantastic Ben, the fiancé, was and Reagan let Kate feel sorry for herself when necessary. Reagan had liked Nick, but she'd kill him with her bare hands if allowed. Kate loved her even more for that.

"You're late."

"I know," Kate said, finishing up a quick text to her sister-in-law, who insisted on sending pictures of her nieces at the oddest times. *How can I not respond to a picture of the girls?* she thought, tilting her head up quickly to smile at Reagan as she slid into the booth.

"It's so scary that you are out there in the world with that phone. I mean you're in public relations for Christ sake, and you are the worst texter. That must be Faith with yet another picture?"

"Why does she do this? Why can't she just email? I love email. Texting seems so urgent, immediate, you know?"

"I do. That's why I shut mine off."

"Yeah, well I don't have that luxury." Kate stood to take her jacket off.

"I am proud of you that you managed to get to the table without bumping into something. We're drinking Pisco Sours tonight," she said, pointing to the board above the sushi bar.

"They're the special!" they both said in harmony, and Kate's shoulders instantly relaxed. They always had whatever the drink special was for the evening. For a sushi place, Hana's really pulled off some incredible craft cocktails. Both of them thought the owner's husband secretly wanted to be a bartender, but he was given the gift of making damn good spicy tuna rolls, and the dream was crushed. Kate put her phone away and checked her selections on the sushi menu.

"So, wedding cakes. Where are we at?" Kate asked, opening a bright pink folder she had removed from her briefcase.

Reagan sighed. "As I'm sure you're already aware, I'm not really a cake person. Ben wants carrot cake. Can we even do that? It's so . . . lumpy."

"You can do anything you want. It's your wedding. I'm sure they can smooth out carrot cake." Kate made a note.

"Should I call the wedding planner lady?" Reagan asked.

"Brenda."

"Right, Brenda. Why can't I remember her name?"

"Because you don't like her and you are trying to avoid all things wedding-related. I'll call her and get a carrot sample in there for next week. You can try a few cakes. Maybe Ben will find something else or we will find smooth carrot. It'll be fine."

Reagan smiled and took a bite of her tuna roll.

"Great. Now let's tackle seating," Kate said, wiping her hands on her napkin.

"Ben's mother is complaining that her side of the family is stuck in the corner of the reception room," Reagan said, rolling her eyes.

Kate pulled out the seating chart and looked up. "It's a round room."

"I know. I told Ben that last night, but she's driving him crazy."

"Okay, well, we could . . . move their table closer to the center instead of off to the side of the circle."

Reagan looked over as Kate starting erasing and re-sketching the table. "Right, but then we have to move my family table too."

"That's fine. What if we move them both in front of you and Ben instead of to the sides like you originally planned? That will make it easier for dancing and Ben's mom will have a better view. Maybe that's why she felt like she was in the corner."

"Perfect." Reagan looked relieved, as if she could not possibly make one more decision. "I love you. I mean, I loved you before all of this wedding business, but I really love you now," Reagan said, stealing ginger off of Kate's plate.

"I love you too." Kate finished drawing the new seating chart. "And, we are almost done. You're doing great. I realize your artistic soul has a hard time with all this structure, but trust me, if we get this out of the way now, all you'll care about on the day is kissing that wonderful man of yours." They had just clinked glasses, when Kate's phone vibrated.

She looked at the screen—Mark.

"Hi, Mark."

"Where are you?"

"I'm at dinner. Why?"

"With who? Have you seen Grady today?"

"Mark, it's eight o'clock on a Tuesday night. I don't meet with him until Friday. What's going on?" She heard a deep sigh across the phone.

Shit.

"A friend of mine just texted me to say he saw Grady Malendar mounting the concrete horse outside of Roka on Hollywood Boulevard. He knows we are representing the senator and thought he'd have a laugh at my expense."

Kate's breathing picked up, and in seconds her Pisco Sour buzz was gone. She waited for Mark to start yelling. It was coming, any minute.

"When was this?"

"Thirty fucking minutes ago." *Here it comes.* "I don't need this Kate. He's your goddamn responsibility." Kate motioned to Reagan that she had to leave. Reagan nodded and called for the check.

"I realize that, but we just met with them yesterday. I mean what the hell does he—"

"Don't . . . don't be cute or clever or sarcastic. Get into the office now."

Kate hung up.

"Was that the lovely boss?" Reagan asked as she signed for the bill.

"It was. This new client is going to kill me. I'm in charge of a child."

Reagan looked interested. "Wait, they have you working with a kid?"

Kate laughed and threw her phone in her purse. "Yeah, a very big kid." She looked around out of habit, and then explained to Reagan just who her new client was.

"Holy crap, are you kidding me? I saw him at some art gallery once, or maybe it was a picture of him at an art gallery. He's hot, Kate." They got up to leave because Kate could actually feel Mark seething. She needed to get to the office before he blew.

"No. He's not hot. He's a pain in the ass and for some reason, karma maybe, he's mine, all mine."

Reagan smiled. "It sure is karma," she whispered, "the really great kind." They pushed through the doors of Hana's.

"What?" Kate asked fishing for her keys.

"Oh nothing, honey," she said, kissing Kate on the cheek. "You've got to get going. Call me if Mark actually blows."

Kate shook her head, kissed Reagan back, and for the second time this week, cursed Grady Malendar.

Chapter Four

"Really? Right out of the damn gate? He's ridiculous," she exclaimed as she entered Mark's office and threw her keys in her bag.

He glanced up from his desk covered in paperwork. "Fix it, Kate. You can fix it. Clean this up and then figure him out. We need to find something . . . redeeming."

"I can't. He's an arrogant, womanizing ass and there's nothing—"

"There's something there, find it. We need him for this strategy. If it wasn't important, I wouldn't be putting you through this."

"He was in the conference room. He was given the plan. He's an adult for Christ sake. How hard is this?"

Mark was patting his desk, searching for his vibrating phone lost somewhere under his reports. Kate may have huffed a little, and then turned to leave.

"Hey, is this personal? I mean are you having a hard time with him because . . . "

"What are you talking about?" Kate asked turning back.

"Because he's charismatic and the women . . . is this too soon for you?"

"No! Mark, I'm a professional, why would you. . . ? Wait, what are we talking about here?"

"I'm just saying you seem over-the-top with this, and I know things with the divorce have been hard on you." Kate stared at him and tried to calm down. *Unfucking believable!*

"Mark, my personal life has nothing to do with my job. This would be a difficult assignment for anyone. You know what, it's fine." Kate said, holding her hands up and backing away. "You're right. I can fix this and I will. I will no longer need a sounding board. Sorry to disturb." She turned and walked out as she heard him calling after. How the hell did he know the details of her divorce? She had only told one person in the office. It had been happy hour and Mary from accounting was her friend, well maybe not a friend, but she was friend-ly. They'd been to each other's homes. Doesn't that mean something? Kate had been two, three, maybe four drinks in, when Mary leaned over and said, "So, what happened with your marriage, Kate? Nick is delicious. What went wrong?"

Kate was just intoxicated enough to knock Super Delicious Nick right off his pedestal. Mary bought another round and whispered, "Oh, come on. I won't tell a soul. Promise," and then she crossed her heart like they were on the playground at school. Kate had spilled most of the sordid details of her divorce and now, thanks to super-trustworthy Mary, her boss clearly knew some, if not all of her mess. Lesson learned, she thought, and who the fuck still crosses her heart?

Kate pushed through the glass doors of the building. She stood for a moment and let some of her embarrassment slip away. She had nothing to be ashamed of; it was shared in drunken confidence and had nothing to do with her job. In fact, it was inappropriate for Mark to bring it up. Kate buttoned her coat, took out her phone, and began doing what she did best.

"Javier, did you hear yet?"

"Already on it, boss. So far nothing too bad, both women had underwear on, so no up-the-skirt shots. Mr. Malendar, aside from mounting the concrete horse, really could have passed for sober. That's at least what I'm hearing and seeing so far."

"Video?"

"There's one up on YouTube, but it's fuzzy, no direct face shots, and some guy bellowing at his wife to carry her own purse. It's nothing. I flagged it as inappropriate so hopefully it'll just get pulled in a batch. I'll check every fifteen minutes and let you know what I find. All right to call you late?"

"I'm living and breathing this, so feel free. Be sure to check blogs too, and I'll have a press release in a couple of hours. I'll send it to you and I want it to all outlets first thing in the morning. If anything at all, no matter how small, comes up, let me know."

"All over it. This guy gets Lakers girls, and I had to walk out on the first date I've had in a month to clean up his mess. Seems about right."

She apologized to Javier before ending the call, and dialed a number she rarely used.

"Hello, this is Katherine Galloway from Bracknell and Stevens. Yes, good evening. Sorry to be calling so late, but I need to order a complete background check on a Mr. Grady Thomas Malendar. Yes, current client and in the system. I'm particularly interested in what he does with his free time. Any potential scandals. I'll take everything you can find. Of course you're backlogged. Yes, I understand. Well, it is time sensitive, so if I can get it any sooner than two months, it would be greatly appreciated. Thank you." Kate disconnected and called Javier back.

"Hi. I've ordered a background check from research, but it's going to take forever. Let's start digging on our own. I need to know more about him, separate from his father. Great. I'll let you know if I find anything on my end." Kate disconnected and started her car. *Grady Malendar, you little shit. You want to play? Well, here we go.*

Up until the moment he looked out over the large concrete mane, Grady was feeling good, carefree even. He'd transferred money that morning and made the drop off because Bryce couldn't get away. Things with his other life were good, running smoothly and put away, at least for a few weeks while he played trained monkey. Sure, the media attention would get thick as his father's election day grew closer, but Grady was confident his dodge and distract skills would keep the things he wanted hidden, well hidden. He would continue to act just as everyone had come to expect and no one would be the wiser.

But there was no doubt when he peered down from his giant stone steed that there was a crowd, a crowd with cameras. His blurry mind was pretty sure a few of them began chanting. This had moved past distraction into out-of-hand. He and tequila never did get along, but thanks to the cool evening air, his brain kicked in and for once in his life, the voice in his head wasn't only his father's. He too realized he was acting like a moron. Time to recover what was left of his dignity.

Grady smiled, blew a kiss, and dismounted. He put his jacket back on, draped his arms over his two lovely dates for the evening, and tried to return to the bar as if it were the most natural thing in the world that he'd just mounted the giant horse statue outside Roka in Hollywood. Grady grew more sober with each hi-five he received en route to the coat check. It was time to drop his dates off and go home. It wouldn't take long for his father or Stanley to call, or maybe they had pawned that job off to his uptight babysitter. Was she going to call? Grady's head ached at the thought, as he phoned for his driver, who was parked across the street. He'd go home, shower, and remind himself of what Plato had said about a man of moderation being a man of character and wisdom. He'd always loved Plato, but found his advice damn near impossible to live by.

As his two dates exited the car with kisses and the predictable "Call me!" Grady took two aspirin and drank a coconut water from the fridge under the seat, hoping they would stave off the headache. His arms were sore, probably from pulling himself onto a horse that was built to deter such things. Rolling his shoulders, he did appreciate how great it felt to climb something. He hadn't climbed anything in a very long time. Growing up, his family home had pecan trees in the backyard. Those trees were huge. Grady closed his eyes and the memory of his father building his tree house settled into his fuzzy consciousness.

"Remember," his dad had said, "no girls allowed."

"Right, no girls," young Grady had said, adjusting to his newly grown-in front teeth.

"Okay, next week we'll finish the windows and pull that small mattress up here so you can sleep in a tree. Every boy should sleep among the trees, Grady," he said, pulling his son into his lap. Grady still had the small hammer in his hand that his father had bought him. "It's wonderful to build things, my boy. I wish I'd done more of it."

"But you built this. That's building, right?"

"It is. It's the best kind of building." He kissed Grady on the top of the head.

"Did you build our house?" Grady asked staring up at the darkening sky through the cut out in the roof of his very own place.

"No, our house was built a long time ago, back when people made things by hand and cared about craftsmanship."

Grady wrinkled his forehead trying to figure out what craftsmanship was, when his father reached over and tousled his sun-bleached hair.

"All right, mister. We need to get back to the house before your mom and Kara eat all the cake and open your presents." Grady jumped to his feet.

Heading for the ladder, he turned back to his father, "Daddy?"

"Yeah?"

"We're builders aren't we?"

His father stooped to help him undo the rope across the entrance. "We are, Grady. You are the master builder and I'm your helper. Happy seventh birthday, son." They hugged, and Grady could remember clutching his father's white work shirt rolled up to his elbows. He wanted to be just like his dad on that night when he was seven years old and his world was as perfect as any boy could hope.

Grady's eyes opened on his present life as the car pulled in front of his house. He took a deep breath and let go of the memory, as he stepped into the cool night.

"Thank you, Tom. Hope I wasn't too much trouble tonight."

"Not at all, sir. It was certainly not a hardship driving Lakers girls around." Tom smiled at him and accepted the cash Grady placed in his hand.

"Have a safe drive home."

"Will do, sir. See you in the morning."

Grady watched Tom leave down his gravel driveway, tail lights against complete darkness. Dark sedans leaving, yet another memory from his childhood.

When the car was gone, Grady turned to his house, the one he'd helped design. He had lived out of a trailer so he could check on its progress every day for a year while it was being built. Lights illuminated the windows of his front porch and the coral tree that grew straight through it. Still a tree house, but much larger. Grady had no intention of cutting down the old tree when he bought the land a couple of years ago, so he simply built his house around it. Maybe it was an ode to his first tree house. Grady wasn't much for looking back, but he thought about being seven at least a few times a year. Before things changed, before his father became human to him. Grady loved his dad, appreciated what he had given him growing up, he just didn't always like his father or the choices he made. He was sure the feeling was mutual. Maybe they needed to work on that, or maybe it was best to just keep moving forward. They'd traveled a long way from that tree house.

Chapter Five

*H*uge overhead florescent lights were beginning to turn on over the tennis courts at the Fountains Country Club on a cool March evening, as Kate pulled into the parking lot. She turned off her car and sat looking out over the expanse of terra cotta buildings and fountains, wondering again why she was there at seven o'clock at night. Grady had asked her to meet him to talk. He had called earlier in the day, interrupting her working lunch, to tell her he was sorry about last night. It wasn't as bad as they made it out to be. Grady was already on thin ice, Christ that's why she had a job. Sad, but true. Last night was just the cap-off, complete with two barely-dressed women clapping as he tried, and succeeded, in mounting a damn stone horse. What was it with men and pairs? Not good. Not only had she received the call that interrupted her dinner with Reagan, but also later that evening Senator Malendar himself called Kate to ask her what her plan was, and what she thought the damage would be. He was calm, like he'd dealt with this before, but it was still not good. Tonight would be different, at least according to Grady.

As Kate entered one of the club patios, she felt a little out of step in black slacks and black shirt. *Perfect, Kate, could you be any less country club if you tried?* She came straight from work and willed herself not to care. The waiter approached and sat her at a round teak table with an umbrella just above the courts.

"Club soda, please," Kate ordered when asked if he could get her anything. The match on court six was over and Grady walked toward her, rubbing his hair with a towel. There was not a woman alive that wouldn't notice him physically, but it was late and she was not in the mood to drool over Grady's beautiful body.

"Katherine Galloway, it's a pleasure to see you—"

"It's Kate, and why am I here?"

"It's a lovely night. I thought we could have a little dinner and—"

"Dinner? You dragged me all the way down here for dinner?"

Some of the charm dropped away and for a moment he looked human, almost confused. "No, I just thought since you came all the way down here that I'd buy you dinner. We can talk strategy."

"We don't need dinner to talk strategy. Here it is: Behave, keep your zipper up, smile, and keep your mouth closed unless your brain is engaged. That's it. You'll be thirty next week; this shouldn't be too difficult. I'll handle the rest. Just act like you have something to lose and you're not a completely spoiled . . . well, ass." That last part was a little harsh, but she was annoyed, out of place, and once again feeling like Grady's entertainment for the evening.

He stared at her with crystal blue eyes that were lovely, glistening behind thick lashes. She did allow herself the briefest moment to notice. They were like the ocean in those pictures of places where Kate would never vacation without a very large hat.

"Wow, I gathered you were uptight, but we can now add frigid and angry, yeah pretty angry. I do have something to lose and I'm not an ass. Spoiled? Sure, but there's all kinds of crap that comes along with that. Can I sit down, or are you just going to spank me for being a bad boy and be on your way?"

Kate held back a laugh as he sat down. Long legs out in front and hands resting over his head. Crazy relaxed, and so comfortable in his skin. It was great skin, and his ease was enviable. He wasn't caving to her usual badass voice. *What did he call her?*

"Frigid?" Kate asked breathing deep. "Did you just call me frigid?"

"Sure did. You give off this angry-at-the-world vibe that seems, well ridiculous. Look, I get that I shouldn't have done what I did last night. Drinking and I don't always make the best impression, but I'm not a jerk. It was a mistake. A 'poor reaction to a difficult situation,' as my father would say." Grady mimicked the headshake and even the voice of the senator. "I see that it makes your job harder and I'll lay low. It's just that sometimes I get . . . "

"Oh, please. Please don't tell me the pressure of being a senator's son is so hard and you just act out—"

"See there it is again, frigid."

Kate glared, stood, and reached for her purse off the table.

Grady put his hand over hers. "Hey, if you're going to babysit, I mean represent me, shouldn't you at least be on my side? Give me a chance to sell you on what a great guy I am apart from the wonderful impression you clearly have of me?" This time he didn't smile, he just looked straight at her.

Maybe he was right; maybe Mark had a point too. She was frigid, in fact it could be said that Kate was in a man-hating mood lately. But this was her job. She needed to make him look good and protect the image for the senator. Oh God, she was becoming that woman, crazy box-living frigid lady. Next she would start only wearing sensible shoes, even to work, and posting nasty comments about the objectification of women in the pages of *People* magazine. *Shit.* Maybe she *was* taking out her issues . . . *issues*—God, how she hated that word. She was divorced, it wasn't an ailment. She needed to get a grip. *Pull it together.*

"You're right. I will not apologize, because you're far too smug, but I do need to know you and help portray you in as positive a light as possible. Right now, after your little equestrian stunt, I'm finding that . . . difficult."

Grady smiled and it climbed right to his eyes. Taking his hand back, he gestured for her to sit.

They ordered dinner and discussed how Kate's firm was going to spin the latest incident. She learned that Grady had just broken up with some super model he'd dated for a few weeks. They would portray him as a heartbroken fool falling back on bad habits. Everyone loves to see the rich rejected and miserable. It would work. In exchange for Kate's help, Grady agreed to keep close to home for a little while. She suggested he read, but he smiled and said, "Now why would a guy like me bother reading? Does *Maxim* count?"

Kate was beginning to see that Grady was a bit of a contradiction. Sure, what she was able to dig up so far showed the craziness of his youth, but he was also extremely well-educated and surprisingly together for a guy that the public thought of as nothing more than a handsome buffoon. She'd just scratched the surface on his background, but at first glance, there was nothing that scandalous. Stupid was all over his history, but she could handle stupid. They needed to focus on the things that gave Grady Thomas Malendar depth. Hopefully it was in there somewhere, and most of the world just never saw it. Kate decided to work on moving away from frigid and closer to hopeful. He listened closely this time as she laid out the plan for the next few months.

"Javier is in charge of blogging and your father's internet presence. He's working with the senator's staff to ensure we can control anything that pops up on the web and also be sure we don't miss any opportunities or buzz words for his opponent. Believe me, we have it on all fronts."

"How long have you been doing this?"

Kate was a little thrown by the question, not knowing if he was making a personal inquiry or if he wanted her resume. "I started at the bottom of a firm in New York, working phones and getting coffee while I was still in college. Once I graduated, we moved here and I started at Bracknell. I was promoted to junior associate shortly after, and I've been a full associate for just over two years." She paused, not sure if she had answered what he was asking. "How long have I been handling this type of exposure?"

Grady nodded.

"About three years."

"We?" Grady asked taking a sip of water.

"I was married," Kate said and added nothing else, hoping she was clear that she didn't want to discuss her personal life.

"Ever have anything worse than containing a spoiled ass?" Grady asked, obviously getting the message.

"Yes."

"That was a joke."

"I know."

"Wow. Do you handle your own PR or does someone else take care of that for you?" He said and then sat back smiling at her.

Kate took a deep breath. She felt better, a bit of weight lifted. She could handle this project. He was funny, she would give him that. It was probably pretty easy to be funny when everything was handed to you.

Chapter Six

Kate married Nick Galloway because he had great shoulders, warm eyes, and a fearlessness that tempted her cautious nature. They both liked to read the paper on Sunday morning and the sex was intense, passionate. They were great together. Well, he was great and she was great at making him feel like there was nothing he couldn't do. Kind of like a cheerleader. Christ, she'd never liked cheerleaders.

Curled in the leather chair of the conference room, Kate was reviewing proofs for the Carousel of Hope Ball menu and press kit. The Children's Diabetes Foundation used Bracknell and Stevens for the ball they held every two years. They used them for some of their daily marketing materials too, but the ball was a huge event that had taken almost a year to plan. All monies raised from tickets and the auction went to the foundation. It was an important night and Kate was always so proud to play a small part. It was a little awkward now because her ex-husband would be there. Type 1 diabetes deeply touched his family, and both of his nieces were affected. It was a cause very close to his heart. She knew Nick wouldn't miss it. It became a little less awkward once Kate reminded herself that the Children's Diabetes Foundation worked tirelessly researching and caring for children dealing with a disease far beyond the coloring books and video games that occupied the minds of most of their friends. They were a wonderful organization. The least Kate could do was stop worrying about her stupid ex-husband, and make sure the foundation pulled off another spectacular event.

Mark was at his wits end with a certain political campaign client and needed a Saturday off. Kate told him she would take care of the rest of the paperwork for the ball. The proofs were due to the printer yesterday, but Kate spoke with them and assured the woman she would have everything emailed back by two o'clock. She had just finished proofing the menu, and made a few corrections, most notably that dessert was missing an "s," making it sand, and not a delicious Key lime torte. Kate leaned back in the chair, adjusted her feet, and sipped her coffee. She held up the cover of the menu that mirrored all of the print work for the ball. It was the silhouette of a child's face, rounded cheeks and rosebud lips. Within the silhouette there were other outlines of children, all different ages. It was meant to show the cycle of a child growing up, often with something they carried since they were born. The outlines were sketch-type and the colors were bright but muted, so it didn't come off as too much. Kate liked it, but made some adjustments to the wording and noted that part of the image was cut off at the fold of the menu. That would need to be adjusted.

The Carousel of Hope Ball was a couple of months away. Mark informed her that she would be working this year, introducing Senator Malendar, who would be one of the keynote speakers. According to Mark, the senator would be discussing the climate for children within the current healthcare system, and policies he would like to see implemented if re-elected. Kate had opened up an email and was about to send some questions about the title font to the printer when her phone vibrated. She looked at the screen and took a very deep breath before answering.

"Hi, Mom."

"Hello, sweetheart. I was thinking we could all have dinner tonight after Chloe's spring performance."

"That sounds like a great idea, but I won't be there tonight. I already spoke with Ethan and Faith. Senator Malendar has a political fundraiser tonight and I need to be there. I can't get out of it."

The line was silent. Kate knew it would be.

"She's going to be a sunflower. Your niece, she will be dressed up like a sunflower and singing *You Are My Sunshine*. You're going to miss that for some chicken-on-the-plate fundraiser? Oh, Katie, come on."

Kate let out another deep breath. The guilt trip was in full force. "I know, and Eth said they would record it. I'll be at your house next week for Easter. I can watch it then. I sent flowers to the school, sunflowers even."

"Well, that's nice, but it's not the same as having her only auntie there for her first spring show. This job, I mean it's one thing when you're working with our community, but this new project seems... distracting. I mean your father says this kid, this guy you're representing is kind of a shyster."

Kate rolled her eyes and took out the banana and package of Toaster Strudel she'd brought for lunch.

"Mom, Dad says everyone's a shyster. Anyway, the job is the same. This is a pretty all-encompassing client, but nothing I haven't dealt with before." Kate added peeling her banana.

"Well, if you say so. I'm just saying that your 'encompassing client' seems like he's taking up quite a bit of your time."

"What are you even talking about?"

"It's Saturday. Where are you?"

"At work."

"See, it's not good for a single divorced woman to be working so much, at work on Saturday. It's just not right."

Jesus Christ! "Mom, this client has nothing to do with me being here on Saturday. In fact, I came in to help Mark with the Carousel of Hope Ball press kit. I actually just finished reviewing the menu. Looks like it's going to be a great night. Did you and Dad donate anything to the auction this year?" Kate tried to change the subject.

"Really? Well, that's a good use of your time, not on a Saturday, but much better than watching after that... that... philanderer.

You need to watch yourself, Katie. You're not living with Nick anymore and a single woman has to be careful."

"Is that so? And what exactly would you know about being a single woman?" Kate spit back and regretted it as soon as the last word left her mouth.

Her mother said nothing.

"I'm sorry. That was uncalled for. I'm sorry, Mom."

Still no response.

"Listen, I'm just tired. Maybe you're right; I shouldn't be here on a Saturday. I'm just going to finish up and head home. Maybe I'll take a nap before—"

"A week at Huntington Lake."

"Sorry?"

"That's what we donated for the silent auction. A week at that cabin place at Huntington." Kate recognized that her mother was pissy, but was moving on. She was certain the 'you know nothing about being single' comment would come up again; when she least expected it her mother would swing back. Save for later and then sneak attack. That's just how she was. Kate tried to appease for now.

"Oh, right. Well that was very generous of you both. I'm sure someone will love that."

"And it's going to such a wonderful cause. Those babies, and their families. Your Nick's little nieces, remember them, so precious."

"Mom, he's no longer my Nick, and of course I remember Sasha and Mellie. It is a wonderful cause. The menus are lovely. Key lime torte for dessert, looks yummy. Listen, I need to get going so I can finish up. Please give Chloe a big kiss from me." Her mother said nothing. "And Mom, have a great time at the recital."

"Oh, I'm sure we will. There will be a void, of course, because the whole family isn't there, but we will manage. Did I tell you Neil is coming after working a double?" Of course, her sainted brother Neil would be there. Kate put her hand on her face and leaned on the table in front of her. Dear God, her mother was a master at the guilt.

"I did hear that. I spoke with him yesterday. That's great. Okay, well have a wonderful time. I'll see you next week."

"Okay. I love you, sweetheart."

"I love you too, Mom."

"Please be safe and remember to fast on Friday. I'm sure I don't need to mention that you should remain abstinent on that day too, because . . . well, hopefully that's not an issue for you right now."

At this, Kate said nothing, but she actually lowered her head to the table and tried to remember if she had Tylenol in her purse, as her mother continued.

"Anyway, please try to squeeze in the celebration of the Lord's Passion, if you can tear yourself away from your very important job. Good Friday is our most somber day, Katie. I don't make you kids go anymore, but you should—"

"Remember what Christ gave up for me. Right, got it. Talk with you later, Mom."

"Bye bye."

Good Friday service, was she kidding? Kate hadn't been to church since . . . she couldn't remember. She was a heathen in her mother's eyes, so Kate wasn't sure why she kept trying. Finishing up her coffee, needing a refill and Toaster Strudel, Kate took her empty cup and her zip lock bag to the kitchen to find the office toaster.

That night, Kate arrived at a fundraiser for Senator Malendar. While she was a little aggravated that Grady had not shown up to the parent center opening at the children's hospital yesterday morning, she was still pleased they had gotten through a week without incident. She stopped by the powder room to check her dress before entering the Agave Ballroom. It was very nice for a hotel event. The ballroom had four sets of doors that were open and leading to a balcony. It was beautifully lit and there were fresh flowers on each of the round tables throughout the room.

Kate set her bag down at her place setting. No one was at her table yet so she turned to get a drink at the bar. The sound guys were doing mike checks, and Kate saw Stanley adjusting the microphone at the podium. Stanley, who never liked to be called Stan, was a balding guy, she guessed mid-forties. He was incredibly well dressed, and seemed to do it with ease. From what Kate could tell, dressed-up Stanley was the only Stanley. His hair was cut very short to his head and his ears were small and round. They stuck out a little, and when he was angry, he looked a bit like a monkey. Stanley was often angry or frustrated with what he considered "the incompetence all around him." Kate smiled in case he saw her, but he was engrossed in shaking hands and passing important people along to the senator.

Kate wore a simple black silk dress. Long, straight across and off the shoulders. It was her "go to" dress. She loved the lines, the feel of the silk, and the barely-there strappy sandals she always wore with it. It fact this dress was the only time she ever wore the insanely high strappy sandals. Her hair was up and she felt together, calm even, when she ordered a sparkling water and lime. She didn't often dress up to the evening gown level, but when she did she was always reminded that she was a woman. She knew that was silly, of course she was a woman, but since the divorce she had forgotten a lot of things.

Grady, who was talking with a man and a woman Kate recognized as his childhood friends, Peter and Samantha, looked over at her and then excused himself and made his way through the crowd. As he approached, Kate was now acutely aware she was female, and slightly annoyed that the temperature in the room went up an easy ten degrees.

"Katherine."

"Grady, haven't we settled the name thing? It's Kate."

"I'm sorry, but that is not a Kate dress. That is most definitely a Katherine. Hepburn, Deneuve, take your pick, but it's a Katherine." He took her hand, kissed her knuckles and lingered. Kate tried to remember if a man had ever kissed her hand. If it had happened, it was never like this. "You look stunning."

"Thank you." That was all she could get out of her mouth. It was one thing to know the magazine cover Grady. No question he was lovely to look at and his tux was perfect, but since spending time with him, Grady had grown on her a bit. There was something in those eyes, behind them, that spoke to Kate far more than his beautiful face. She had clearly not been a good judge of men in the past, but this one did seem like a decent guy. She was about to ask where he was yesterday, when a blonde in a bright dress with a sizable slit took Grady's arm. He looked awkward for the briefest moment, but Kate was prepared and doing her best to be gracious.

"You must be Maddie, that's quite a dress. I'm Kate from Bracknell and Stevens."

"Oh, you work for Grady? For a minute, from the look on his face, I thought you were moving in on my guy." She giggled; there may have been a little snort, and Grady's cheeks actually tinted. *This was going to be fun.* "How did you know my name? Have you been talking about me?" She made some weird pouty face at Grady and he started to say something, but Kate jumped in.

"It's part of my job to know who Mr. Malendar is with during the campaign. Maddie Brinks, you are twenty-four, your family has been close friends with the Malendars for years. You went to UC Santa Barbara, majored in fashion design, and you currently own a little boutique in Los Angeles. Um, "Madly Chic," yes that's what it's called. You and Mr. Malendar have been dating for approximately five hours, so it's super cute you're already keeping an eye out for him." Kate smiled her best girlfriend smile. Grady began to smirk and turned toward Little Miss Mile High Slit.

"Wow, you're good. She's good, isn't she, babe?" she said.

Grady was now into a full warm and wonderful smile. He looked right into Kate. "She certainly is. She's the best."

"It must be great to have such good employees looking out—"

"She's not an employee." Not looking away from Kate.

"Grady, it's fine. I'm sort of an employee."

He turned to his date, as if she were a toddler, and explained. "Maddie, Katherine works for one of the largest PR firms in the country. We are her client, I'm her project."

"Oooh really? Katherine—"

"Kate, please call me Kate."

"Kate, where'd you go to school? Have you worked with a lot of celebrities or only politicians?"

At this point Kate was distracted by the drinks being passed around, as the senator and his wife were about to toast and welcome their guests. Grady should probably be down there, at least available to his father. He must have read her mind because they started walking toward the main table. Kate liked work and was more comfortable with speeches and guest lists. Work didn't have a lot of hand kissing and she liked it that way. As they took a seat at their table, Kate answered Maddie, who still wanted to know about the celebrities.

"Columbia, I went to Columbia, and I'm not at liberty to discuss our clients. Maddie, it was a treat meeting you, but if you'll both please pardon me, it looks like the senator is about to toast." Kate smiled at Grady, who looked perfect and poised, and she moved toward the center of the room.

Grady had schmoozed and even spent a painful half hour talking with Senator Grafton about his new parrot. After surviving that, and the rubber chicken dinner, Grady managed a dance with Samantha and even sat with his mother and her bridge friends for a while. Maddie tagged along, but after all of the talking heads had finished talking, Grady had driven her home, telling her he was heading home too. She had offered to tuck him in, which was the farthest thing from his mind. He kissed her on the cheek and knew he would wait maybe another week before making a clean break. It was explained that his father wanted him to have a "significant other" during the campaign, but Maddie was not that other. Grady was restless after dropping Maddie off, so he returned to the fundraiser. Sam and Peter would still be there, and Kate. Kate would still be there and, well shit. He wanted to see her.

By the time he got back things were winding down. Most of his father's staff and a few select friends had moved from the ballroom to the senator's suite. Grady walked into the large presidential suite, which was bigger than most LA apartments, and saw her first. His gaze fell on her instantly, and why not when she was wearing that dress? Her hair was piled on her head, messier than it was earlier in the evening. A few strands curled at her neck. She was talking to her boss, Mark, and the small crease between her eyes appeared. It was there every time she focused or was mentally prepping her argument. He knew that now. He noticed things about her. *When had that started?* Grady was now used to Kate's serious and often starchy personality. It was stimulating, and for the first time in a long time he was on his toes and enjoying it.

He grabbed a bottle of water from the bar that was now en suite, and as he looked up from twisting off the cap, someone made Kate smile, and the air changed, just like that. Her face was warm and soft. She put her tongue to her teeth and did this little crinkle with her nose when she laughed. Genuine, so unstudied, and alive.

"Hey, you're back," Samantha said, slipping her arm through his.

"I am."

"Any particular reason?" Sam noted his line of sight. "Or someone in particular?"

Grady caught on. "Actually, I came back to see you. Where's Peter?"

"Sulking."

"Yeah, he seemed pissed tonight. Hugely successful playwright pressures?"

Sam chuckled. "That must be it. Hey, would you mind giving me a ride home?"

"You've got it. I'm probably going to leave in a few minutes. I just wanted to say goodnight."

"Uh huh," Sam said as Grady's gaze drifted back to Kate. "She's very sweet."

"Huh, not the word that comes to mind. She probably likes you, so she might be sweet with you. When she's with me, it's more like sour."

"Well, you can bring that out in people."

"Thanks, Sam."

She patted him on the back. "I'm going to get my coat and I'll meet you by the valet in twenty minutes?"

"Sounds good. I'll be right down." Grady kissed Sam on the cheek and made his way over toward the balcony, to Kate.

She was now sitting with her back to everyone. Her arms were perched on the railing as she held out a piece of paper she was reading. He didn't even need to see her face for his stomach to do that weird flip it had started doing since she kicked him the first day they met. As he got to the balcony, someone called her name and Kate turned. Her hair fell softly around her face and she wore glasses, something new and in contrast to her flowing gown. She uncurled from the chair, noticed him, smiled, and then walked toward Mark, in bare feet.

Grady hadn't seen this Kate yet. Sexy and completely unaware. Working, but still having fun with her job. Beauty, brains, and those glasses. He was slipping into unfamiliar territory. It was time for him to head home.

He found his father, said his goodnights, and tossed a wave to Kate as he left. He needed to keep his distance. Distance had always been his unwavering friend.

Chapter Seven

*K*ate left the hotel about a half hour after Grady. While unlocking the door, her heart stopped as her phone vibrated with a text telling her to get down to the Cal Medical Center. It was urgent, that was all Mark said.

She locked up, turned around and ran to her car. On the drive, she received bits and pieces of information. Grady had been in a car accident. He was fine. His friend Samantha had been injured, but she was stable. A million questions swirled through her mind as she pulled her car into the emergency room parking lot. She grabbed a pad and pen from her car, gathered her dress, and walked through the buzzing doors as quickly as she could, thankful she had found flip-flops in her car so she wasn't going to have to run interference all night with crying feet.

Kate met with Mark and the senator's staff in an unoccupied break room just off the ER. She collected information and was chosen to address the press that had already assembled outside. She wasn't thrilled that she needed to meet the press in an evening gown, but there was a woman, Grady's dear friend, in a hospital bed, lucky to be alive. Kate really had no room to complain. She had a job to do.

Kate walked through the main hospital lobby on her way out to the front entrance where the press was cordoned off, anticipating a statement. Her brother Neil was standing just inside the hospital talking with two other uniformed police officers.

"Hey, Sis." His arm outstretched, he pulled her into a hug. "You okay?"

"Sure. I'm fine. I wasn't in the car."

"I know, but I heard Grady's name on my radio and just came down to make sure you were all right."

"Are you working tonight?" Kate asked noticing his jeans and sweatshirt.

"No. I was, well, I was close and I just wanted to check. Looks like everyone's fine. His girlfriend is pretty banged up, and I think he needed stitches, but you probably already know all of this, big shot." Neil bumped his shoulder into hers.

"Yup, that's so me, big shot." They both laughed. "I'm not feeling very tough in my princess dress here."

"You look beautiful. How was the shindig, well, before Mr. Fancy Pants wrecked his car?"

Kate shook her head. "Look at you with that clever wit, huh? If you read the report, super cop, you know that Grady was not at fault, so while his pants may be fancy, he didn't wreck his car all by himself."

"Yeah, I did see that. No drugs or alcohol either."

"Oh, and not his girlfriend. She's a family friend."

"Thanks for clarifying that." Neil smiled. "So, you better get out there, the natives are getting restless."

"You realize that phrase is a touch racist, right?"

"What?"

"The natives, Native Americans?"

Neil looked confused. "That's ridiculous. It's a damn expression. A saying. Everyone is so sensitive these days." Neil wrapped his arm around her and squeezed. "Well, good to see you, even at two in the morning. Get out there and be politically correct."

"Good to see you too, officer." Kate lifted up and gave her big brother a kiss on the cheek.

She stepped through the automatic glass doors of the hospital and into the cool early spring air. Greeted by a dozen microphones and several blinding lights, Kate had met worse, but not without her navy blazer. It was her best friend in these face-to-face dances with the media. Kate took a breath. She told herself Super Girl was still Super Girl even without the cape, and then the battle began.

"Kate, how's it going?" James from *The Tribune* shouted from somewhere in the crowd.

"I don't make a habit of standing around hospitals at two in the morning, so considering, I'm fine, James, thanks for asking." Kate smiled and more shouting ensued.

"Gentleman . . . and lady, hello, Carey." Kate and Carey nodded to each other in acknowledgement that they were both in a sea of men. Kate continued, "I will make a statement, take a few questions, and that will be all for tonight. It is late. The senator and his family are tired. I ask for your respect."

"At approximately 11:45 this evening, while returning home from a fundraiser for the senator, Mr. Grady Malendar was in a car accident with what we are being told was a 2010 pickup truck. He was in his Porsche. The accident was a result of the pickup running a red light and hitting Mr. Malendar on the passenger side as he moved through the intersection. Mr. Malendar's light was green; the other driver was cited at the scene. Mr. Malendar and his passenger were taken by ambulance to this hospital. His passenger, Ms. Samantha Cathner, is a family friend and Mr. Malendar was escorting her home. She has suffered a minor concussion and a broken arm. Mr. Malendar, aside from a cut on his forehead and a few bruises, is unharmed. That pretty much covers it. I'll take some questions."

"Were alcohol or drugs involved?"

"No. Well, let me say alcohol and drugs were not involved with either Mr. Malendar or Ms. Cathner. We have no knowledge as to the state of the other driver other than he was unharmed in the accident."

"Are Grady and this . . . Samantha Cathner, involved, are they dating?"

"No, they are not dating. They are friends, grew up in the same neighborhood."

"Ha, that's assuming Grady's grown up."

"Not necessary, Bill. If there are no more—"

"Did Grady drink at the fundraiser?"

"Were you at the fundraiser, Kate?" another reporter shouted before she could answer.

"Okay, that's enough. Mr. Malendar did nothing wrong, period. If you all came down here looking for dirt, I'm sorry to disappoint. In fact, I challenge any of you to find one incident where my client has ever driven under the influence of anything. I thought for a minute I was dealing with news organizations seeking information about the welfare of a U.S. senator's son following a car accident. Clearly that's not what's going on. We're done here."

Kate turned amid several more questions about Grady, none of which she hadn't heard before and of course *the horse*—the horse was still haunting her. Security began pushing back the reporters as the doors zipped closed behind her. She took a deep breath.

"Nicely done. The vultures didn't stand a chance."

Kate turned to see Grady leaning against the wall in the darkness of the waiting room, out of sight lines. He was a pro, she knew this, but at that moment, in the middle of the night, looking at him in the darkened corner, she felt . . . she felt something. This was not an easy world he lived in and there were vultures, as he called them, hovering, waiting to attack. It actually felt good to spare him from this onslaught, especially since he was still shaking when she had arrived.

"All part of the job, Mr. Malendar."

He laughed as she approached.

"Christ, you look awful," she said and reached to move the hair off his forehead so she could see the stitches. She had brothers, it was instinct, but as soon as her hand touched him, she knew it was a mistake. She was too close and all the warning bells went off. Kate stepped back too quickly and she was certain Grady noticed her discomfort, but he seemed to let it go.

"I checked with Sam and her family. She's stable and they have the driver of the truck in custody, so . . . " Kate was rambling because she needed to focus on the job, her tasks, and not the touch of Grady's face or the warmth in his tired expression. "You should probably get home, get some rest."

"I know. I called a driver, but I want to wait and see Sam again before I leave. They're putting her cast on now." Their eyes held in the dim light of the waiting room.

Kate could still hear the rumbling of the press.

"Thank you," Grady said. "Your comments, your statement. It's nice," he seemed to stumble a bit and Kate's heartbeat picked up. "It's nice that you're on my side, it seems genuine. I mean, I'm sure it's your job, but the way you handled it was, well, you're good at what you do, Kate Galloway."

"I am on your side. It is my job, but I'm a person, you're a person."

Grady laughed. "That we are. Thank you, Kate, for noticing."

She felt foolish and a little lost in his eyes.

"Right," she smiled. "Well, anyway, you are welcome. I'm glad you're all right and Samantha is being taken care of. It's late, so I'll let you go. I'm going to head home. Good night." She touched his hand, she had absolutely no idea why, but there she was touching him again.

"You, of course, checked my driving record before offering up that challenge, right?" he asked, breaking the awkward buzz, and Kate released his hand.

"Yup, even the naughty things senators' sons do that get expunged from their records. You're squeaky clean. I don't feed the vultures unless I'm sure. Get some sleep Mr. Malendar." She continued down the hall.

"Atta girl."

Kate heard him chuckle as the wood doors of the emergency room closed behind her.

Atta girl? Did I really just get an atta girl? It was a stupid comment, but she smiled and felt that weird something again.

Chapter Eight

Grady took a break from the campaign for almost a week following the accident. He was sore, but mostly he needed to focus on some of his things for a while, ground himself in reality. He wasn't prepared to miss Kate, but he did. Found himself Googling her because he wanted to know more about her, her life outside of work. There wasn't much to find. He should have known someone like Kate wouldn't flaunt her life on social media.

Grady walked through the front doors of Bracknell and found himself excited, silly he knew, but there it was, he was excited to see her.

Kate was in her office, so he smiled at her assistant and let himself in. She was reading something and looked up just briefly, and then back again. Grady caught her eyes for a moment and felt his whole body respond.

"Nice to see you, Grady. You look rested."

"I am. Good as new," he said walking over toward her desk and standing as close to her as he could without seeming creepy. Still no perfume, he noted, just pastry again. Grady wondered if she stopped at a coffee shop on her way in. Where did the pastry come from? Then he noticed the napkin on her desk.

"Is that Toaster Strudel?" he asked.

Kate looked up quickly, put the last bite in her mouth, and threw the napkin away.

"Yes," she mumbled before finishing chewing and taking a sip of her coffee.

Grady got closer, leaned in. "You realize that stuff is full of preservatives, right? And it will kill you?"

Kate just stared up at him and licked her finger.

"Are you trying to throw me, Mr. Malendar? Don't mess with my Toaster Strudel, okay? You think your rich-guy organic-foods-only intimidation routine is going to work with me?"

"Kate, I'm not sure what you're talking about," Grady said, adjusting his orange tie, and resting one hip on the edge of her desk. Her legs were crossed under her desk and she was wearing black high heels. They were high, and Grady's mind wandered to them wrapped around . . . Christ, he almost fell off the desk.

"Stop using my name. What's with that? Cut it out." Kate swatted at him with a folder. He snapped out of his lust haze and stood back up.

"You don't like your name?" Grady asked, feigning confusion.

"Very cute. I don't like you saying my name all the time. It's . . . odd, like you're trying to remember my name so you keep saying it, or like you're making a presentation. Stop."

"I was raised that you use a person's name. It makes things personal, puts them at ease."

"I'm at ease, you can drop it now."

"Really? This is at ease? Hmm . . . "

"Yeah, well as at ease as I'm going to get while I've got your file in my office. Please sit so we can go over the revised schedule and some of my research." Grady came around her desk, leaned on the corner closest to her this time, and looked over at the file. She looked right up at him, and he noticed her eyes, while blue, had flecks of green. What was wrong with him that he kept getting this close to her? He was like a stupid moth and she was certainly a flame.

"Do you have a problem with personal boundaries?" Kate asked.

"What? You want to show me what you've dug up on me and I'm simply showing an interest."

"Can't you show interest on the other side of the desk?"

"Do I make you uncomfortable, Kate?"

She laughed. "Seriously?" Kate stood and brushed right up the front of him, not budging. "No, Grady you don't make me uncomfortable."

His breath caught. She smiled and then looked down as she moved past him. *Apparently two could play at this game,* Grady thought.

"I like my space. Let's move to the table." Kate suggested as those damn heels clicked past him.

They both sat at the small round table in her office.

"Okay, here is the new schedule for this week. Blue represents your father's activities and your commitments are in green." Kate slid two copies of the schedule across the table to Grady. "Any questions?"

Grady shook his head while he read what his week would look like, and then set it aside. "Nope, looks pretty standard."

"Okay, I have another goal for us this morning."

Grady put on what Samantha always called his Happy Camper smile.

Kate ignored him. "Mark wants us to put together an ad featuring you, so I need to figure out what that's going to look like. Tell me about your daily schedule."

"My daily schedule?" Grady found the novelty of any type of commercial about his life humorous and relied on his sarcasm once again. "Um, okay, well let's see. I start each morning with a cup of coffee and a quick count of my pile of money."

Kate looked up from her notes.

"Then I shower, meet some of my entitled friends for a morning of tennis. We retire to some bar or restaurant for food, booze, and loose women. Then—"

Kate was fighting a smile, he could see it, so he finished strong. "We all usually get lucky because after all, we're so good-looking and loaded. So that leads to dinner, dancing, a quick trip to the jewelry store to buy my soul mate a bauble, and then back to my place for an endless night of passion." Grady kept a straight face, sipped his water. "That about covers it, now where did you want to schedule in some super-senator's son time?"

Kate sipped her own water and looked down at her notes, but he saw the corners of her mouth give her away. "Well, that seems like quite a life. I'm just wondering when in all of that gluttony and debauchery you find time to deliver groceries to the Dante House and," she lifted his left hand, the one that Grady was trying to keep out of sight, "color eggs with the kids that live there?"

"What?" Grady said pulling his hand from hers. Damn egg dye. *What the hell was with that stuff? It was like being branded,* he thought. "I'm not sure what you're talking about. This?" He held up his hand. "This is from my pool." Grady knew it was weak, but how the hell did she know about the Dante House? Were they having him followed?

"Your pool?" This time Kate let a laugh go.

"Yeah, some kind of reaction to the chemicals. I was testing them yesterday and, yeah I don't know what happened."

"Rainbow reaction? Just on your fingertips? That sure is strange." Kate was still laughing, and pretending to take notes. She put her pen down, folded her hands. Grady knew the jig was up.

"Seriously, this isn't a joke. I have a job to do here and with all due respect, you're being ridiculous."

Grady finished his water and refilled, buying time while he tried to think of something to say. Her gorgeous, full-throated laugh was not helping. Who knew that was in there? It was sexy, and her mouth, *sweet Jesus, that mouth. Focus you idiot!*

"Grady?" Kate said when he came up with nothing but visions of what and where he'd like to see Kate's mouth. Not helpful at all. He looked up.

"Dante House, tell me about it."

"I have helped them out a couple of times. I went to college with a girl that got the shit beat out of her by her hailed and celebrated football player boyfriend. I guess I have a soft spot, but it's certainly not a habit. There's no need for that to be part of my wind-up son package. It's private. They're, as I'm sure you already know, a battered women's shelter. They don't need the attention. In fact, it's dangerous."

"Okay, but you do need the attention. Is there anything else you do, any other ways you give back?"

"No."

"Nothing? What about other things, philanthropic pursuits, $500-a-plate feed the children events, maybe?"

"There it is again, Kate." Grady smiled.

"Right, the bitter me. Sorry. Moving on."

"You know there's actually a little undercurrent of self-righteousness in there too. Do you have an issue with money, Kate?"

"No, I do not Mr. Malendar. I was joking. My apologies."

Grady nodded, leaned back in his chair and folded his arms across his chest, watching her, because it was quickly becoming his favorite pastime. Kate's eyes fell to his chest, panned up his shoulders, and he could have sworn he heard her make a little sound. She seemed to lose her train of thought. *Interesting.*

"Okay, let's get back on track here. From what I've learned, you give money to the Boys and Girls Club. You also helped out with their field day event at the beginning of this year. It would be great for voters to see you—"

"No. Voters are voting for my father, not for me. Focus on what he does, it's extensive, and just let me do what I do well."

"Which is?"

"Smile, shake hands, you know what they say, woo the ladies."

"Yeah, I'm sure you're a huge asset among the female voter demographic, but your father needs to pull in more than just lonely debutantes looking for a quick ride in your sports car—"

"It's a Porsche. Well, it used to be. She's in the shop now."

"She, the car's a 'she.' Of course it is. No one cares."

"Now I'd have to disagree with you there. Do you have any idea the engineering—"

"Uh huh, could you please focus? My . . . *our* plan calls for drawing attention to the depth of who you are as a person. There's not really much to work with, but there are some little glimmers of light. I understand that we can't spotlight Dante House, but we might be able to blow up some of these small gestures."

"Kate, listen, people are comfortable with my current image. No one wants to hear about the twenty bucks or the few hours I spent chasing kids around. Let's drop this, believe me, my good deeds are few and far between."

"Well according to Amy at Big Brother—"

"You've already spoken to Amy? Jesus, because she has nothing better to do than chat with you about what a good guy I am? They do real work there. Move on."

Kate kept hitting a wall and Grady could tell it was frustrating her, but that was all he was going to give her. He understood that most people he dealt with exploited every dime and minute they gave to the "less fortunate." He had no intention of being portrayed as one of those rich, out-of-touch douche bags. He liked how the public knew him, he had crafted it carefully, and now he just had to convince Kate that pitching Grady Malendar as a concerned citizen was a waste of his father's money and her time.

"Okay," Kate said flipping through her notes. "How do you feel about speaking tomorrow morning at the Women's Under-40 Luncheon. It's a group of female entrepreneurs. Your father needs exposure with younger career women."

"I'm sure I'd be outstanding in that capacity." Grady smiled.

"Okay. You're scheduled to discuss your father's policies on small business loans and work/life balance. Are you aware of what those policies are?"

"I am."

Kate must have thought he was joking because she handed him a stapled set of notes. "Okay, well just in case here are some key talking points. Things Stanley feels we should be pushing in this demographic."

Grady took the papers, flipped the first page. "Well, if Stanley thinks we should, then by all means, let's hit it."

"Look Grady, it's important for someone like you to—"

"Someone like me?" Coming from her, the condescension stung a little. He found himself wanting to show her, only her, who he really was, but that was not going to happen.

"I meant someone with your . . . reputation. We need to—"

"What you need to do is get me in front of the camera so I can smile and, what did you say, use what little I have to impress the voters. What I do in my free time is my business. I've agreed to lay low, stay out of trouble. I'm being a very good boy, Kate. Is it time for cookies and milk, yet?"

Grady was kicked back, sleeves rolled, with a taunting smile playing at his lips as he tried to dodge and distract like a teenager. He was annoying, but something about his demeanor made Kate wish she were playful. His ease was enviable.

And then, as if she'd slipped into an alternate universe, she suddenly saw her brother Ethan, "the other brother," as he was often called, walk by the conference room window in his black cargo pants, black T-shirt, and SWAT vest.

Potentially Playful Kate ran from the building. Guarded and Responsible Kate replaced her in an instant. Grady must have noticed because he turned to look at Ethan, who was now at the glass door with a "funny seeing you here" expression.

As Kate stood and straightened her skirt, she knew in the pit of her stomach that Neil must have told Ethan about her current "project." Ethan was sent as badass ambassador. Years of living in the smallest testosterone network in the world told her she was right. *Oh, this was rich.*

"Ethan." Kate said opening the door. "Why, what are you doing here?"

"Hey, Katie. What? I can't come say 'Hi' to my little sister?"

Kate put her hands on her hips.

Ethan's smile dropped. "Fine. I'm here making a delivery. I guess the department is donating to the Carousel of Hope Ball.

Dad, er, Chief as we call him in the work world, asked me to drop this off," he said, holding up a large manila envelope. "Anyway, I just happened to walk by and see you with . . ." He was never good at subtlety, so Ethan let himself into the room.

Kate turned to Grady. "Ethan, as I'm sure you already know, this is Grady Malendar."

Grady stood, smiled a dazzling rehearsed smile, and extended his hand.

"Grady, this is Detective Ethan Flanagan. My brother."

Grady briefly caught her eye and then shook Ethan's hand. "Pleasure," he said effortlessly.

"Likewise," Ethan said, giving Grady his best cop look. The two men locked eyes and Kate decided this would definitely be added to her most awkward moments list. They could not have been more different.

"Okay, well—" She tried to move things along.

"I voted for your father. Are you helping out on his campaign?" The now overly-friendly Ethan asked.

"Appreciate that. Yes, back on the circus tour. Kate here is helping to make me a more wholesome guy." Grady laughed, Kate smiled, and Ethan gave a fake laugh she had never heard her entire life. It had more than a hint of crazy.

"I'm sure that's no easy job, but our Katie's up to the task. She's a pro." *Our Katie? What the hell? Was he getting ready to challenge Grady to a dance off? This was ridiculous.*

"Eth, um, we're in the middle of a meeting and you probably have to get back."

He was still locked on Grady, who was now looking everywhere but at Ethan.

"Ethan?"

"Right. Sorry. I didn't want to just walk by without saying hello. And, I got to meet your new friend, so that's nice."

"Client, my client."

Ethan looked at her and clearly read the "you're a dumb ass" look she was sending his way.

"I'll walk you out."

Grady was still standing and glancing at his expensive shoes.

"Good to meet you, Grady." Ethan shook his hand again. Hard.

"It was interesting, Detective." Grady returned the handshake and returned the glare.

Ethan smirked and walked out. Kate motioned she'd be just be a minute and whirled toward the door fit to be tied.

"What the hell was that? I'm at work, Eth. Save your Neanderthal bullshit for the station, will ya?"

"Did you see his socks?"

"What?"

"His socks. I saw them when he stood up. They're colorful, with, shapes. What's up with that?"

Kate shook her head in amazement at the absurdity of the conversation. "Argyle. They are argyle. It's a thing, an accent. Some men are into accents, Ethan. Black is not every man's 'go to' color."

"It's not right. Anyway, Neil told me about the accident last week. You at the hospital in the middle of the night."

Kate rolled her eyes, but Ethan continued. "You staying out of trouble?" Ethan smiled and Kate forgot to be mad. He was closest to her in age and usually the one in trouble. Growing up, she had always been the good girl, but Ethan used to ask her if she was staying out of trouble. When she was younger it made her feel a bit rebellious, like maybe she was capable of hanging with his crowd. Even as an adult, if Kate ever felt like getting into trouble, Ethan would have her back. He often infuriated her, but brothers were nice to have.

"I wasn't in the accident, as I'm sure you already know. I was just there to make a statement. Yes, I'm staying out of trouble. Thank you for stopping by to see me. I'm sure it had nothing to do with your need to perform your death grip handshake on my client."

"Your 'client' looked awfully cozy when I walked by. I'm pretty sure there was a little hand touching there."

"I . . . I don't even know what to say to you. We were not touching hands. But let's just say we were. Let's say we had just gotten our clothes back in place when you came around the corner."

"Oh Christ, please, I'm a visual guy, Sis."

"Let's say that. I was, what's that you call it, oh yeah, 'getting some' with my client."

Ethan was now covering his face with his hands to extinguish the image of his sister "getting" anything.

Kate pulled his hands down and went up on her tiptoes so they were almost eye-to-eye. "So? So what? I'm a grown woman and I do not need a bodyguard. I can do what I want."

"So you are," he gestured between Kate and the conference room door, "with him"?

"No!" Kate was clearly not making any progress. "I don't have time for this. I have to get back to work."

"Okay, I didn't mean to get you all riled up." He kissed her forehead. "I'll let you go, but Katie—" Kate was back at the door to the conference room, but she looked over at Ethan. "He's not for you. Not in your league, so be careful."

Kate laughed, a little. "That is actually quite insulting, but since you're an idiot, I'll let it slide. I love you anyway, now go away."

"I love you too. Go be important."

Kate returned to the conference room. Her face flushed with some combination of anger and embarrassment. She shut down her personal life, and that sometimes included her family, so Ethan showing up and the thought of getting anything on with Grady had thrown her off. She sat and took a sip of water.

"Okay. I'm so sorry. Where were we?" She looked up at Grady and he was blowing into a folded piece of paper. As he blew, the paper turned into a cube. He handed it to her.

"Oh wow, I left you so long that you've resorted to origami?"

"Very good, Kate. I only know two or three things. If you and your brother had been a bit longer, I was going to start working on a swan."

Kate smiled and set the paper balloon down on the table.

"Do I want to know how you know origami? Family immersion trip to the Orient maybe?"

Grady smiled. "Ah, see, I love the quick wit. No, as I'm sure you already know, the Malendars have never been to Japan as a family, but I have. Didn't learn origami there though. Picked up the art of paper folding from a girl I dated in college. She also taught me how to fold towels properly."

"Wow, important woman."

"She was."

"What went wrong?"

"It was," he pretended heartbreak, "it just wasn't meant to be. She dumped me."

Kate picked up her pad and tried to get the conversation back on track, but she smiled and in spite of herself said, "Really? Did she see the warning signs?"

"Why, Kate?" He faked a gasp and placed a hand to his chest. "What signs are you referring to?"

She shook her head and ignored the question.

Chapter Nine

Kate stepped out into the courtyard of the Pasadena Playhouse, leaving Grady chatting with his family. When he had asked her to attend the premiere of his friend Peter's new play, she knew it wasn't necessary. Mark said she didn't need to attend. Nothing was going to happen at a play premiere with Grady's family and friends. In fact, if Kate went, she would be the only member of Bracknell and Stevens in attendance. She didn't need to be there, but he had asked, said he wanted her there, that they would have a great time. She knew it wasn't necessary, practical, and yet she had agreed anyway. What had she been thinking? Kate stood in the night air in a gorgeous blush-bead trimmed dress she really couldn't afford, but bought anyway a few days ago on her way home from work after Grady's invitation. If she were honest with herself, she had been excited, but now she was just confused.

It was intermission and she needed some air. The playhouse glowed through the evening darkness. Kate wrapped her arms around her bare shoulders and looked up at the clear sky. So many stars. She took a deep breath and allowed herself to relax. Her face hurt from smiling. She moved through the tiled arched walkway, past a couple taking pictures. She didn't want to check her phone, didn't want to work. That was a first. Grady and his family, his friends, the bantering and teasing. What was she doing all dressed up and pretending? It felt like pretending, as if she was one of them, with him. Kate leaned against the stucco wall, careful not to snag her dress, and she saw the lobby lights dim indicating there were ten minutes until the second act.

"Kate?" Grady called out into the courtyard, since he couldn't see her in the walkway. She watched as he put his hands in his pockets, and then her heart tripped as he too looked up at the sky, enamored by the stars. Who was Grady Malendar? Why couldn't he just be the idiotic rich snob she assumed him to be?

"Right here," she called to him. He turned toward her as she emerged from the shadows.

"Everything all right?"

"Yes, everything is fine. Incredible sky, I just needed some air," she answered.

"It's kind of cold out here, do you want my—"

"No!" Kate snapped, and Grady froze midway through taking off his jacket. "I'm sorry."

Kate tried to soften her response. "No thank you. Please do not give me your jacket. I'm fine and besides, it's time to go in."

Grady looked a little surprised and shrugged back into his dark navy blazer.

"I'm . . . I guess I'm sorry. Didn't mean to offend you—"

"It's fine. It was nice. I'm just not sure why I need to be here, so I'm a little out of sorts, that's all. Thank you. It was nice."

Grady smiled and tried to defuse the stifling awkwardness. "Yeah, well that's me . . . nice. Shall we?" He gestured toward the door.

Kate took a deep breath. "Yes, definitely. Sure." She walked in ahead of him. As they were walking to their seats, Grady spoke into her back. She could smell him. When had she started smelling him?

"Listen," he said quietly, "if you want to cut out now, you can. I promise to behave. I mean, you didn't have to come if you didn't want to. I get that this is above and beyond and you probably have other plans." When they arrived at their row, Kate turned to face him.

"It's not that I don't want to be here. The play is great and your family, friends, they are all lovely."

"Then what's the problem?"

They both sat in their seats, shoulder to shoulder. The lights began to dim and Grady turned to look at her. She could feel his breath on her skin, his leg touching hers, and she felt like she was melting into her seat.

"Kate?" Grady put his hand on her knee and then at her look, quickly pulled back. "If you want to be here, then what's the problem?"

Kate looked at him, his face glowing from the warmth of the stage lights. "I do want to be here. I'm a little thrown by that. This feels . . . it's nice, but it doesn't feel like work. I'm used to, comfortable with, work. Does that make sense?"

"It does."

"Why are you smiling?" Kate whispered.

"I'm not smiling. Eyes front, Galloway, it's rude to talk during a play. Wouldn't want to make a scene."

By the time the play was over, Peter Everoad and Samantha Cathner, Grady's two best friends, were engaged. He'd proposed during the second act, right up on stage during opening night. It was the stuff of fairytales and Kate had to admit it spoke to the tiny part of her damaged heart that was still a romantic.

She also found it interesting that somewhere inside of Grady Malendar there must be more than fast cars and body shots, because she was certain those were tears she saw glistening on his eyelashes as he hooted during the final applause.

After the play, while it was a shame to cover up her gorgeous shoulders, Kate finally accepted his coat. Grady liked the way she looked in it, all tiny and mismatched. They walked around down-town Pasadena and got ice cream. He went with the Rocky Road, and Kate of course had vanilla. Grady had always found vanilla a boring flavor, but watching Kate lick her ice cream cone and run her tongue along her lips, he realized he'd just never seen it eaten properly. There was nothing boring about watching Kate eat vanilla ice cream.

"That was really stunning. Did you know he was going to do that?"

"Nope. I'm not sure Peter even knew he was going to do it. Those two have been circling each other for years."

"Are you happy for them? I mean, I'm sure you are, but they are both your best friends. That has to be weird."

"It was for a while, but once I stopped thinking about myself I was very happy for them. They belong together. Pete's a compli-cated guy and Sam gets him, so it's good. I love them both. I'm glad he finally took the plunge."

"Do you think they'll get married in Pasadena? Doesn't Peter live in New York? I wonder how that's going to work?" Kate was thinking out loud and continued licking her ice cream. She seemed almost giddy in her memory of the proposal.

When she smiled, her whole face changed and he wondered if she knew. It was a real, genuine smile, and she went all human on him. Grady was mesmerized by all the different sides of Kate Gal-loway. The dance of her eyes suddenly made it hard to keep jabbing, joking. Jabbing was fun and kept them both where they belonged, but he wanted more dancing eyes, almost needed a clos-er look. He was certain, just as sure as he had been when he touched the stove burner for the first time at his sister Kara's third birthday party, that a closer look, while warm, would burn. *This wasn't a date*, he told himself. Even if it felt like the very best, most stimulating date he had ever been on. Even if she smelled like something he'd yet to figure out, but wished he could bottle. Even if when she looked at him he saw possibilities—he wanted more, to *be* more. Even with all of that, this wasn't a date. She may be in a soft moment right now, but she would snap out of it any minute. She'd realize she was working, he was her project, and she'd remember she didn't have ice cream with guys like him.

Until that moment though, Grady was going to enjoy this Kate Galloway, as much as she'd let him. "Would you like to see my house?"

Kate almost dropped her ice cream and Grady loved the shock on her face. "I . . . I'm not sure that's such a good idea."

"Oh. Yeah, I was just thinking since we are meeting the first set of volunteers there tomorrow that you might want to see it first. Check me out and make sure I don't have a wall of shot glasses or porn in the bathroom." Grady smiled and Kate blushed. Damn, the blushing was fun.

"Right. That is tomorrow. Okay, sure. Let's go clean up your act. Why am I picturing posters and a pinball machine? You don't have a pinball machine, do you?"

Grady shook his head. "I have a ping pong table, but it's in the basement. No pinball," he said as he opened the door to the car that had pulled around to take them home.

"Well that's a relief." Kate held her dress and slipped into the dark leather seat. Grady closed the door and as he circled the back of the car, he realized he'd never brought a woman to his house. Ever. Before he could tell himself this was a mistake, he told himself it was business, work. *Yeah right.*

Kate walked up the front path of Grady's home and tried not to gasp. She was normally great at faking interest, or pretending to not be shocked, but everything about this man defied prediction. She couldn't figure him out and in some sick part of her brain that made him all the more interesting.

The house was white, maybe whitewashed was the term, with wood planks. Kate guessed it was a ranch style. The entryway where they now stood as Grady took out his keys had a giant tree growing up and through the roof as if the tree was more important than the house. Kate gestured to it.

"Did you—"

"Think to cut that down before I built the house?" Grady opened the large all-glass front door and motioned her in. "That probably would have been the easier thing to do, but the tree was here when I bought the land. Didn't seem right to cut it." He threw his keys on a concrete table near the door while Kate tried to keep her mouth from falling open.

"I'm sure your contractor appreciated that," she said, trying to make conversation because every cell of her body was buzzing. Grady smiled and the buzzing got louder.

"Yeah, he's a good guy, so he understood. Can I get you a drink?"

"Water is fine," Kate said, walking through the entry and following Grady into the kitchen. It was unlike any kitchen she had ever seen. There were two utility sinks and a huge stovetop all set in some kind of stone. A giant antique-looking butcher's block sat in the center. Grady took two waters out of one side of the refrigerator, which also had glass doors, and from what Kate could see, food. Real, like *I cook,* food.

"Okay, I'll give you the ten-cent tour," Grady said, handing her a water. He loosened his tie, rolled his sleeves up his forearms, and took a sip of his water. "All right, we are obviously in the kitchen. I guess I should tell you that everything in this house is repurposed, which is a fancy way of saying used."

She smiled.

"Nothing is new?" Kate asked.

"Well, the electrical, plumbing and the appliances are new. But the materials to build the house and most of the furniture is used."

"Huh," Kate said looking at the floor.

"The flooring is from an old barn. The windows are each a little different and were recovered from a number of the homes destroyed in New Orleans. There's a pretty cool one in the bathroom that's stained glass, but it doesn't open properly, so there's the trade-off with old." Kate smiled again. She was flooded with images of him in this space. Living a life she would have never guessed when she first met him. It was all so strange. How could he possibly be all of this underneath? She caught herself chewing on her thumb and stopped.

"Why used? Just to conserve?"

"I like old things," he said, leading her into the living room that was a huge open space with a leather sectional couch, and what looked like a large pulley under glass for a coffee table. "I knew I wanted to build my own home, but I didn't want that new feel. I wanted the energy of an old house, so I decided to try and create that here. It took me two years, but it really turned into a great space."

They turned toward the back of the house, which was all glass. There were sliding doors that seemed to disappear into the walls as Grady pushed them open. Outside was a patio, a small pool, and what looked like 1960s patio furniture.

The night sky stretched endless, and when Kate turned to look at him she was lost. In him, in what he called his space. All of it was overwhelming and she needed to get out, needed to leave before she did or said something stupid. Her heart was racing. He wasn't moving, just facing her, looking at her under the stars. She could feel his breath, and if she didn't turn and run this instant, she would put her hands on his chest, finally look deep into the ocean of his eyes, and lose herself in a kiss she knew would ruin her.

"Grady," Kate heard her voice say. She was staring at his chest, she could see his breath moving in and out.

"Yes, Kate." He wasn't moving. Her eyes moved up his neck and met his gaze. He wasn't looking at her like Katherine Galloway. Those weren't work eyes, or sarcastic "Let me mess with you" eyes. These eyes, they were "I want to see what you look like in the morning, tangled in my sheets," eyes. Kate couldn't breathe. She wasn't what someone like Grady wanted, she wasn't that woman. She had played this game before and been burned.

"I need to leave," Kate said on a whisper.

"I know." And he did, it was all over his face. He saw her, saw her fear, and maybe sensed some of his own. She wasn't ready, would probably never be ready, for what was dancing between the two of them.

In that moment, both turned as if running to save themselves. Kate politely said goodnight, from a distance, and Grady opened the door to the town car for her. When the driver pulled away, Kate closed her eyes tightly and put her head back on the seat. Less than a half hour ago, she was innocently touring Grady's house, checking it out before tomorrow. Nothing could have been easier. Until less than five minutes ago, when easy had turned into being surrounded by a man she found herself wanting. And not just a "wow, he's attractive" sort of want. This was a "strip my clothes off, don't worry about the buttons, and take me right here" kind of want. It washed over her, a feeling she hadn't felt in a very long time. In fact, Kate was pretty sure she'd never had this particular feeling, and now she was safely locked in a car heading home where she belonged. Thank God!

Chapter Ten

The next morning, Kate was up early and outside Nordstrom with Reagan when the store opened at nine o'clock. It was Find Reagan's Wedding Shoes Saturday. They'd met for breakfast and were now fueled and ready to go. Reagan had some ideas she had pinned on Pinterest and she was showing them to Kate as a lady in a white coat wrestled the door locks open.

"So are you going flats or heels? There's both here."

"I know, I couldn't decide. Pinterest is evil. Anything is possible. Look at these, they're real glass slippers." She turned her phone to Kate.

"Ouch." Kate grimaced.

"Right? But they look incredible."

"I think it's probably more important that you have feet for your honeymoon."

Reagan laughed in agreement as they stepped off the escalator and into the shoe department.

"The dress is floor length, so you could really go either way," Kate said, picking up a pair of ballet slippers with encrusted crystals.

"True, and Ben is a good six or seven inches taller than me, so I don't have to worry about looking like Athena next to him."

The clerk asked Reagan if she could help. They found two comfortable chairs and the fun began. After a couple of hours and two store changes, Reagan decided on flats and heels. She would wear the heels for the ceremony and pictures, but wear her satin flats for dancing and the reception. They also found her an outfit for the honeymoon plane ride. She and Ben planned to spend two weeks touring Italy. Reagan had been once before, but it would be Ben's first time. Sometimes Kate thought Reagan was more excited about the honeymoon than she was about the wedding. Looking at her Italy itinerary over salads, Kate couldn't blame her.

"You're sleeping on the train for two nights of the trip." Kate sighed. "So romantic."

"I know. I'm just stupid for the whole thing. I'm so happy already. It doesn't seem real." Reagan's eyes started to tear and Kate took her hand across the table.

"But it is real, honey, and you deserve every bit of it. Ben is just the luckiest guy."

Reagan smiled. "Messy apartment, clay under my fingernails, and all?"

"All of it. You're an amazing woman and he sees that, so major points for him."

They both smiled and decided on dessert. They didn't normally go for dessert at lunch, but they had new shoes and a honeymoon outfit—definite reasons for a celebration.

Kate sipped her coffee and took a bite of their shared cheesecake. She was quiet for a moment.

"Hello?" Reagan waved her hand in front of Kate's face.

She looked up. "Oh, sorry. I'm not sure where I went. What were we talking about? This is delicious," she said, holding up another forkful.

"Is he cute?" Reagan asked.

"I think we should try Faire Frou Frou in the valley for your silk and lace. Two weeks in Italy and you're going to need . . . wait, what did you say?"

"The son, the client, is he cute?"

Kate's face flushed, it was silly. "Really, Reagan? Are we ditching fifth period in school again? Cute? We're thirty-two, no one is cute anymore."

"So, is that a yes?"

"He's . . . rich. That brings with it a certain look."

"Oh, boy. That hot, huh?"

"Will you stop? He's a good-looking man. You said you've seen him, or seen him in magazines. He's . . . well he looks like the pictures. He's attractive, but he's also sarcastic, at ease, and painfully confident. He drives me . . . "

Kate stopped. Reagan was smiling her "I know you" smile as she put a bite of cheesecake in her mouth. Kate hated that smile. "Fine, he's beautiful, better than the pictures. Happy?"

Reagan nodded as she pulled the fork out of her mouth. "So he's luscious and rich and he annoys you because he's always so at ease, confident, and that's a bad thing, why?"

"He's not . . . we are not . . ."

"Oh, but I think you are. Kate, for the last month we've met for food or shopping, what, nine or ten times? You've mentioned him in one way or another every time."

"What are you talking about? I didn't mention him today. You brought it up. I was discussing what Ben was going to see once he got you out of your dress. You're the one that—"

"You're attracted to him. You're thinking about him, I can tell. He's pushing your buttons and getting under your skin, but you like it and why not? You've been holed up in your girl cave long enough. What a way to emerge!"

"Okay, enough. Cut it out. Do you want this last bite?"

Reagan slowly shook her head as her mouth formed into a knowing smile. Kate could tell Reagan was no longer interested in the cheesecake; she wanted details.

"It's not like that. He's a client. I'm working for his father, so please lasso in your romantic Bohemian heart, because that's all this is. I think we should hit that little accessory boutique on our way to Frou Frou," Kate said, and took a sip of her coffee.

"Oh, please. Don't change the subject."

"I'm not changing the subject. We have things to do."

"You're blushing. Your cheeks are pink. I haven't seen that in a very long time."

Kate put her hands to her cheeks. They were warm. Damn her fair skin. "That's a blush of annoyance," Kate said.

Reagan dismissed her explanation. "Have you kissed him yet?"

"No! Wait, *yet*? What makes you think . . .? Believe me, there will be no kissing." Mainly because Kate was sure she would go up in flames, but Reagan didn't need to know that. Kate tried to stop it, but at even the suggestion of kissing Grady, her mind flooded with images. Blue eyes, soft lips, the dark evening sky, urgency and heat. Lots of heat. Where the hell had that come from? Her face was probably five shades of scarlet by now. She looked up and Reagan's smile was now stretching right up into her beautiful brown eyes.

"You're totally picturing kissing him right now! Oh God, it's inevitable. When it happens I want all the details. Sliding tongues, heavy breathing, I want it all. I love kissing. It's my favorite part of the whole naked business."

Kate snapped out of her lust fog. "You are crazy. Nuts. There will be no sliding tongues. Who even talks like that?"

Reagan laughed and pointed at her. "Blushed again! Tongues, was it the tongues, Kate?" Reagan was having great fun now moving her head back and forth in an air make-out session. "His hands, and those lips, I'm sure the lips are yummy."

Kate couldn't help it, she started to laugh. "You're ridiculous."

"Laugh now, but it's coming. I know it. Maybe we should all go to dinner. You, me, Ben and Mr. Yes, Please. That would be fun."

"For the hundredth time, crazy lady, we are not dating. He's a client. Great lips or not, that's where it ends."

"Really, then, why were you all dolled up in that gorgeous dress last night? Why did his car pick you up?"

Kate replayed the evening in her mind. The car, the ethereal glow of the Pasadena Playhouse at night, the chill, Grady and his friends wrapped in the most romantic marriage proposal she had ever witnessed. It messed with her mind, felt like a fairytale. Too bad Kate didn't believe in fairytales anymore.

"Work. That was work. It was an event. The senator was there, his son, the entire family was there. They're actually great people and the playhouse has this patio, I guess it's a courtyard, with a fountain and old tile. It was all very 1920's. The whole night felt unreal. Grady's friend, Peter, is a playwright and his other friend, Samantha, is the artistic director. They all grew up together. Peter proposed to her, and Reagan, my God it was incredible." Kate looked up to Reagan's soft expression.

"There's a light in you, Kate. It's dim, subtle, but it's there. It's coming back." Reagan sighed.

Kate held her breath. She didn't have room for light or love. She was sensible. People only got one shot at the fairytale, if they were lucky. Kate's had started out exciting enough, but it was over now and it hadn't worked out.

Reagan seemed to sense her panic and changed the subject, for now. "Okay, well, enough about how the other half lives, let's go get me some naughty panties." Reagan tossed her napkin at Kate.

They paid the check and Kate's pulse returned to normal.

Grady arrived home and went straight for the shower. He was filthy. As scheduled, he had spent the morning at a campaign volunteers' appreciation breakfast. His father was there and they served the volunteers as a way of thanking them for their work. It hadn't been bad, but then his other life came calling. He hadn't expected a call, nor was he expecting a shipment on a Saturday, of all days. No one was around, his partners were all busy, and even their normal go-to crew was nowhere to be found. Grady made excuses to his father and cut out early. The delivery guy was short-handed too, so Grady ended up helping him move crates and the day got away from him.

Hair still wet, Grady moved to the kitchen to prep a well-deserved dinner. He rubbed olive oil on a roaster chicken he'd picked up on his way home. Salt and peppered it, then placed it in a skillet with some potatoes and carrots. He threw the whole thing in the oven and turned the television on. Not the news, he never watched the news. His channel surfing brought him to an Antique Roadhouse marathon. He loved this show. Dropping the remote on his coffee table, Grady grabbed a water from the kitchen, and returned just as some guy with a long goatee was inquiring about the value of his old AM/FM radio. Thankful for the distraction of the show, Grady sat and propped his legs up on the coffee table.

He couldn't get her out of his mind. What the hell had he been thinking? Why did he give a shit whether she knew him, really knew him? Christ, he was going soft. She spent less than thirty minutes in his home and now she was everywhere. When he looked out his back patio all he could see was her standing there in the moonlight looking at him like he might actually have a chance. Like she was about to kiss him, or would have let him kiss her. This was insane.

He wanted her. It was as simple as that. The thought washed right over him as she walked through his house. He had no idea what to do with her. Actually, he had a lot of ideas on what to do with her, they came to him daily now, but none of them would ever find a door in his world to let her in. He felt as if he was standing outside a store that he never knew existed, and she was in the window. He wanted, but wanting and having were two very different things. *Shit!*

To hell with lying low, he was going out. He had friends, women. There was no reason for him to sit around this house pining over some woman he met last month. This wasn't him. Grady picked up his phone to make fun, single guy, non-thinking plans when he saw the text from Kate:

Great work with the volunteers today. Hope you're having a calm and peaceful night in. No climbing! :)

He must have read it three times before something in his male brain said, "That's a damn smiley face, you idiot. Why are you staring at it like it's a naked woman?" Grady dropped the phone and then picked it up again. He should respond. Christ, it was like he was in high school again. He started with a simple, "Thanks," and then thought that sounded too, well simple. He hated texting, it lacked personality, but she was obviously reaching out, professionally anyway, so he needed to say something. In the end, he decided to just be himself:

Just lying here in bed, alone.

Grady smiled and hit send. "That'll fix your cute little smiley face that's driving me crazy," he said out loud to no one. Yep, he'd lost his damn mind.

He looked up and there was a lady on Antique Roadhouse wanting to value the enamel on silver gilt she was told was Romanov. Grady turned up the volume, eager to hear how the show turned out, and went to the kitchen to grab his dinner. It was official. He was staying in for the fourth weekend in a row.

Chapter Eleven

Madison Elementary was hosting the regional spelling bee this year. Once again, Kate agreed to be the reader. It all started when Faith, her sister-in-law, Ethan's wife, who was a fourth grade teacher, called her a year ago with a crisis. Mr. Plimpton, the theater teacher with the melodic exacting voice, had some type of nervous breakdown and apparently started eating at the drywall in his apartment. When Faith called, Kate was on her second pint of Ben and Jerry's Chunky Monkey and not feeling so great herself.

"Kate, the spelling bee is tonight and without a reader they just can't . . . think of how disappointed everyone will be!"

"Isn't there someone else that can do this?" She had asked, muting the television.

"You have a really great voice and we need that—someone who can articulate. Please," Faith had begged.

When Kate said nothing, Faith started to back out, masterfully. "It's fine, if you're busy I understand. Mr. Hardgrove can read. I mean, his voice is a little scratchy, and we always need him to repeat the words during practice, but . . . I just thought if you weren't doing . . . don't worry. It'll work out."

What the hell else was she doing? Sitting on the couch, over a year after her divorce, and eating herself to death? She wasn't at the drywall level yet, but give it a few more months and she could very well be there with Mr. What's His Face.

"Faith, I'll be there," Kate had said, getting up from the couch.

Faith thanked her incessantly, and hung up.

That night had stirred something in Kate, and since then she had been the reader for many spelling bees across the city. She loved it. She wouldn't give it up for all the Chunky Monkey in the world. These children dressed in their finest and despite insecurities, braces, poorly-fitting pants and just general adolescent angst, they got up, walked to the microphone, and gave it everything they had. They were inspiring every year. They showed her that the little things matter, and during a time in her life when she really needed it, they helped her hang on. Still did.

As thirteen-year-old Suki Bahati came up on stage to receive her trophy, Grady saw Kate stand to clap, and he too was already offering his own standing ovation in the back of the cafeteria. His sleeves were rolled up above his elbows and he was clapping and hooting. He couldn't have cared less about the two reporters that had followed him in earlier and were now making a beeline for him. Kate turned to the crowd and saw him. He wasn't hard to miss among the proud parents and spelling bee participants. Not a whole lot of single guys at spelling bees, which was a shame because he was having a blast.

Grady almost jogged up to the officials' table.

"That was incredible." He spoke directly to Kate, who was wearing her black-rimmed glasses again. The ones that conjured up a very sexy librarian fantasy he never even knew he had. "I mean, I've been to sporting events and been on the edge of my seat, but that was brilliant. Look at her parents, they're beaming."

Kate tilted her head. "Grady, what are you doing here?"

"Your assistant said you'd be here . . . "

Suki's parents now recognized Grady and her father approached.

Grady extended his hand. "You must be incredibly proud, Mr. . . . ."

"Bahati," Kate prompted him.

"Yes, Mr. Bahati, so proud. That was sensational to watch. Mrs. Bahati," he gently kissed the mother on the cheek, "congratulations. So exciting." Both parents thanked him for coming and presented their very smart, but incredibly shy daughter. At that moment the reporters made their move and stepped right in front of Suki.

"Hey, Grady. How's the head healing? Spelling bees your thing now? I don't think there's an open bar, and these girls look a little underage."

Grady had learned to mask his distain for ignorant reporters long ago. He took a quick breath, moved around both men, and stood next to Suki and her family.

"Gentlemen, settle down. This is a school function and I'm here to congratulate Suki Bahati. Now if you'd like to take her picture with her parents that would finally be a good use of your time. I'm not the story tonight guys, but this fantastic young lady deserves some attention, as do all the spelling bee participants." With that he winked at Suki, who smiled from ear to ear, and then he stepped aside. He didn't shake her hand or pose for pictures like a good politician's son would—the moment was too normal, too real for that kind of bullshit.

The reporters began asking questions about the spelling bee and took several pictures. Suki and her family would be in the paper, probably the front page, with some spin about Grady, but he didn't care. They deserved the attention. He cupped Kate's elbow. "You ready to make a run for it?" he asked, and began moving her slowly toward the door.

"I'd advise against running. Have you been drinking?" she asked.

He huffed, and feeling like a teenager, breathed right in her face. "See, minty fresh."

She looked at him sideways, but he grabbed her bag and had her out the door. "And no, I have not been drinking Grey Goose either. Please, a little faith."

"Where are we going? Better yet, why are you here?"

"Do you have your car?"

"I do," she answered.

Grady signaled to his driver and the black Lincoln Town Car disappeared out of the school parking lot. "Great. Where does one go after a spelling bee?"

"One goes home to do one's laundry."

On a Friday night? Grady thought, but did not say. His expression must have given something away because Kate shot him a look.

"Something of which I'm sure you know nothing about. Let me help," she mocked, clearly enjoying herself, "you know those clothes that magically show up, perfectly folded in your always dust-free dresser? Laundry. That's how they get there. I don't have a fairy godmother, so I do it on my own. Usually on Friday nights."

Grady was now smiling as Kate's ears turned pink again and he could tell she was pissed at herself for sharing too much information. She shook her head and walked toward her car.

He followed her and couldn't resist. "Wow, Kate. Your social calendar is really staggering. I'm wondering, coupon clipping on Saturday nights?"

"One more time, what are you doing here, Grady Malendar?" she asked, stopping in the middle of the now almost-empty parking lot to face him.

"I called your office, Sabrina said you left early for the spelling bee. I was intrigued, so I asked questions and stopped by. I didn't know you were the ringleader, announcer-person."

"Reader," Kate replied, keeping her eyes steady. She was serious, so he stopped teasing. "Reader, right. Great job by the way." He smiled.

"Thank you."

"Anyway, I really got into it and before I knew it I was on my feet clapping. It was truly one of the coolest things I've ever seen."

"And that certainly says something, Mr. Man of the World."

"Don't be mean. I'm serious."

"I can see that. It was nice of you to do that for Suki and her family. They were quite taken with you."

"Yeah, well first impressions can be deceiving." Kate's look softened, but she quickly averted her eyes. He knew how she felt, because looking at each other was sometimes too much these days. "Anyway, it's about time those vultures focused on something important, and Suki was fantastic."

"I'm surprised. You got me. Never would I have expected Grady Malendar to see the value of, let alone enjoy, a spelling bee."

Her words hit him, just a little, but he recovered. He couldn't blame her—the Grady Malendar she knew so far would have never been at a spelling bee. Hell, he would never track any woman down, let alone one that did laundry on Friday night and worked for his father. That was the persona he fed people, and even though he found himself wanting to explain, he couldn't. There was too much at stake, and while he really enjoyed Kate, he wasn't willing to risk much these days.

Even with all of that, he was still defensive, and said, "Yeah, well you don't know Grady Malendar, now do you?"

"I suppose I don't. Just what I read in the papers like the rest of the plebeians." Their eyes caught one another for just a second. "Listen, aside from the fact that we're standing in the parking lot of a not-so-desirable part of town," Kate said walking to her car, "I really need to get home. So, since you apparently sent your car away, get in. I can drop you . . . " He opened her door for her and took her bag. He could tell she was taken aback, as if she was uncomfortable with anyone helping her, let alone a man. The look on her face made him feel . . . well, let's just say that he felt like helping.

At the office she was a sophisticated, organized, pulled-uptight ball of fire. He was drawn to that, but this Kate, hair pulled back, glasses on, standing in the dim light of the parking lot—she was so genuinely vulnerable and beautiful that he was stuck for words. He wanted to reach out and touch her face, hold her . . . *Shit!* Grady closed Kate's door and tried to shake some sense into himself as he rounded the back of the car.

"Hungry?" he asked, climbing into the passenger seat.

"Um . . . I could eat. Why are we always eating?"

"You must catch me with those deep blue, 'I'm not taking care of myself or eating anything other than packaged pastry,' eyes."

She laughed and he was right back to staring at her every feature, trying to figure her out.

"I actually know a great place close to here," Grady added, putting on his seatbelt.

"You know a place to eat in this part to town?"

"I do."

"Then lead the way because this I have to see."

Kate started the car and as she turned to back out, he said, "And for your information. I do my own laundry. It wasn't the laundry that shocked me, Kate. It was your sad little Friday night ritual that threw me for a loop."

Kate snickered. "I'll bet you have a cleaning lady."

"I do, in fact. I'm not really a toilet guy." They turned left and headed farther downtown.

He could tell Kate was struggling to make sense of him, and he had to admit he liked the game. She drove as he navigated. Part of him reveled in the simplicity of the whole situation. No complications, options to weigh, or ramifications to consider. It was a meal with a smart sexy woman. They stopped in front of the glare of an obnoxious neon sign, and Grady couldn't wait to share a small piece of his world with Kate. He could tell by the look on her face that she was already surprised.

"Do I want to know where we are?"

"Lulu's Chicken and Waffles. Ever been here?" he asked, getting out of the car.

Kate opened her door before he could get around to do it for her.

"Can't wait for me to be a gentleman, can you?" Grady asked, closing the car door for her.

"It's weird. I never did the door thing well. Sorry."

Grady took his coat off and draped it over her shoulders before she had a chance to refuse. She was wearing a thin white blouse and looked cold. They walked into small, old, and family-owned Lulu's. Brandon, Lulu's tall basketball player-looking youngest son, met them at the door, shook Grady's hand, and seated them at a corner table. Grady asked when he was leaving for college, and Brandon explained he was heading to North Carolina in August. Grady congratulated him, and waived to Fred, one of the cooks who peeked his head out to say "Hi." Grady loved this place, loved the family.

"Come here a lot?" Kate smiled.

"I do." He looked at his menu.

"Grady."

Their eyes met over the red laminated rim.

"Doesn't really seem like your scene."

He put the menu down. "Well, see, Kate, that's where you're wrong. This place has great food and even better people. This is exactly my scene. Maybe I'm sharing, Kate, helping you with your research."

She looked playful and then ducked back behind her menu. There it was again, the pull to be himself, share his life.

"Okay, so what's good?" Kate asked a few moments later.

Grady peeked over the menu again. "Why do you do that?"

At his question, Kate dropped her menu, looking a bit self-conscious. "Do what?"

"Bite your thumb? Is it a nerve thing or do you do it when you're thinking?"

Kate shook her head and lifted the menu again. "I have no idea. I don't realize I'm doing it. Why do you notice these things?"

"Of course you know you're doing it. I mean, the tip of your thumb is by your teeth, near your mouth."

Kate dropped the menu, this time looking frustrated. "Look, it's late, I'm hungry. Let's just leave it at . . . I bite my thumb when I'm thinking. I don't actually bite it, but let's not go round again. There, that's why."

"Nah, I think you only do it when you're nervous. Are you nervous, Kate?"

"You do not make me nervous, Grady. Christ, there I go saying your name all the time."

"It's nice, right? Personal. I like the way you say my name, Kate."

"Cut it out. I'm not here for your entertainment. Not all of us live the carefree wealthy bachelor life. I have thoughts, I worry and I question. That's what people who work do. Life makes us bite our thumb sometimes. You, Mr. Games All Day Long, wouldn't understand."

Kate went back behind her menu while Grady tried to focus on what he was going to order, while his stomach growled at the delicious smell of fresh waffles drifting through the tiny restaurant.

Kate closed her menu and crossed her hands on top of it. "I'm having the two-piece with the collard greens and sweet tea."

"Excellent choice." Grady said and then they ordered.

As they both took a sip of the most perfect sweet tea in all of California, Grady couldn't let her last comment go.

"So let me get this straight. You grew up in a blue-collar family; you work for a living and know how to save money and balance that chip on your shoulder. You are solid and in the real world your life is incredibly complicated. I, on the other hand, was given a trust fund and therefore lack all substance and complexities? Did I get that right, Kate?"

"I didn't say you lacked complexities." Kate smiled. "Look, I'm just tired of you picking at me, commenting on my commoner uptight habits. You have no idea what it's like to be me, as I know nothing about being you. We have a common goal, helping your father get elected."

Grady laughed because sitting with her at Lulu's, he had actually forgotten all about the election.

"Don't we? Isn't that the goal here?" Kate asked.

The food arrived and Grady poured syrup over his waffles.

"I suppose it is the common goal, Kate. You're right."

"Wow, can I get that in writing?"

Kate smiled and took a bite of her chicken.

Chapter Twelve

Kate liked Senator Malendar. She believed in him as a politician, but she knew little about him as a father. From the view in her office Kate could see Grady and the senator discussing something. While the conference room glass insulated their conversation, she could tell it was heated. Grady was seated and the senator was pacing, more agitated than Kate had ever seen him since they started working his campaign. When she first looked up their exchanges were quite animated, but now it seemed as if Grady was in a trance. He nodded as the senator, his father, leaned over the table and appeared to be right in his face. His voice was raised and Grady was staring right through him. She felt like she should do something, but she didn't move. He was a grown man, they both were, and it wasn't her place. Maybe that's exactly what Grady needed, but she found herself wondering what could possibly have prompted such an outburst. Was there something she didn't know? *Had something happened?*

The senator grabbed his jacket off the high back chair as Grady stood. He smiled at his father and the senator held his shoulder in a gesture that looked forced, but reconciliatory. Both men looked as if whatever had been so heated was now resolved. Kate was curious.

She grabbed her pad and walked toward the conference room just as the senator left in the elevator. As she pushed through the heavy glass doors, Kate decided to act as if she had not seen a thing. Grady was now seated again with his back to her as she took a seat across from him.

"Okay, I've been on the phone most of the morning and I think we have things pretty set for next week. I do have some questions about the carnival on Friday. Will you be bringing a date?" Kate asked, looking down at a yellow pad.

Grady's chair swiveled to face her and he gave a smile. "To my parents' backyard carnival? Is that customary?"

"Well, it's a family-type thing. There will be a lot of families, couples, and I just wanted to know if you would be bringing someone. I want to be prepared. Maybe Maddie from the fundraiser?" Kate glanced up long enough to see Grady's smile widen.

"Yeah, that didn't really work out, but you already knew that."

"I . . . you know, you could have patched things up. There was real potential there."

Grady matched her sarcasm. "You think? Nah, it's important that my pretend girlfriend during a campaign at least know there are two senators from each state."

Kate smiled and looked down at her pad again.

"So, with Mensa Maddie gone, I'm not sure the other ladies I associate with would fit in with the carnival crowd. In other words, no, Kate, I will not be bringing a date. Can I bring my dog?"

Their eyes met on his question.

"You have a dog? How did I not know that? What kind of dog? How long . . . " Kate began to write. She wasn't sure what the hell she was writing, but she couldn't look at him sitting across from her in jeans and a long-sleeved gingham shirt rolled up above his exceptional arms. *God, he has great hands too.* Her mind was not her own, it flooded with images of Grady walking his dog, Grady on the beach, or Grady curled up next to her on a couch she didn't even own. She noticed everything about him and suddenly found herself wanting something, someone she wasn't even sure existed.

"Are you taking notes on my dog?" Grady looked over at her pad. "I just got him last night. He's a mutt, will that look bad for the campaign?"

Kate caught the sarcasm and enjoyed the distraction of returning it. "Well, actually adopting an inner-city dog may be just the thing your father needs. Does this dog have all his shots?"

"Taking him to the vet today."

"Make sure you get a license too. We don't want a scandal at this point, Mr. Malendar."

His laugh, had she ever noticed his laugh before? How his eyes squinted almost closed? Kate had to pull herself together. She flipped through her notes and tried to find some order. What was their meeting about today?

"I'll be sure to provide you with copies of all documentation."

Kate sat back in the soft leather chair.

"A dog. Did you go to the shelter? I'm surprised that wasn't a photo op."

"I do manage to sneak around occasionally, but no he was hanging around the construction site . . . er, I was just hanging out, meeting a friend for dinner. The foreman mentioned the dog, Bo, that's what I named him, had been around for a few days. I need a dog, you told me to stay closer to home, so it was meant to be, right?"

"I suppose it was . . . meant to be." Their eyes held and Kate knew he felt it too, but he didn't look nearly as petrified as she felt. Being together, their easy bantering, it was no longer annoying, it was fun, she looked forward to it, and she could tell from the look on his face that he did too. She needed to back this up. They had months left with the campaign and this was not the time for butterflies. She took out Grady's schedule for the coming week and handed it to him, hoping to redirect both of them back to the job at hand.

"Did you watch the game last night?"

Kate flipped through the first page of her schedule. "What game?"

"Um, baseball. Yankees . . . Red Socks . . . big game?"

"No, I'm not really into sports. No game. Why are we discussing baseball? We should be discussing, oh yes, here it is. The town meeting. I'm told you will be speaking, a brief question and answer—"

"What do you mean, you don't like sports?"

Kate looked at him. "I mean, I grew up surrounded by men, so I tolerate sports, but I'm certainly not watching them in my home." She showed him the town meeting on his copy as a way to redirect, and then scooted closer in to the conference table. Grady nodded at her gesture, but continued talking about sports.

"Wait, back up here. Last week, at the play, you were rambling off stats and talking current games and projections like a pro. I remember vividly because I didn't figure you for a baseball fan. How can that person not like sports?"

"Oh," Kate chuckled, "that's just the job. Governor Spellman looked bored before the play started, and I know he is a huge baseball fan. It's my job to schmooze and make people feel important. Doing my homework is part of that. Mark said your father needed his support, so I brought out the baseball. Doesn't mean that's who I am behind the curtain."

"The curtain. There's a curtain?"

"Of course there's a curtain, this whole business is a curtain of sorts, isn't it? Were you thinking you were the only one hiding yourself?"

Grady looked genuinely surprised. Maybe he didn't think she knew he was playing a game too?

"Yes, Grady, you're hiding. I'm not sure what it is you don't want me or anyone else to know, but I know your dancing Dumbo thing is a front. I also know more than I ever wanted to know about Wheaton Terriers. I can do some Ju Jitzu and I might remember how to make curry. Actually, probably not, but I can tell you what goes into it and where to find the closest Indian market." She marveled at her own odd skill-set and slid the preliminary questions Grady would need to review across the table to him.

"Wow, I'm a little speechless here. That all goes on in front of the curtain? Why?"

"Why do you insist you're shallow, self-centered and ridiculous?"

Grady said nothing.

"No answer, why am I not surprised? I just told you why I do what I do. Research. I need to get to know what people are interested in for the connection. Nothing does that quite like learning or taking an interest in their hobbies, jobs, and friends. It helps me get close."

"Oh I get it, so the cold babysitter thing you're working with me, I won't see her again? Next time you'll be in tennis whites showing me your moves?"

"No, I will not be showing you my moves. You're . . . different."

He smiled.

"I can't play tennis. Bad knees. Most of your other hobbies are dangerous or close to illegal, so I'm going to pass."

"Fine. Miss out. Do I get to see what's behind the curtain then, Kate?"

"Grady," she warned.

"Not what I meant. I mean the real you, off-hours you. I got a little at the spelling bee. I had to steal that piece though. What do you really like to do? Do you even know? You seem to spend an awful lot of time at work."

"Of course I know and . . . no, you will not get to see the real me because we have to prep for your glittering performance at your father's town meeting and you are my client. You did get to see the spelling bee and I do love doing that, but that's enough about me. We're here to discuss you."

He pressed on. "I'm not feeling very connected to you. If you're looking for me to open up, I think the best way—"

"Ah, fine." Kate closed her folder and took a sip of her water. "I crochet. I learned in college. I like very cold beer from the bottle. I clean my oven and my refrigerator when I'm stressed. I like cold pizza much more than warm pizza. I watch reruns of *Law and Order* and . . . I sing Motown, mostly Gladys Knight and the Pips, in the shower."

"Are you Gladys or the Pips?" Grady asked, not missing a beat.

"Usually, Gladys, but sometimes I can't help myself and I try to sing both. 'Midnight Train to Georgia' is especially hard to resist. You know, the train, *hoo hoo*." Kate gestured the train horn with her right hand. "The Pips have some great lines, but it's never a good idea to try their moves in the shower." She laughed and caught herself.

"Can we move on now? I need you to really focus on the top four questions. They're going to be the ones that . . . "

He just stared so she stopped.

"What?"

He kept staring.

Kate checked her teeth with her tongue. Nothing. "What?"

He smiled. "Sorry, my mind was still back in your shower. Give me a minute."

Kate was sure she blushed, and there went the temperature again.

Grady looked at the paper she had handed him. "Behind the curtain is, well it's surprising. There's a whole hell of a lot more going on than you let others believe. And I'm usually pretty good at reading people, Kate." He looked up. "I'm starting to think I had you all wrong." He held her eyes for a moment and she was suddenly aware of her chest breathing in and out. At the odd sensation, she broke eye contact and cleared her throat.

"Okay, enough of that," Grady said, and looked again at the questions, obviously trying to ease the tension that seemed to grow between them more and more these days. Kate followed suit and looked at her copy of the town hall questions. "I've made some in-roads with the YMCA and the Veteran's Youth Program. Both seem very interested in having me speak at their events and will send representatives to the town meeting," he continued.

Kate asked him a few questions and just like that they were back to business.

Chapter Thirteen

*E*veryone was already gathered around him in Mark's office when Grady noticed Kate enter and stand near the door. They had been at this for almost an hour, so Grady rubbed the bridge of his nose and finished off the last bit of coffee in his Starbuck's cup. After the news Kate had called him with last night, Grady found himself wishing there was more than coffee in his cup. There was a lull in the bickering, so Grady tried again.

"For the last damn time, I am not gay," he said quietly.

"Okay, so you say. I mean if that's your story, I'm fine with that," Stanley said, rolling his eyes.

"Well that's just great." Grady stood and made eye contact with Kate. "Stanley, I'm so happy you're fine. Can we be done here?"

"No. As much as I would like to be done, we still have a situation. These pictures—the ones on the front page of every rag in town— they sure look like you're gay and they are not going away."

Grady was about to explode.

His father put a hand on Stanley's shoulder, gesturing for him to take a seat. He looked at Grady. "Okay, so help me understand these pictures one more time."

"Christ." Grady took his seat again. "You know how Harvard

has the Hasty Pudding production? The theater department has celebrities get in on the acts? Do you know what I'm talking about?"

"Yes," his father said.

"Okay, some guys at Stanford were mocking them. Putting it up
on the Internet, sending them their version of the Harvard tradition, like a *Saturday Night Live* sketch. It was actually pretty clever.
Literary references and the like. Anyway, one of the guys in their
theater department was in my frat. He needed a bigger guy and
asked for my help."

"And you didn't think this would come back and—"

"Dad, I was twenty years old. I was in college. It seemed harm-
less. Did I think some asshole would profit from it over ten years
later? No, I did not."

"Right, well that's exactly what has happened. I've told you
your whole life that we need to be careful, more careful than the
average family because people find things to—"

"Careful, we need to be careful, or just not get caught? Which is
it, because I'm not sure any of us are always careful, are we, Dad?"
Grady could feel the anger flood his face.

"Don't start," his father warned.

Grady knew the entire room could feel the unspoken happening between them, but he was suddenly fed up with the double
standard.

Senator Malendar continued, "Okay, this is an issue and we
need to deal with it. It's not time to play poor Grady, neglected
son."

Grady glared, but said nothing.

Kate spoke up. "Excuse me, sir. I don't mean to interrupt, but
I've gone over the information and I think I have an idea." Mark
looked a little nervous, as if he had no idea what Kate was going to
say. Grady didn't either, but he hoped whatever it was would put
this crap to bed quickly.

The senator gestured for her to share her thoughts.

Kate walked toward them. "So, there's nothing shameful about
being gay."

"Jesus Christ, I'm not—"

Kate put her hand up to stop Grady. "Let me finish. As a campaign, we are offended that the other side is making this out to be a scandal. Explain that it was a spoof, a skit, and then turn it on its head. Grady Malendar respects the gay community and is in no way threatened by an innocent skit. He and the senator both find it absurd and insulting to their gay friends, and the community as a whole, that his opponent would use such obviously innocent and fun pictures as something disgraceful."

All eyes were on Kate. No one said a word, and she continued. "This could lead to an awareness campaign, acceptance of alternative lifestyles. The gay community, at least the out and progressive gay community, are a large part of that youthful vote you are looking for, sir. This isn't an embarrassment, it's a young man not intimidated or homophobic."

It was quiet for a moment longer and then Stanley crossed the room and hugged Kate, who looked shocked and a little squeamish. Grady had wanted to punch Stanley before, but this moment was really testing his control.

"Yes, I don't know why I didn't see it first," Stanley said, clearly relieved.

"Because you were too busy preparing me for some kind of homosexual exorcism there, Stan-ley. Super cool that you're all pro-gay now. Gotta love politics!" Grady said, shaking his head and laughing at the stupid insanity of the world he grew up in. "It's a great plan, Kate. You really are a wonder, perfectly suited for this zoo." He stood and didn't care that she looked hurt. "Now, are there any other tidbits of my personal life we need to comb over, or can I get the hell out of this cage? I have things to do, real things."

The senator shook Kate's hand while he was saying, "Sure, Grady. Thanks for—"

That was all Grady heard as the conference room door closed behind him.

Kate finished her meeting with Mark, and spent the majority of the morning putting the finishing touches on the statement that was read at a two o'clock press conference. Grady would ideally have been there, but the senator decided he would address the media himself and spare his son any further hassle. It was a kind gesture Kate didn't often see in politics. The response to the senator's statement was almost instantaneous, and Bracknell spent the rest of the day fielding calls of support and donations to the senator's campaign. It was a good day. Kate accepted praise for her work, but she was exhausted and still felt restless and maybe a little angry. She had offered a suggestion, one that worked, and Grady still found a way to cut her off at the knees. Kate closed her computer, rubbed her eyes, and was finished for the night. She shut her office light off and headed out as her phone rang. She knew the number and let it go to voice mail.

Kate pulled out of the garage and thought that maybe she would pick up Chinese for dinner. For the first time in a while, toaster food didn't sound good. Her phone rang again. Same number.

"Katherine Galloway," she answered.

"I'm sorry." Grady said in a tone she had not heard since this project had started. She said nothing. "It's not your fault and it wasn't fair of me to snap like that. I'm not going to waste your time making excuses. I'm simply calling to apologize. I'm sorry, Kate."

Kate swallowed a lump in her throat as she pulled up to a red light.

"You certainly don't need to apologize to me, Mr. Malendar. I understand how frustrating . . . "

"Don't! I'm sorry. Please don't start that shit with me. Your Mr. Malendar routine. I can't take it."

"Grady, it's not a big deal. You're entitled to snap. This is a crazy time. I get it. You don't owe me anything. It's fine."

The line was silent.

"I do need to discuss this with you at some point. Your father's statement worked, but we need to be on the same page if there are any follow up questions from the press. We can talk about it in the morning. Have a good night."

"Would you like to have dinner?"

"Excuse me?"

"I'm asking if you would like to eat, Kate."

"I'm not sure that's such good idea."

"Come on, let me take you to dinner. You said you have to discuss today's events with me. I'll buy you a meal and you can give me my lines. It will be very . . . front of the curtain. I promise."

"It's probably best if you just lay low at least for tonight. Where on God's earth could we go for dinner tonight that wouldn't create a media frenzy, positive or negative? I know this is ridiculous, but it's still a situation. The press will be all over you, waiting for your next conquest. Male or female."

Grady laughed and Kate smiled into her phone.

"That's why you're perfect. No one would ever believe that you and I were . . . " He stopped mid-sentence, and must have realized his comment was a veiled insult.

"I don't even want to know what that means," she said.

Kate felt her face warm and she discovered she actually wanted to go to dinner with him. She wanted to see him. "Grady, thank you for the invitation, but I'll just talk with you tomorrow." She hung up before he could say anything else and began to hyperventilate as she rounded the corner to her apartment. Suddenly she was filled with a strange intrusive weight. She wanted her strudel, strudel was just fine.

Her phone rang.

"What?" she said in her most unprofessional voice.

"Please, just listen. I know I can be a pain in the ass. Have dinner with me and we can put this behind us? I'll be on my best behavior. How about I cook at your place?"

Kate said nothing, this guy was incredible . . . the balls. *My place, would we call it a place? What are you doing Kate?*

"Kate?"

She took a deep breath. "Fine. My apartment in an hour. I have the basics, but you'll need to bring anything extra to make dinner. I don't cook."

She could feel him smiling through the phone. "Absolutely, don't worry about a thing. Just text me the address. I'll bring everything. Hey, Kate, what kind of beer do you like?"

"Well, that depends on what you're making." *Flirting? Jesus, Kate, are you flirting now?* "I don't eat mushrooms," she said, and then hung up before she was stupid enough to say anything else. Her heart was racing, her hands were clammy, and she was in trouble. *Shit.*

Chapter Fourteen

*W*hat was she thinking? She didn't even have a real home to cook dinner in. Boxes, strategically arranged boxes, that's what she had, and Grady Malendar was arriving any minute. She must have slipped into some sort of exhaustion coma because she truly didn't care. Her hair was still wet and she moved her lips, feeling the Chapstick she'd put on after getting out to the shower. Everything was heightened. She noticed the fade in her jeans and the shine of her toenail polish. She remembered the salon lady saying the bright red polish she had chosen was called Lady is a Tramp. Her mother, who was in the pedicure chair next to her, had snickered and clearly disapproved. Kate decided then and there that the *Lady is a Tramp* would be her "go to" color from then on out.

Kate was hovering, pacing, not sure what to do, and then the doorbell rang. She didn't even bother to look in the peek hole. Grady stood in the open door, with several paper bags hanging from those damn arms again, and that smile. He was trouble in a linen shirt, but she stepped back anyway and let him walk right into her insanity.

"Wow, I love what you've done with the place," he said, taking the bags around some boxes and into the kitchen.

"I'm still unpacking." Kate said, grabbing the beer dangling from his full hands and suddenly realizing she was hungry as she saw the bread peeking out of the bag.

"I didn't realize you just moved in."

"Yeah, well . . . beer?" Kate asked as she put the bottles in the fridge.

"Please." He began unpacking the bags. Fresh vegetables. She hadn't seen those in a very long time. Wasn't she supposed to be tending to him? Well, not him exactly, but his image? Why was she beginning to feel he was trying to take care of her?

"So you and your husband have been—"

"Oh no, we are not jumping into that. You promised food. I need food and we are here to discuss potential questions following the senator's statement, remember?"

Grady nodded. "Can I have one question? Just one? I make my own marinara sauce. Come on."

Kate sighed and gave in. "Fine, one question."

"There's a little pressure here. Hold on. And this doesn't count as my question—do you chop?"

"I suppose." He handed her one of the knives he'd pulled out of the block and gently guided her in front of a cutting board full of carrots and onions.

"Great, you chop," he said wiping his hands on a towel. He grabbed his beer and sat up on the counter. *What are you, five?* she thought, but did not say. She had not sat on a counter in a long time, probably since she was a kid. It looked like fun. Grady was nothing if not fun. She envied that part of him. It seemed so simple in theory, to just have fun. She set her focus back to chopping—it wasn't something she did often, so she actually needed to pay attention.

"Okay, here goes. It's a two-part question."

She stopped chopping and looked at him.

"Like a compound word, two parts."

She was walking a fine line. She barely knew him and yet she found herself comfortable sharing at least part of herself. She said nothing, didn't protest, but didn't encourage, and returned to the cutting board.

"Right, here we go." Grady took a sip of his beer and continued. "I'm assuming you're divorced. How long have you and . . . "

Kate laughed, she couldn't help it. "Nick," she said filling in Grady's implied blank.

"Nick, right. How long have you and Nick been divorced?" Still chopping and not looking at him because her heart was racing, Kate said, "Yes, we are divorced. Just over two years."

It was silent for a moment, the only sound was the knife slicing through carrots.

"Part two. Have you lived anywhere else since you moved out?"

Kate set the knife down. "Oh, aren't you cute?"

"Well, my mom really thinks so, but . . . "

"You don't need to dance around me, Grady. Just ask what you need to ask. Have I been living out of boxes for almost two years? Yes." Kate glanced quickly at him and then returned to chopping. "Ever been divorced?" she asked.

"No." Probably the first one-word response she had ever heard out of his mouth.

"It's not fun." She was finished with her task. Kate gestured for the towel from Grady and wiped her hands. "Done."

He hopped down from the counter and reviewed her work. "Nice chopping. Were you in love with him? I mean, of course you were, are you still?" With that he moved to his cans of tomatoes without looking at her.

For one moment Kate thought about laughing him off, but it was a genuine question and there was not a hint of sarcasm. She wasn't sure why she answered. His two-part question was over. She didn't need to say a word, but she did anyway. Maybe it was partially for herself. "Yes, I was in love. But no, I no longer have any feelings for Nick."

"Hmm," he said, and began sautéing the carrots and onions. "So what do you think—"

"Grady," she warned.

"Right, too personal. Hand me that olive oil."

They ate and she tried to steer clear of anything beyond typical first-date questions. Wait, this wasn't a date, she thought, but then admitted that's what it felt like. A first date, maybe even more than that. He was in her home, cooking them dinner. That was a date, all things considered, so why didn't she hate it? Why was she asking him if he wanted ice cream instead of showing him the door?

Grady talked a little about the traveling he did after he graduated and Kate talked about her job.

"Why do you give it so much?" he asked.

"What do you mean?"

"Your job, that place, the people you work with? Why is it all so important? I mean, there's more to life than a job, right?"

"Well, I suppose there is, but I need to get paid. Besides, I love my job. I need to be there and I give what's required."

"I'd say you give it quite a bit more than what's required."

"Doing my best work is important to me. I would think as my client, you would appreciate that."

Grady smiled. "I'm not your client and I get that a job well done is important, but what about your life, the rest of you?"

"What does that mean? My life is . . . great, it's fantastic, really. You should have seen me a couple of years ago." Kate attempted a laugh and messed with the napkin in her lap.

"I would have liked to have seen you a couple of years ago."

What the hell does that mean? He's into nut jobs? "Why?"

"I don't know, maybe you were a little more reckless, free?"

She looked at him and could not figure out where this was going. "Reckless, by your definition? I can guarantee I've never been reckless. I was born grown up. I'm sorry that bores you, but I'm probably the perfect antidote to your free spirit."

She smiled hoping they would move on.

"You seem very . . . in control. I'm intrigued by that."

"Don't be."

"But I am. You're so wound up and sort of obsessed with creating pictures for other people and yourself, maybe. I understand being driven, but it feels like you're hiding, and you know what, Kate?"

She was annoyed now. "Oh great, another pearl of wisdom?"

"I think you want to be found. I think beneath all this, this pencil skirt, tightrope-walking, you're probably breathtaking. I'm guessing you're brilliant when you're flustered and spinning out of control."

She didn't know what to say. Kate felt warm and he was looking at her like he saw something she had never imagined being. She did what she always did in uncomfortable situations, she dismissed it.

"Yeah, thank you for that, but you invited yourself to dinner so we could discuss . . . wait, why did you come for dinner?"

Grady laughed, and Kate still had that wrinkle between her brows.

"I think it was just dinner and something about questions that may come up. I wanted to have dinner with you and you said we couldn't go anywhere in public because I'm a pariah now, so I came here and made you dinner. How was it by the way?"

"Well whatever the reason, I'm not paying you for therapy or an image makeover. You're paying me, remember? So maybe we should use this time productively. Let's review the statement your father gave earlier today. It's brief. Nothing too painful." Kate stood and as she brushed by Grady on her way to her briefcase and the statement, work to quiet her mind, he took her hand. Not a grab, a hold. His fingers traced her palm and interlaced with hers. She stopped dead, but kept looking toward her briefcase, willing it to rescue her from warmth she knew she should not want and could not have.

"Kate, the dinner, the sauce, how was it?"

She looked at their hands and then at him.

"It was— it tasted— it was very good. A great sauce. Maybe you can give me the recipe. I used to enjoy . . . "

His thumb moved over the palm of her hand and the hum of energy was too much. Kate pulled her hand away and finally made it to her briefcase.

"Careers are cold if that's all you have, Kate. I've seen it first hand."

She turned, folder in hand. Her pulse was pounding as she found herself straining to control her emotions. "That may be, Grady, but your career never wakes you up in the middle of the night to tell you it doesn't love you anymore." *Shit*. "Can we please do something productive here? I don't want to drink beer and play let's hold hands. I want to work, work may not be your favorite thing, but I like what I do, I understand it. Now—" She sat and handed him a printed paper. "Give it a read through. At the top are the highlights of the senator's statement. Below that are possible follow-up questions you may receive over the next couple of weeks. After that this should die down, but whatever you do, if it's brought up again, keep it casual and don't get pissed." She looked at him, hoping Grady couldn't see the vulnerability, her need to hide behind the work. She hated that he was right about her, but he was.

"Sorry, yes, this looks good. General. I'm glad you didn't mention names. No sense in dragging perfectly normal people into my shit storm. I'm dialed in. It's good," he said and took a deep breath that allowed Kate's own breathing to return.

When there was nothing safe left to say, Kate handed Grady his jacket. Thanking her, he leaned in to kiss her on the cheek. It was unexpected, and when Kate turned away, she ended up turning into him and his lips gently slid beyond her cheek to the corner of her mouth. Grady's arms stilled her and he gently moved back to her cheek, kissed her gently there, and she felt the room spin. His closeness made her feel like she was slipping, easing into a warm bath. He lingered by her cheek and then his lips moved to her ear as he pulled away.

"Kate." It was just her name, she'd heard it a million times before, but his voice, the dinner, the relaxed comfort of his body, it was all unnerving. She pulled back and Grady seemed a bit stunned himself.

"Grady. Christ, why do I keep saying your name? It's you. Your strange name game is rubbing off on me."

At that, Grady smiled and Kate opened her door.

"Thanks for dinner. It was really, well, it was nice. Thank you."

Grady moved past her to leave. "You're welcome, Ms Galloway. Always a pleasure meeting with you." His thousand-watt smile was back and Kate couldn't help herself, she laughed at his formality. "I will see you tomorrow at what should be an incredibly exciting carnival in honor of my now hip and cool father. Is this a casual, wear-shorts type of thing?"

"Yes, there will be rides, bands, the more casual you and the senator look, the better."

"Got it. Maybe I'll even bust out a baseball cap, eh. Really commoner myself up? Although we are in snooty Pasadena, so it will be a struggle to leave my Rolls Royce at home."

Kate laughed again. "Do you own a baseball hat?"

"I own several actually, and for the record, I do not own a Rolls Royce. Will you be wearing, eh, casual wear, Kate? Shorts?"

Kate swallowed and gripped the doorknob. "I will."

"And suddenly there's a reason to show up. Goodnight, Kate." Grady smiled and walked away.

"Goodnight," she said to no one as she closed her door. She leaned with her back to the door and slid into a seated position on the floor. Looking out over her sea of boxes, Kate could still smell Grady's sauce—he'd put the leftovers in the refrigerator—and something shifted. Suddenly her space felt infused with him, garlic, spices, great bread, and his laughter, their laughter. Kate was sure she wouldn't be able to smell anything else for days, and she wasn't even sure she wanted to. Grady, her evening with him, lingered, and even though he was no longer in front of her, the shift stayed.

It happened again. *Well, of course it did, you idiot, you went to her house for Christ sake!* This was nuts, but at the door, as he was leaving, he wanted to pull her into his body, taste her lips. Actually, from the moment he stepped into her disheveled space, he wanted to pull her into his arms, protect her. Which was ridiculous, because Kate wasn't some shrinking flower, she was a force all her own, but in her space, faded jeans and laughing, he wanted her. It was primal, weird, caveman kind of crap, and Grady didn't know where to put those feelings. He remembered being at Marcie Probst's birthday party when he was in the sixth grade. That was the birthday party where, closed away in some closet, he figured out girls were very different than boys. That adolescent moment when things changed, and the boy in him, the future man, took center stage. It felt like that, standing with Kate, her face soft and relaxed. Her bare feet, rumpled hair, all of it called to him, just like Marcie's glossy bubble gum-scented lips.

Christ, he wasn't a child anymore. He was a—what was he now? He was in the shadows, pretending, and something about the light in her eyes made him want to pull back his own curtain, maybe even roll down the windows and kiss a girl.

As he slowed at the traffic light, and turned left up to his house, Grady knew that wasn't possible. He was in too deep with his current life, he had responsibilities, and for better or for worse, he would honor those and keep his secrets safe. It was the only way. So no matter how much he wanted to climb into Kate Galloway's eyes, run his fingers along the delicate line of her neck, he couldn't. It would never work. Women always wanted more, and Kate was definitely a woman who wanted it all. She was relationship material and those never worked if they started with a lie.

Chapter Fifteen

Movie night was a tradition dating back to junior year of high school. Any time Kate and Reagan didn't have dates, which was often, they would order pizza and rent movies based on the theme for the evening. When she returned from New York, they added a few other worthy friends— Beth, Reagan's soon to be sister-in-law, and Poppy, who also went to school with Kate and Reagan. Poppy was now an attorney and stupid in love with Kate's older brother, Neil, who of course, was oblivious. All four women took turns hosting, and tonight was Kate's night.

"Kate? Everyone's waiting for you. Did you get lost on your way to the dish towels?" Reagan was always funny, but Kate didn't look up. "Kate," she tried again. "Kate, damn it! Why the hell are you staring into the washing machine?"

"It's interesting to note that when the washer hits the spin cycle my very distinct pieces of clothing—things that I recognize during most of the wash—all spin out of control and mash into one big blur." She was still staring down into the glass top of her washing machine, the swirl, so Reagan walked up next to her and stared into the swirling clothes too.

"Uh huh," Reagan said after a little more than a minute. The concern in Reagan's voice was strong enough to penetrate Kate's hypnotic gaze.

"Maybe I'm finally slipping over the edge, but suddenly this washer is a metaphor for my life." Kate finally said.

"Okay. Metaphors are good. What are we looking at here, honey?"

"Hey, guys are you weaving those dish towels?" Beth's voice came sailing around the corner.

Reagan looked up and grabbed the towels off the dryer. "Here they are," Reagan shoved them in her direction. "Give us a minute. We'll be right in."

"Oh, yeah sure. Everything okay?" Beth asked.

"Yup, we're great. Just checking on the laundry."

Beth disappeared, the cycle stopped spinning, and Kate looked up at her best friend.

"Kate, are you okay?" The concern was growing in Reagan's face, Kate could see it.

She had to rein it in. She wasn't going crazy. Was she? "After I left Nick I really thought I'd sorted it all out, you know?"

"Honey, you did. You've been doing great."

"Then why am I still living in boxes? Do you ever wonder that? I mean do any of you, when you come over for movie night, when it's my night? Do you wonder why I'm still living in boxes almost two years later? Do you guys talk about it when you leave?"

"Kate, divorce is hard, and no, we don't talk about it. It's just the way it is. We don't give a crap if you're still living in boxes. We love you."

"I know, and I didn't care either, but then he came over and made dinner and asked about—"

"Wait, Nick came over?"

"No, Grady. Grady came over and for some reason the boxes seemed weird. He made dinner. I chopped. A real dinner, and we had conversation. It felt like, well it felt like someone opened a window or pulled up the blinds. All of a sudden the boxes didn't fit. Does that make sense?"

"Oh sweetie, it does. It really does. Maybe you're outgrowing the boxes. Maybe you're ready to—"

"No, I'm not ready for anything."

Reagan said nothing as they turned their backs and leaned on the washing machine. "Maybe a dining room table, but that's it," Kate said.

"Okay, well a table is a great start."

"Reagan?"

"Yes?" She touched Kate's arm.

"Stop talking to me like I'm standing on a god-damn ledge."

They laughed.

"Just give it time. One box at a time. It's great that you had dinner though, right?" Reagan asked.

"No, it's not great. I was doing just fine with the boxes and my Toaster Strudel. I don't want to know what dinner tastes like here in my little box cocoon."

Reagan laughed and put her arm around Kate.

"Well, let's go watch Channing Tatum take off his clothes in the comfort of the boxes."

Kate finally looked at her.

"The pizza just arrived." Reagan continued to lure.

Kate smiled and decided that she might not be skilled at picking great men, but she lucked out in the friend department. "Lead the way."

Grady didn't often have dinner at his family's house, but his mother had called him herself to ask if he would join them and his sister Kara for "some family time before the big carnival tomorrow." Grady was in the car when she called, and he nearly ran off the road. How many people were invited to family time before the big carnival? But it didn't matter if he thought it was too much. His mother wanted him there, so he would be there.

The entire dining room was covered with mailers and large stacks of pre-printed labels when Grady arrived. Kara was sitting at the far end, by the window, already well into a glass of wine. He looked at her and she rolled her eyes.

"What the hell is this?" he asked, and Kara smiled a fake, large, what they both called her "campaign smile," and said nothing.

Grady's mother came through the double doors that connected the kitchen and the dining room. "Grady! You're here. Perfect. I thought we would start with you on labels and Kara on the postage machine."

Grady set the flowers that he'd brought for his mother down on top of a stack of labels.

"Oh careful, of that. Here let me put those in some water," his mom said, as she took them and promptly flew back into the kitchen.

Grady looked at the table and then at Kara. "What the hell is this?"

"Not sure. I can't tell if she's drunk, but she wanted to have us over for an . . . " Kara put her perfectly manicured fingers up in quotes, "old fashioned stuffing party." She dropped her hands with a huff. "I think she's finally lost it. You know, her elevator has never exactly been fast, as Nana used to say, but I'm pretty sure it no longer even goes to the top." Grady smiled at the reference to their favorite grandmother, and looked at the contents of the table. He remembered, as a kid, stuffing envelopes for their father, but they weren't kids anymore.

"Who the hell still stuffs envelopes?" Grady asked, picking up a stack of envelopes and flipping through them.

"Yeah, I don't know, Grady, but dad went to pick up the Chinese food. Since when does he get his own food? I feel like we've been invited to a hopped-up rerun of *Leave it to Beaver*." She got up to refill her glass.

"Does that make me Beaver?" Grady asked, and Kara laughed in the kitchen.

Shit. He didn't have time for this.

When Bindi Malendar, senator's wife and Grady's increasingly delusional mother, glided back out into the dining room, Grady braced himself.

"Thank you so much, dear. The flowers are beautiful." She said placing the large crystal vase, now brimming with deep purple freesia, his mother's favorite, on the large round table in the entryway. "So what do you think about my plan?" she asked, smiling a spring picnic smile.

Grady turned to her and tried to say this as carefully as he could. "Mom, why are we doing this? Dad has staff and volunteers for this now."

He clearly failed, because his mother looked shocked, although he was never sure what was real or fake anymore. "I just thought it might be fun for the two of you to participate. You know, help get your father re-elected. Like old times." Grady couldn't tell if she was drunk either. He almost hoped she was.

"Mom, I've *been* campaigning for dad. Giving speeches. I'm not going to sit here and stuff envelopes the night before I have to put on my best face at the carnival thing tomorrow."

"Me neither," Kara said, walking back into the room as if on cue.

Their mother sat down looking sad and trying to work up her fake cry. Grady touched her shoulder.

"He's worried, he thinks he might lose. I just wanted to do something to help," she said, turning her glassy eyes to Grady and Kara.

"I understand that he's nervous, but this is not the way to help, Mom. His campaign is working really hard to pull this one out for him. Everything will be fine." He looked over at Kara, who flashed him the smile again. She was absolutely no help. "So, why don't we get this cleaned up and put away? I'll drop it by the office on Monday and the volunteers can do these."

His mother acquiesced and they set the table for dinner. Even with Chinese, his mother insisted on using china. Grady looked at Kara and often wondered how either of them were even remotely normal.

After dinner and endless talk about television spots and projections, Grady walked Kara to her car, and when he returned, both of his parents were asleep on the couch. His mother's head rested in her father's lap. They always looked human to him when they were asleep. Just an average couple curled up together. No lights, no cameras, and no phony homogenized bullshit put forward to lure in as many votes as possible without ruffling too many feathers. When they were awake and back to being Senator and Mrs. Malendar, the human part was buried. It was hard to believe the woman standing by her father at the podium was the same woman who used to chase him through the sprinklers when he was three, or let him fingerpaint on the patio until the housekeeper carried on in Spanish and told them both to get out.

She was the first person he would call when he needed something, had a story to tell, or got in trouble. Except for the day he was a junior in high school and ditched class. He came home early, unexpected. He would never be able to tell her what happened that day, so a secret was born between them and their relationship changed. His family changed. Lies and secrets, even just one, had a way of wiggling into even the tightest of bonds and shaking a foundation. Grady kissed his mother on the cheek, dimmed the living room lights, and locked the front door on his way out.

Bo was at the door, tail wagging, when Grady got home, and he had to admit it was nice having someone waiting for him. While Bo ate, Grady checked his email. Eric, his friend from college, had texted him earlier. There were some last minute "hiccups," that's what he called them, but from the looks of the email sent about an hour ago, everything was ironed out. By early next week the project would be done. This one had been a long time coming, their biggest yet.

Bo joined Grady on the couch. It was nice having a dog, calming. Grady wondered what other simple pleasures in life he had been missing. He wanted something. He wasn't sure what yet, but something felt different. Grady got up to get some popcorn when his phone vibrated.

"Hello, Kate. Is this you calling to tell me, lights out?" Kate laughed and Grady's pulse picked up.

"Nope, just calling to touch base and let you know that according to the latest polls, your father is already up a point."

"Really? That's great news. I left their house a little while ago and my mother was going a little Valley of the Dolls on me, so I hope someone called them."

"I think Stanley and Mark are on a conference call with your father now."

"And you were assigned the lucky job of calling me, your charge."

"No, no one told me to call. I just thought you would want to know." Kate hesitated. "I wanted to call, see how you were."

"I'm good, Kate. Sitting here with my dog and practicing being a homebody. How are you?" *Did you want to come over and climb into my bed? Yeah, probably best to leave that part out.*

"That is very good to hear. I'm good. I just finished watching Channing Tatum take his clothes off."

Grady almost choked on his water. "Is that so? Is he still there?"

"Nope. My friend Reagan, who wants to meet you by the way, and my other two girlfriends, took *Magic Mike* with them. Girls' movie night, it's a tradition."

"I see. Kate, have you been drinking?"

The line was silent.

"Maybe a little. I'm not working. Mark just called and I thought I would just let you know. It's not like I'm drunk or anything."

Grady laughed because her words were just a bit slurry and he wished he were there to witness Tipsy Kate. "Relax, Kate. Having a good time is not a crime. Even for you."

"Right. Exactly. Anyway, I'll let you go. I'm happy that the numbers are heading in the right direction." There she went again making everything about the campaign. Even with a few drinks and *Magic Mike*, Kate's default was always work, and for some reason that made Grady sad.

"Okay. Well, thank you for calling," Grady said.

"Sure. Goodnight."

"Goodnight, Kate."

Just as he was going to hang up, she cleared her throat and said, "Hey, Grady? Are you still there?"

He smiled. "I am, Kate."

"Oh, well, I was thinking maybe I should get some furniture. You know, start with something small. Maybe a table."

His smiled deepened and his heart squeezed in his chest. She was letting him in—just a peek behind the curtain.

"I think that's a great idea, Kate."

"Yeah, well we'll see. Goodnight."

"Sleep well, Kate." She hung up and Grady had a feeling he knew what it was he wanted, and not just in his bed.

Chapter Sixteen

The Malendar's Pasadena home was huge. White columns in front, football fields of lawn, tiny balconies and a circular drive, huge. She had not yet stepped foot inside, but she would bet money there were chandeliers, lots of chandeliers. Kate had worked with a lot of successful people, she had assisted Mark on a couple of corporate big-wig projects, dug a politician out of a scandal, she had once even worked on a civic campaign for a prince, but she had never seen anything like Senator Malendar's home. It wasn't even a home, would this be an estate? Kate had no idea as she pulled her Prius up to one of the three valet stations.

"Welcome to our backyard carnival! Please check in up the stairs," the female valet said, blonde ponytail swinging as she handed Kate a round plastic tag and hopped behind the wheel of her car. Kate laughed a bit at the silliness of calling something like this "our backyard carnival," but simple everyman was the strategy, and Kate supposed technically this *was* the senator's backyard. She turned to show the valet how to work her car, but she had gone. A young guy in a red and white striped shirt and suspenders gestured her to the white marble stairs, and Kate had to admit she was awestruck. She wondered if anyone could tell she bought her shorts on sale at The Gap.

Should she have worn her hair down? Maybe more makeup was in order, even though it was an early evening carnival? Just as she started feeling stupid, a couple pulled up in a Rolls Royce, a god damn Rolls Royce. *Stop staring and get it together, Kate.*

She walked through the double front doors and there it was, what Kate imagined was the first of many chandeliers. She smiled, checked her bag with the coat check, and received another token that she slid into her back pocket. Her shorts were navy blue and she wore a silky blouse with lots of swirling colors. She thought it looked festive, fun, at least she did until she saw the woman in head-to-toe Gucci who walked past her. She was used to this and not sure why she all of a sudden felt insecure. It may have been that she was in Grady's parents' home, but she didn't want to let her mind go there, so she walked through the open back patio doors onto a marble platform that had stairs on either side cascading down to a green lawn that looked like something from *Pride and Prejudice*. Kate tried not to gape, but this was really something. The lawn was alive with rides, the smell of food on a stick, gourmet food of course, and people, lots and lots of people. Kate saw Javier talking to Elaine, Bracknell's photographer, who was staging her first few shots. Seeing them reminded her she had a job to do. This wasn't a dream, or a movie set. Where was Grady Malendar, her charge, as he'd called himself?

She grabbed a frozen lemonade and walked down the stairs to her right. She checked the kissing booth first, which seemed like a place Grady might hang out. She laughed to herself.

"Careful, Kate. No laughing on the job." She turned to see Grady in red chinos and a denim shirt, untucked and rolled at the sleeves. He was holding a corn dog. She looked down and he was wearing Converse. No Gucci, not an ostentatious thing about him.

"Technically, I'm not working unless you decide to man the kissing booth. Is that a real corn dog, or some sort of handmade sausage wrapped in organic corn cake?"

Grady laughed. "It's legit. Frozen when they got here and I saw the guy fry them in a vat of grease. Want a bite?" He held it out to her.

She was going to decline, but fun danced in his eyes and she wanted . . . well, she wanted a little fun. She leaned forward and bit into the corn dog. It was incredible, very carnival, and authentic. She moaned as the warm juicy bite filled her mouth. Kate was hungry, she realized, and then she mumbled, "It's delicious," as she finished chewing. Grady's eyes were fixed on her mouth when she looked up, and Kate wondered if she had made too much of enjoying his—*Oh, God!*

"You have mustard. It's right—"

Kate lifted her hand at the same time she touched her tongue to the corner of her mouth. It was just a lip, and a tongue, but Grady's gaze stayed on her mouth and she was suddenly uncomfortable. First she had made porn sounds over a corndog and now she was licking the corners of her mouth. She was certain her cheeks flushed once again. Kate swallowed and stepped back.

"Thank, thanks." Kate looked around at the crowd, wondered if anyone saw what was probably nothing, but for some reason felt a lot like something. A hot and dangerous something. Her tongue instinctively touched her bottom lip and Kate quickly pulled it back into her mouth. This was ridiculous.

"Now about the kissing booth," Grady said, and then laughed at the look on Kate's face.

"What?"

"Just wanted to bring you back, looked like you went somewhere there. Kissing booth, I will not be manning the kissing booth, so you are off duty. I intend to be on my best behavior."

Kate looked at him a bit sideways. "Really? Not going to climb on any rides, get into some carny gambling or a fistfight?"

"Nope. Now there is a fire breather over by the barbecue, that may be something to try."

Kate laughed.

"That's a great sound."

"The music?" she asked.

"Your laugh."

Their eyes locked and Kate wasn't sure what was going on. Grady was charming, true statement, but these days she was immune to charm. Was he flirting, or just naturally this way? Whatever it was, Kate felt like an inquisitive child. She wanted to step closer, get a better look, figure it out. Ignoring his comment, she started walking.

"Please tell me there's cotton candy," she said over her shoulder.

"Hello? What's a carnival without cotton candy?" He pointed to the red and white food tents and a few moments later, a slender man with a driving cap handed Kate a paper cone piled high with a pink sugary cloud. She grabbed a piece between two fingers and closed her eyes as the sweet crystals melted onto her tongue. Oh Christ, her tongue again. Never had every damn thing felt so seductive.

The sun began to set and Kate was thrilled with the turnout and the pictures Elaine was able to get for the senator's website. Kate was wrapping things up and laughing at Javier's version of a circus carney.

"Step right up, step right up," he called out to the crowd, smiling joyfully.

Kate felt the wind pick up, and as Javier and the other crew left, she turned to see Grady staring at her. Her entire body felt his look. It was electric. Like one of those glances across a crowded room that only ever happened in the movies. There he was, looking at her like . . . like a man looked at a woman that was not his PR professional. Kate suddenly felt naked. Her mind took over and she wondered if anyone else saw what was in Grady's look. This needed to stop. She walked over and stood next to him smiling, as the guests moved toward their cars.

"Stop," she said quietly.

"Sorry. I'm just—"

"Grady, listen. We have to work together and—"

"Three and a half months."

"Excuse me?"

"Three and a half months, that's what's left of our working relationship. Election Day and then we no longer work together."

Kate tilted her head to look at him. "Okay, right, well you said it. We have three and a half months and it's great that we are getting along, but this can't be whatever, whatever that look, that thing you did with your eyes— It just can't be."

Grady seemed to be trying for hurt or put off, but he quickly had a smile on his face.

"Yeah, that too," she pointed to his expression. "That 'Isn't Kate entertaining' smile. Cut that out too."

"I didn't mean to make you uncomfortable. It's just that you're kind of dazzling tonight, I mean really, flushed cheeks and out of your comfort zone gorgeous."

Kate looked toward her car. "I'm not uncomfortable," she said barely above a whisper, walking to the driveway.

Grady stepped closer to her, but this time kept his distance.

"Where the hell did I park?"

Grady took her keys out of his pocket and held them in his open palm.

"The valet closed up about an hour ago and left the remaining keys with us." Kate took her keys from his hand and damn it all, she could feel the pulse. It was as if he was plugged in somewhere. She had never felt that kind of energy. It was time to leave.

"Right, okay, great." Kate spotted her car parked at the end of the circular drive. "So, this was—" she looked toward the house, anywhere but at him, because Grady was staring right at her with his soft evening, just-been-to-a-carnival eyes, and she couldn't take it for one more minute. "This was great, a huge success, and I think we—"

He was smiling at her again.

"Oh Christ, I'm going. I'll see you tomorrow."

"Do you want me to walk you to your car?"

"No!" she snapped and he laughed. "No. Thank you, Grady. I can find my way to the end of the drive. Even one this size." She smiled and turned to leave before he offered or said anything else.

"Kate?"

Dear, God. Please get me to my car before I jump this man and ruin my entire career and destroy my poor sad healing heart. God, are you listening?

Kate looked over her shoulder. Grady had his hands in his pockets and the light of the moon was on them both, painting the scene as if what was coursing through her body needed any more encouragement.

She tried for casual. "Yeah?"

"I had a great time."

She stopped walking toward her car and turned to face him. It was such a simple thing to say, but that was just it. Grady never did anything the simple way. Standing there in the moonlight, he had a good time, no a *great* time.

Kate smiled, certain she was a safe distance away. "I did too. It was great. Thank you."

"Any time."

Kate turned toward her car again.

"Hey, Kate."

She turned again, still smiling. "Yes, Grady?" she said playfully. Lord, she thought she'd forgotten how to be playful.

"Will you, by any chance, be wearing those shorts to the office tomorrow?" And the real Grady was back. Kate laughed, shook her head, and kept walking toward her car.

"No?" Grady called out into the night. "Okay, I'll take that as a no. Good night, Ms. Galloway."

"Good night, Mr. Malendar," Kate said into the night, and got into her car.

Chapter Seventeen

A week later Grady was on the Metro Gold Line heading toward Boyle Heights. He wore faded jeans, his favorite boots, a sweatshirt, and his beat up Dodgers cap pulled down over his eyes. Grady had perfected the art of blending in, disappearing if need be. When he was younger, he used his skills to sneak out of the house, or go to a music festival his parents forbid. Now that he was older, Grady used his covert skills to fly under the radar, to do things he didn't want anyone to see. It was really easier than people thought. No one would expect to find Grady Malendar, playboy, senator's son, on the Metro, let alone emerging from the Mariachi station. That's exactly how he wanted it. They had no business knowing where he was going. Since the start of his father's campaign things had become a bit more difficult, but Grady liked a challenge. He saw it as a game.

People exited and entered the railcar at each stop. Grady sat in a corner and read. Lately he was into the Ottomans, so he was half way through *1453*, a book about the holy war for Constantinople. Very few books gave a detailed description of the actual battlefield during one of the most important wars of the Middle Ages, and Grady wanted the details, craved them. He noted he had three more stops, so he finished up the chapter he was on, slipped the book into his backpack, and stood, holding the cool metal railing for balance.

Today was an important day. It had been a long time coming. He wouldn't participate because thankfully, it wasn't about him. He would arrive early, as always, and be gone long before the media and the crowds showed up. Today Grady felt normal. It was a privilege that had escaped him most of his life. He understood the benefits of his birthright, and certainly wouldn't want to be poor, but he often longed for something in the middle. His family and wealth provided opportunities, but they also robbed him of truly participating in life as an observer, a student. Because he drove a certain car, or knew a certain family, people formed judgments, decided who he was before he ever had a chance. Sometimes before he even arrived and shook a person's hand. He enjoyed engaging and learning from others. His life and the choices of his family made that difficult at times.

Sliding doors, scarred with peeling stickers and a few permanent marker symbols, opened, and Grady stepped out onto the platform. He rode the escalator up. As he approached the exit, into the brisk morning air, he looked up at the colored glass eagle wing above him. The morning light spilled through the sculpted overhang and made him smile. The Roads Foundation had renovated the Mariachi station three years ago, and Grady still marveled at the delicate work that married the history of LA's culture and modern conveniences.

He pulled his backpack over both shoulders and headed around the corner to Al and Bea's Mexican Food for a breakfast burrito. He planned to take it to go and warm his hands on the wrapped tortilla as he walked a mile to the finished construction site. The morning was a still peace. Storefronts were rolling up as the people of East LA began their day.

When he arrived at the front gate, Jason was outside to let him in.

"I'll never understand why you walk in this part of town." He smiled, patted Grady on the back, and leaned in to smell his breakfast. "Smells good, but that shit'll kill you, man."

They walked through the gate. Jason pushed a button and it closed behind them.

"When did you get so old?" Grady said, finishing the last of his burrito and throwing the wrapper into the metal can. "What'd you have this morning? Oatmeal, maybe a little flax seed?"

Jason looked awkward and Grady laughed.

"Holy hell, that's what happens when you get married. Next you'll start drinking your beer from a glass."

"I'm just watching out for my health, you know after thirty . . ."

Grady shook his head and Jason stopped.

"Whatever, man. You're just pissed Kelly chose me back in college and not your sorry ass."

"Oh, yeah, I'm sure that's what it is." Grady pulled open the front doors to the building, wiped his boots on the ragged mat, and felt that feeling—the one that stopped him and climbed into his soul every time. He looked at Jason, now serious, and they both smiled. Eric and Bryce came through another set of doors holding a small spool of red ribbon and a box. They set everything down on the bookcase near the entry. The bookcase that, very soon, would hold brochures outlining the center's services and a guest book. Eric and Bryce took turns patting Grady on the back.

"Good to see you," Bryce said, pulling out four crystal glasses and one opened bottle of whiskey.

"You too. How's Sophia?" Grady asked, taking one side of the ribbon and handing the other to Eric.

Bryce beamed and his eyes went sappy soft. "She's incredible. Almost two months and just . . . well, you saw the pictures. She's her mama. Gorgeous already."

Grady patted him on the back and turned to Eric, who had unraveled some of the ribbon across the entryway. "We're the only two left."

"I know, but Felicity is moving in with me after the holidays, so you better get your shit together. Seems fitting you'd wait until last."

Grady smiled. "Waiting, who says I'm waiting? There will be no settling down for me, believe me. You'll all just have to live your long-buried bachelor lives vicariously through me. I'll keep the flame burning." They all laughed.

"You sure about that, man? I had lunch with Peter last week and he said you had some feisty babysitter that was giving you a run for your money," Jason joked, and when Grady's face turned a bit pale, all three men hit hi-fives and laughed.

Grady shook his head.

"We ready to do this?" Grady asked promptly, taking the focus off his very sexy and very feisty babysitter. Bryce handed each of them a glass. "Whose turn is it to cut?" Grady held out the scissors.

"You're up," he said, handing them to Eric.

"All right." Eric stepped forward and grabbed the scissors. "Glasses up. Four guys, one great idea, and a thankful community. I proudly, before all the other big wigs get in here, declare this much-needed parent facility open for business."

He cut the ribbon, all four men clinked glasses, drank, and looked at each other. Their first private ceremony had been almost twelve years ago. It was for a wellness center for students not on the Stanford campus. A small, five hundred-square-foot clinic. They had forgotten ribbon on the morning of that first dedication, so they'd used dental floss from the facility for their private opening. Looking around now, Grady felt whole. They had come a long way and were now standing in a ten-thousand square-foot space with thirty-five private rooms for the parents of the children staying at the Los Angeles Children's Hospital. The parent facility allowed the families to stay close, but not have to sleep in stiff hospital chairs or on couches. They would have clean rooms, hot meals, and collective areas to share common concerns with other parents. All of it free of charge. In a few months they would have webcams installed in the children's rooms so parents could keep an eye on their child from the facility. All four men did the one-armed hug thing and put their glasses back in the box Bryce held out. They might have gone another round had they met at night, but eight in the morning was the only time that worked for all of their schedules. Macallan whiskey, specifically a 1949 bottle, was the tradition dating back to their very first project, so morning or not, they dedicated with whiskey. All four men walked toward the door to lock up.

Grady turned to his friends. "Until next time."

"You sure you don't want a ride? Christ, man don't you have a couple of cars?" Eric asked.

"Nah, I like the esthetics of the Metro."

"Really? Yeah, you're alone there, my friend." Bryce said, buttoning up his coat. A beep unlocked his car. "Be safe. See you next week. New project time. Any ideas?" he asked.

"I have a few." Grady smiled.

"He always does," Eric said, throwing his briefcase into the passenger seat and climbing into his own car. Both men waived and drove away, leaving Grady and Jason to lock the outside fence.

"You pull out and then I'll lock up," Grady said.

Jason was staring at the building.

"It's incredible, you know?" Jason said, looking up at the steel-beamed entrance.

"Yeah, it turned out. I love the glass." Grady added.

"It did, but that's not what I meant. What you do, it's incredible."

Grady bumped his shoulder. "Aww, are you gonna get all girl on me again?"

"See, you always do that, always dismiss it, but we're getting older now and this is some shit. Admit it. We're making a difference. Don't you think it's time you took your rightful place?"

"Oh Christ, we're not that old. Get in your damn car. My rightful place? Maybe you need to cut down on the flaxseed. I'm happy right where I am, doing what we do."

"You sure?"

Both men looked at each other.

"Because it feels like hiding, feels like you just ... I mean how long? You deserve to come out of the shadows," Jason said.

Grady's face was stone serious, but he knew Jason wasn't going to let it go at that. He knew the conversation would come up again soon, but Grady wasn't providing any answers today. "I need to get going, so pull your car out so I can lock the gates behind you and give you these keys."

Jason let out a sigh and got in his car.

As he pulled out, Grady walked to his car window and handed him the keys. "Talk to you later. Smile for the cameras and shake the nice senator's hand."

Jason shook his head and they both laughed. He drove away and Grady began walking toward the Metro.

Chapter Eighteen

S he hadn't seen Nick in several months, and it'd been a very long while since she'd seen him in a tux. So Kate was a little fuzzy as she approached the stage at the Fallen Officers Charity Banquet, after almost bumping into Nick on the way up. This was an important evening that had nothing to do with her, or Nick for that matter. This would be easy, she told herself, as she stepped up to the podium.

The Charity Banquet recognized police officers lost in the line of duty and honored their families. The proceeds often went to scholarships and other assistance. Kate had volunteered for this banquet since she was a teenager, but tonight all she needed to do was welcome the supporters, most of them cops or families of cops, and introduce the senator. Stanley had decided, given the increased stress between the LAPD and the community, that Senator Malendar needed a spot at this year's banquet. Mark had made arrangements for Senator Malendar to present one of the scholarships.

The simple act of an introduction turned out to be far from easy. In fact, the high jump Kate had to do during their senior track meet, because Melissa Hunt was sick, was easier than what was about to happen next.

Nick and Kate had been divorced for nearly two and a half years now, but when she adjusted the microphone, he was the only person she saw. His just-a-little-bad-boy look, that smile where his lips curved down into almost a frown, were so familiar, and she wondered why he still looked so good. Shouldn't he look like shit? Feel like shit? Where was karma when she needed it? Kate didn't have butterflies or feelings of affection, but she wasn't angry or resentful anymore either. As she smiled and welcomed the audience, Kate realized Nick was simply a familiar face in a sea of other faces. That was all. Her view eventually opened up, and she smiled at the other three hundred people seated at round tables. Kate gripped the podium and the rehearsed speech flowed from her mouth. She hugged Senator Malendar following an eloquent introduction, and when she turned to leave the stage—that's when she saw it.

She had made a point not to look at Nick's table again during her speech, apart from her initial familiar moment, but as Kate turned, something drew her attention. She sort of stumbled down the two stairs into the dark corner off stage. The entire room was eyes up to the senator, but Kate couldn't look away.

She was now touching Nick's hand, and Kate saw it again.

She was the cheater; *she* slept with another woman's husband. Kate could tolerate them as a couple, Christ she had even told him to be with *her* during a much more together time in her mind. But . . . there was no way it seemed right that *she* was now going to be his wife.

Kate tried to breathe. Peering from the darkness, she checked again. The damn thing was on her left hand. It sparkled under the hotel chandeliers. *They were engaged? He'd asked her to spend his life, the same way he had asked her* . . . Kate felt like she was going to pass out. She was definitely suffocating as she pushed the handle on the exit door and ran as fast as her high heels would take her. Kate needed her car, and if she wanted to keep what was currently her crappy job, it was time to leave. She ran past the reception area without a word and beat the doorman to the front door. Pushing through, she took a gulp of air as if her life depended on it. She looked up and everything was swimming. The stars were a swirl of light and she tried to focus. She needed to find her car and get home behind closed doors. She would not fall apart here. Maybe she wasn't going to fall apart at all, but whatever was going to happen once the world stopped racing through her head was not going to happen here, it couldn't. Tears began to creep into her eyes. *Walk, Kate!*

"Kate." *Oh, Dear God, could this get any worse?*

Grady caught up with her and attempted to turn her toward him. She pulled her arm away and kept walking. Where was she walking to again? She couldn't think straight. *Right, breathing.* Tears continued to threaten, and she would have given anything to just disappear.

"Kate, you can't just walk . . . "

She turned, so sick of listening to what she could and couldn't do. He saw the look on her face and stopped. *Tears, apparently tears shut Grady up. Good to know.*

"Please," she held up her hands and kept backing toward the parked cars. "Please just leave me be. Just this once, please walk away. I don't want to argue, I don't want any of your witty banter, please . . . " She turned, wiped her eyes, and attempted to find the guy in the red jacket that held the keys to her escape.

Bless his soul; the valet approached with a smile that faded when her face came into the light. He adopted a big brother look and ran to get her car. Kate sat on the bench, waiting and trying to keep herself together just five more minutes; the shelter of her car would be there so soon. Grady sat next to her and she shot him her very best warning look.

"No wit, and no arguing, I promise."

Her head dropped back and she closed her eyes.

"Kate . . . "

"Please stop saying my damn name," she moaned.

"Fine, I promise I'll be quiet, but I'd like to go with you. We could have some coffee, I'm a master of the French press."

Kate glared at him.

"Right, sorry, no charm either. I'll just sit like a eunuch, I swear."

"I want to be alone, I just want to be left alone. I need a minute." She dropped her head into her hands, leaning her elbows on her knees.

"I get that, and I'll leave you alone soon enough, but it's been my experience that it's not good to be alone right when shitty things happen. I'm not sure what the hell happened back there, but the initial shock of shitty things, when experienced alone, only leads to trouble."

Her car arrived. She took a deep breath, sent another warning look to Grady, and got in on the passenger side of her sensible Prius. Grady was quick enough to tip the valet, and slipped in to drive.

They drove in silence, as Kate rolled the window down and willed the wind to dry her tears and take her pain with them. Married, he was going to marry her. Kate felt like her chest was going to cave in. *She* would be his wife, *she'd* have his children, *she'd* be . . . Oh God, *she* would be enough.

"Pull over," she said.

Grady immediately pulled to the side of the road. Kate opened the door and threw up. Twinkling black sparkly shoes, and there she was on the dusty, dirty, shoulder of the highway, bringing up stuffed mushrooms. Tears mixed with the gross taste in her mouth, and Grady handed her his handkerchief. *Who the hell still carried a handkerchief?* Next came a bottle of water he'd pulled from somewhere in the car.

"Rinse and repeat. If you need to blow your nose, go right ahead."

She couldn't look at him. He was the client. She was supposed to be keeping him together, making him look good, and here she was a total wreck. At that moment, Kate didn't have the energy to care. He touched her head, pushed the hair off her face, and she looked up into eyes that held nothing but kindness and sympathy.

The kindness was a surprise, and she hated the sympathy. She was fine. *Damn it, Kate. Be fine.*

"I'm fine."

"Yeah, you are. Sure you are."

She put the lid on the water and swiveled back into the car. Grady closed the door and went back to the driver's seat.

"You know what you need?"

"I am truly afraid to ask."

"Will you just let me take care . . . Can I be in charge for a few hours?"

"I don't think—"

"Trust me, there will be ice cream involved." He smiled very gently. He was being so careful.

"Probably not a good idea to eat after I've just—"

"That was anguish throw up, not food related, so the food rule doesn't apply."

She almost smiled. "Excuse me? Did you just say anguish throw up?"

"I did. Falls under the reasons we throw up that have nothing to do with alcohol or bad eggs. Like when I found out Peter's dad killed himself, or the day I came home early from school and found my father with some woman and they were both on the same side of the desk— anguish throw up. So much pain, the body can't handle it, so it yells, 'Everyone out!'"

Kate stared at him. There she was, sitting on the side of the road, feeling about as low as she had been in a while, and she could not take her eyes off of him. It had nothing to do with his looks. He was sharing himself, a piece of his own pain. It was so honest, and for a moment she forgot everything. The moments of light he was capable of, when the charm and bullshit slipped away, were brilliant.

Grady smiled. "So—me, in charge, just for tonight?"

She nodded. He touched her hand. She was not prepared and jumped a little.

"Rest, Kate. Just close your eyes. I've got this."

She closed her eyes as they silently glided down the freeway. Kate could hear Grady's muffled voice on his phone. She felt another wave of nausea, but took a deep breath and again willed herself into fine. The memories continued to crowd her mind. They were relentless and took her back to the last time Nick asked her to come home.

He had arrived at the office with flowers, of all things. It had been about three months since she had moved out. Three months since she had woken up in the middle of the night to find Nick sitting on the side of their bed with his face in his hands. Three months since he'd told her that he had slept with Rachelle, he'd been sleeping with her, he felt this weird attraction to her that he just felt awful about. Kate left that night in a flurry of disgust and then three short months later he was in front of her with the stupid flowers. It was over. If she was ever going to respect herself again, it had to be over. This wasn't the first time Nick had slept with Rachelle, the year prior he'd slept with her in what he termed "a drunken stupor." Kate bought it that time; they went to counseling and mended their marriage. They weren't great, but they were better. The night before the hands-in-the-face routine, they had talked about maybe starting a family. That blew up with his pathetic confession.

The memory was still so fresh. The look on Nick's face, his warm brown eyes, so sad, like a little boy caught covered in mud. And Kate remembered not caring. That was the beginning of her numb phase. Funny, she would kill to be numb right now, but the memory continued.

"There were other problems, Nick. It wasn't just you."

"How can you say that? It was me. I deceived you, that's what you said. I broke your heart, I know."

"You did. All I'm saying is, it's over and we can't go back. There were other issues in our marriage, and obviously I wasn't enough for you. I need you to forgive yourself and let me go. Stop trying to make this work. You don't want to be married to me. You want to feel better; you want the guilt to go away. I can't help you with that, but somehow winning me back is not going to fix things. I love you. I still remember how you smell, your arms. I hope to God someday I stop loving you, but you will forever be a bruise on my heart. You need to listen to me." Kate had actually taken his hands, she needed him to hear her. "This will not work. It's broken. Please, please, let me go. Kiss me, wish me well, and find a way to like yourself again. If you love her, then go do that, be with her. I do not want to love you like this anymore. I want to move on."

"Kate, you were enough. I just, aw shit, I don't know. I have problems, it's the job. She understands the—we're the same. I know I hurt you, but I love you. I've always loved you."

"Oh, Nick. You're fooling yourself."

"No, you're wrong. We can get over this. I'll transfer out of there; maybe I'll take a desk job. I've changed. Please don't throw this all away."

"Changed? Nick, I know you think you love me, but that's not enough. Have you slept with her since we separated?"

"Kate . . . I . . . "

"That's what I thought. Let it go, Nick. Please, for both our sakes, just stop."

He never tried again after that day. It was for the best and it had been years. Most of the pain had healed or was buried. Kate told him to leave and create a life with *her*. She gave him permission, and he did. She honestly didn't feel anything for him anymore, but something happened when she saw that ring, the permanence of it. It was like somehow, even though she never saw Nick anymore, unless by the occasional accident, he was alone and she was alone. They were both broken together. Now he was getting married, starting over. He was not broken anymore and she was. That's how she felt looking at that ring. Kate was drowning in herself; it really had nothing to do with either one of them. It was her. Why was she still broken?

She wiped her eyes and noticed the car had stopped. Grady rolled the window down.

"Good evening, Mr. Malendar."

"Hello, Spencer."

"The suite is ready as requested sir, we will escort your guest up using the back elevator."

"You're a prince." Grady smiled and handed the tall bald gentleman a hundred dollar bill. Grady rolled the window up and turned to Kate.

"These gentlemen will take you in."

"What? What's going on? Where are we?"

Grady touched her hand. "Kate, you promised, I'm in charge. Now you're going to have to trust me here."

Kate's brows crinkled, but she was honestly too tired to argue. She exhaled. "Fine. What am I doing?"

As if on cue, the doorman opened the door.

"Ms. Galloway, welcome. Your bag has been brought up to your suite, if you'll please follow me."

Kate looked at Grady. He smiled, kissed the hand he was still holding, and handed her her purse from the backseat.

"Sleep. Relax, Kate. This place practically demands it. I'll call you tomorrow and we can go over the rest of the weekend."

Kate was out of the car when she turned. "Weekend? Wait a minute, I gave you control for an evening. No one said anything about the weekend."

Grady laughed. "Rest, Kate. Your laptop is up there. I know there's always work to be done, but this is called pampering. You'll enjoy it, I promise."

Kate shook her head. "This really isn't necessary. Why are you still sitting in the car?"

"Now how would that look, Grady Malendar entering a hotel with the dazzling Katherine Galloway? I'm surprised at you. You're slipping."

"I thought I wasn't a threat, remember? No one would ever think—"

"Yeah, well that was then and this is now. You can never be too careful. That's what you're always telling me."

"I don't think this is a good idea. I'm fine and I . . ."

Grady turned to the bald gentleman. "Spencer."

"Sir."

"Ms. Galloway is ready now. Sleep tight, Kate." A bit stunned at being cut off, Kate gave up and followed the two men in deep burgundy suits through the back door of a beautiful historic-looking hotel she had never been to before, white stucco, awnings, and incredible dark green vines. An older, mustached gentleman who proudly introduced himself as the manager met her inside. Kate noticed he wore a tiny Virgin Mary pin on his lapel and smelled like her grandfather. Chaps cologne maybe? Whatever it was, he was warm and lovely. He personally escorted her down Saltillo tile corridors, under heavy adobe arches and past a massive fireplace. All the while he explained the history of the hotel and that it used to be a monastery. He then opened the door to her suite and Kate was certain her mouth fell open. Her mind registered that the room was a stunning combination of white, wood and tile. Thick white stone walls, with deep window alcoves and wood framed crank windows. The floor was the same tile and the entry had a little table with a bowl of fruit. The manager introduced her to Cecile and Gretta. They would be her "room attendants" during her stay.

"If you need anything, Ms. Galloway, please push this button, there's another by your bed in the other room, and one of us will be right in," the shorter of the two women said in a soft melodic voice that instantly relaxed Kate as she nodded to their instruction.

"Well, I will leave you to the ladies at this point and let you get unpacked. Ms. Galloway, and do not hesitate to contact me for anything. My name is Guillermo Correra."

Kate offered her hand, and he took it with both of his thick square hands and looked at her through soft, weathered, dark eyes. "Welcome to the Santuario del Corazón. It's a true pleasure having you with us."

Kate believed him. She'd been to dozens of hotels, she'd had great service and knew the job of providing customers with excellence. This was different. She wanted to crawl into his lap, have him read her a story or push her on the swings. It was a bizarre re-action, but she felt protected. How could Grady have possibly known what she needed at the very moment he found her outside waiting for her car? Reading people was her job.

"Thank you so much." It was all she could manage as Guillermo turned, adjusted the flowers on the coffee table in front of a huge rust-colored couch, and closed the door behind him.

Chapter Nineteen

Something happens to a woman when her husband is unfaithful. Songs and poems are written about heartbreak and betrayal, but they only serve to flower up the ugly truth. The young girl, the one inside every grown woman, the one dancing around in her mother's shoes, she dies. The wide-eyed innocent who looked up at the man she loved and professed her devotion, she leaves and the woman is never the same. Even when she heals, kicks out the bitterness and the pain, she is changed. Some will say she becomes more of a woman, stronger, but Kate simply lost herself, her whole self.

She was starting to find her way back. That was the first thought she had when she awoke to knocking at the door. It took her a moment to realize she was still in the hotel suite. Kate hopped out of the massive four-poster bed she slept in last night, and shuffled to the door.

"Good morning," Grady chirped, as Kate squinted into the morning light and pushed the hair out of her face. He walked past her with bags and a smile that told her he was definitely a morning person.

"Why?" she croaked, and then cleared her throat. "Why am I always opening the door to you holding bags? Do you just carry them around with you?"

"I do. You've discovered my secret. I'm a bag man." Grady laughed, put the bags on the counter, and began removing several boxes of cereal.

Kate walked toward him, picked up the box of Fruit Loops, and asked, "Do I want to know?"

"You said you've never tried sugar cereal. That's tragic, so I thought we might remedy that this morning."

Kate put down the box and turned to go into the bathroom. She smiled. Just when she thought she had him, knew what she was dealing with, he pulled out another surprise.

"Wait, where are you going?" Grady asked, pulling two gallons of milk and paper bowls out of the remaining bag.

"Teeth, I need to brush my teeth and put some clothes on."

"No need to do that on my—"

Kate held up her hand. "Don't, please don't finish that sentence." The bathroom door closed.

When Kate emerged from the bathroom a few moments later in tan shorts and a white oversized button-up shirt, her hair was pulled off her face in a ponytail. She'd washed her face, but had not bothered to put make-up on. She hated make-up. Besides, it was Saturday, she was in a beyond-compare hotel suite with her equally gorgeous client, who was clearly taking pity on her because she had a small nervous breakdown because her ex-husband was going to marry the woman he was banging while they were married. Mascara would not make any of that better, so Kate didn't see the need.

Grady had made coffee in the little kitchenette, but was nowhere to be found.

"Hello?" she called.

"In here. The dining room?"

"This place has a dining room?" She hadn't even noticed the second arch leading out of the entrance when she collapsed into bed last night. She took her coffee and walked barefoot through the tile arch and there, sitting criss-cross on top of a very large Spanish-looking table, was an incredibly handsome man surrounded by what looked like two dozen boxes of cereal. Grady was in jeans, his hair still had a morning swirly in the back, and he wore a faded navy blue T-shirt. He too was barefoot, flip-flops on the floor by the table. Kate laughed for the first time since leaving the benefit the night before.

She stood next to Grady, sipped her coffee, and asked, "Are we eating all of these?"

Grady looked at her, barely able to move amongst the boxes.

"Okay, here's my plan. I've left a space up here for you to sit too. I have bowls and milk and a very large trash can. We are going to eat our way through this cereal and find you a favorite sugary cereal."

Kate nodded, handed him her coffee cup, and began climbing into her spot. "I mean, we should probably be working on your speech for the Cactus League Luncheon on Monday, or attending your father's discussion on immigration this afternoon, but yes, this seems like a priority." Kate shook her head and smiled. She was giving in or giving up, she wasn't sure which, but she sat on the table facing Grady and crossed her legs. He smiled, and she was suddenly wide awake.

"Good. Okay, now you're going to like the second half of this little activity."

"Oh, there's a second half? Do tell."

"Well it's technically research, which will appeal to your incessant need to work on the weekends. With each box of cereal, every sample, we are going to ask each other one question."

"We?"

"Yes, we. It's only fair."

Kate shook her head.

"Let's not start the morning off this way. I brought sugar, you want to know more about me so you can exploit that for my father's gain."

Kate laughed.

"And I want to know more about you because—"

"Because?" Kate asked, raising her eyebrows.

"Because I should get some reward. I did all the shopping."

She laughed again and gave in.

"Okay, here goes," Grady continued. "We are going to ease into this. I don't want your system to go into shock when you taste what you've been missing all these years. I give you Honey Nut Cheerios." He handed her a paper bowl and a plastic spoon. "Now for the purposes of research, we're using 2 percent milk. When I was a kid we drank whole milk, but I just can't get that stuff down anymore, so 2 percent it is." He looked at Kate, who had her spoon poised and ready. "I suppose you had blue milk as a kid?"

Kate nodded. "Skim milk all the way. I still drink it."

Grady gave a dramatic sigh. "A travesty. Let's begin."

"Wait. Don't I get to ask my question first?"

"After your taste-test." Grady said with a full mouth. "Mmm, Honey Nuts are in a class all their own. These are delicious."

Kate took a bite.

"Well?" Grady asked.

"Not bad," she mumbled over chewing. "I can taste the honey, sort of like a graham cracker. Not sure I'm too excited about the weird film floating in my milk, but not bad."

"Okay. Good start. Ask away."

"Why did you major in history?"

Grady thought a minute.

"Huh, I wasn't expecting such a personal question. I guess it's the context. I like seeing my life within the context of history. It's comforting, gives me perspective."

Kate put her spoon down and swallowed the bite of Honey Nut she had just put in her mouth. "Who the hell are you?"

Grady laughed and poured himself a little more. "That's a loaded question. Is that really a question?"

"I'm really not sure what to make of you. One minute you're dating cheerleaders and the next I get this." Kate set her bowl down and suddenly looked serious. "Grady, both of these guys can't possibly exist, so I'm wondering, do the cheerleaders get to try cereals? Do they see what I'm seeing right now?"

Grady seemed to stumble for a moment. His spoonful of cereal hovered near his mouth, and a drop of milk dripped down into the bowl. Kate didn't think it was possible to catch him off guard, but he quickly recovered and said, "No. I do the cereal routine for special guests. Usually only in hotels, actually."

"I'm serious."

"I know, but now is not the time for serious. We are surrounded by all of this delicious sugary mess and you've already gotten an answer to your question. Toss your bowl because we are now going to try another one of my top ten. Fasten your seatbelt, Galloway, because you are about to experience marshmallow stars and clovers."

Kate laughed and reached for her next bowl, but Grady held it and asked his question.

"When you were a little girl, what did you want to be when you grew up?

"Seriously?"

"Do you want the marshmallows, Kate?"

She sighed. "I . . . I wanted to be a lot of things. When I was really little I wanted to be a PE teacher."

Grady laughed.

"Hey, no laughing. I really did. I remember having these fantasies about organizing the locker room the way I wanted it and having all of my own balls. All different kinds for all of the sports. I even imagined that the balls would have a *property of* stamp." Kate laughed at herself and then looked at Grady, who smiled and handed her the next bowl. She took a bite.

"Eh," she said. "These are not my favorite."

"Are you insane?" Grady said, chomping through his bowl. He looked like a kid waiting for Saturday morning cartoons.

"I'm just not feeling it. The cereal part is kind of bland and the marshmallows are weird. It's not blended."

"It blends in your mouth, that's the cool part."

Kate shook her head, leaned over and dumped the bowl in the trashcan. Grady had a longing expression as if someone had just run over his puppy.

"Unbelievable. Maybe we should have had your taste buds checked before this."

Kate laughed and said, "Okay, next question."

Grady added a little more to his bowl.

"Ready?" she asked.

He nodded.

"What is your relationship like with your sister? Are you close?"

"Look at you go with the personal questions, Kate. I think you want to know me. Is this a date?"

"I ate the yucky marshmallows. Answer, Grady."

"Let's see, are Kara and I close?" He paused for a minute. "Yes, I would say we are close. We are two years apart and when we were younger we were very close. She was a tomboy, if you can believe it, so we did a lot together. I remember one time we tried to run away and she insisted on taking her cat. It was the middle of the night and we put the cat in a pillowcase. By the time we got to the door the damn thing was howling. Woke the whole house up."

They both laughed.

"Kara has grown into something I'm not quite sure I can relate to most of the time, but that's recent. She studied to be a chef, you know?"

"I didn't know that," Kate said, finishing up her coffee, hoping it would wash the Lucky Charm taste out of her mouth.

"Yes, but then she gave it up. My parents hadn't known, so when they found out they were pissed. Kara was never really the same when she came home." Grady seemed to go off in his thoughts for a moment. "Anyway, the answer to your question is, yes. I am close with my sister."

"Do you ever think about getting married again?" Grady asked, and Kate could tell he was expecting her to sidestep.

"No," she answered, as truthful as she knew how. That was the game, right?

"You never want to, or you never think about it?" Grady asked, while he seemed to look around for his next box of cereal.

Kate made an obnoxious buzzer sound and said, "Oh we're sorry, Mr. Malendar, but this is a one question per bowl game."

Grady shook his head and poured the next round. They went

on like this, back and forth, for the next two hours. Grady eventually learned that Kate didn't completely rule out getting married again, but she had not thought about it at all since her divorce. Kate learned that Grady cutting his knee open, when he fell in the wash behind his house, was the scariest thing he'd experienced as a child. Grady showed her the scar from twelve stitches.

Kate shared that she went to both of her proms with guys she barely knew. She was never asked, so her dad set her up with sons of the guys on the force. One of them didn't dance with her once. That little gem was her answer to, "What was your most humiliating moment in high school?"

"I should have just stayed home or gone with my friends. Oh, if I only knew then what I know now," Kate added.

Grady agreed and told her that he didn't walk in his high school graduation because he got into a fight with his father about Stanford and took off for two weeks to drive through Mexico. All in all they got through ten different cereals, ten sets of questions, and maybe a few extra. Kate finally settled on Fruit Loops as her favorite sugar cereal, citing the crunch and the rainbow milk as a bonus. Grady agreed that "Loops," as he called them, were in his top three, but told Kate nothing would replace his Honey Nut Cheerios. She laughed herself silly when he explained that he had a favorite bowl and spoon that he used and still ate them for breakfast every morning.

The following morning, Kate answered emails and finished Grady's speech, but also made time for a massage and a pedicure while Grady left for some mystery "details" he needed to take care of. When he returned, they hiked through Vista Hermosa Park. Over a late lunch, on a little bench at the top of their hike, Grady listened to the closely-guarded story of Kate's first marriage.

He checked her out of the hotel, after she said goodbye and thanked the staff, and his driver delivered Kate to her apartment. The weekend, as promised, had pampered her and it was fun. Fun, one of life's little treasures Kate had forgotten all about. Grady was smart and generous. She felt safe with him and was pretty sure he did with her. It was so strange to find that the person she was responsible for sheltering, making look good, was actually doing the same for her. Kate didn't know what to do with all of the feelings floating around inside of her, but she was certain of one thing while she unpacked her bag and started a load of laundry. Real life was very real and nothing about her time with Grady felt real.

Chapter Twenty

The report was in her email when she got out of the shower on Sunday night. Kate put on her pajama bottoms and a tank top. She made some of the Chamomile tea the spa had sent home, opened her laptop, and sat on the floor by her large living room window to catch up on what the real world had been doing while she was playing make-believe. Even after a shower, she could still smell the hotel, feel the oils from the spa on her skin. The first sip of tea burned her lips, so she set it on the window ledge and pulled up her work email. Kate scanned the screen. Basic stuff, meeting minutes from the week before, a couple of new meeting requests, the latest poll numbers showing the senator now only two points behind his opponent, and then her eyes landed on the subject line: Complete Background (Malendar, G) CONFIDENTIAL. Kate clicked on the email, opened the attachment, and sipped her tea again. Her stomach growled, and after a weekend in la-la land, Toaster Strudel seemed downright boring. Maybe she would order take-out.

The report filled the screen. Background, demographics, organizations, things Kate already knew. Some affiliations from college she didn't know about, tax information and contacts.

Criminal background check, nothing. Incidents or altercations, nothing. Possible scandals, fraternity connection during college and possible exposure (i.e., photographs, experimental drugs). Each heading listed resources and additional information links. Kate knew most of it; there was nothing that would help the campaign, and thankfully nothing that would hurt it either. It seemed that on paper Grady Malendar was pretty clean. Most of his mess came from his own doing, surface really, but always shy of real trouble. Kate skimmed the rest of the report, past tax reports, and then she stopped dead, teacup en route to her mouth, when she saw the Businesses/Corporations section. She put her cup down and clicked on the link titled "Roads Foundation."

"I found large sums of money each year on Mr. Malendar's tax returns from 2002 to present that appeared on the surface to go nowhere. Looking for possible tax fraud exposure, I did some digging and found the sums are sent to a trust, which is linked in a very clever but entirely legal way, to The Roads Foundation. The Roads Foundation was founded in 2002 and is headed by three prominent LA businessmen, Jason Black, Bryce Saunders, and Eric Dampier. All three went to Stanford with Mr. Malendar and they appear to have remained close friends. Mr. Malendar is not listed on any of the foundation paperwork, board of directors, etc., but it is clear he funds the foundation's annual budget. I see no exposure issues," the report said.

The Roads Foundation, *The* Roads Foundation, one of the largest foundations in Los Angeles, hell, California. They were everywhere. There was not a community center, hospital, inner city arts program that didn't mention the generosity of The Roads Foundation. They spent tens of millions of dollars every year on Los Angeles and the surrounding areas. They never gave to political campaigns, they had no government connections at all. No special interest, no crap. Jason Black, the president, was brilliant and completely innovative. The Roads Foundation was the gold standard around the country. They just finished an entire parent living facility at the Los Angeles Children's Hospital. The senator was there last week, at the dedication. She remembered because Grady was supposed to be there, but he never. . . *Holy Shit!*

Kate needed strudel. She stood up, pulse pounding now, and walked to the kitchen. The cool rush of the freezer calmed her bouncy nerves. *Unbelievable,* she thought, opening the plastic wrapper and popping two frozen blocks into the toaster. She walked back into the living room, mind spinning, replaying the last few weeks, and grabbed her cup. Returning to the kitchen, she made another cup of tea, took a strudel out of the toaster, and sat on the counter. She'd been doing that a lot lately. It was actually a great place to think. Kate scanned her memory, was there anything, any way she could have known? How is it that no one knew? More importantly, why was he hiding?

Halfway through her second strudel, she remembered. Bo, the dog, Grady had said he got him when he was at the construction site. He was meeting a friend for dinner. He had stumbled over his words, he never stumbled. One more time . . . *Holy Shit!* Kate jumped off the counter and dialed Grady's number.

"Wow, that was quick. Miss me already?" he answered on the second ring.

"I need you to come over."

"Really?"

"This isn't a joke. Can you be here soon?"

"I . . . yeah, is something wrong?"

"No, I just need to talk with you and it can't wait."

"Okay, I'm fifteen minutes away."

"Great." Kate hung up, decided to take the plastic off her new dining room table, and called to order some real food. It was going to be a long night.

The doorbell rang twenty minutes later. She opened the door to Grady holding two bags from Malaysian Mama's.

"The kid was coming up the walk at the same time. I just saved him a few steps," he said, walking into her house, glancing at the table with a smile, and bringing the food into the kitchen.

Kate closed the door. "I owe you money, Bag Man. How much?" Kate asked, sitting on one of her still-wrapped dining room chairs.

"Really?" Grady said coming out of the kitchen. "You're not going to let me pay for the food I'm sure you bought so I wouldn't have to eat pop-tarts?"

"Toaster Strudel, there's a big difference."

He laughed and took a seat next to her. "New table."

Kate's face flushed. *Stupid.* She got up and grabbed her teacup, planning on putting the relaxing effects of Chamomile to the test.

"Yeah, I bought it at that place in North Hollywood," she said, sipping her tea and curling her feet beneath her.

"Mid-Century?"

"Yes, they were great. It's repurposed. Used to be an old bank door."

"Really?" Grady ran his hand over the wood and Kate's face grew warmer. "It's beautiful. What's the occasion?"

Kate was still looking at his hand, so when she looked up, their eyes met. "Sorry?"

"The table, why did you buy a table?" Grady asked.

Kate took another sip and decided Chamomile was no match for Grady Malendar.

"To move on?" Grady asked, looking right through her. Soft eyes that were so much more than their color. She was really starting to like what was behind them even more. The way he looked at her.

"I guess. I needed a place to sit."

"It's a pretty big table."

"Yeah, well I have friends that come over and . . ." She was picking at the plastic covering her chair

"Kate."

She looked up.

"I'm glad you bought a table, really glad to see you're moving on."

"Thanks."

Grady broke eye contact and stood.

"I'm starving, what's in the bags?"

Kate snapped back. Why were they talking about her table? She needed to talk with him. Why did he always manage to take her off task?

"Fish-ball soup, those sliced chicken things. What are they called?"

"Lor bak?"

"Yes, those, and some curry."

Grady came in with the bags and paper plates. Kate forgot he knew his way around her kitchen now. She grabbed napkins. The sun was setting. Grady took a candle out of a box he passed, lit it, and put it on the table.

"Nice," he said taking a seat. Kate opened the containers and pretended not to notice that every time she was near him lately she felt something. Bursts of it really, floods of feeling she held back, kept under control. *Work, Kate, for God's sake. Work!* Right, she had called him over for a reason, but now she didn't know how to bring it up. It wasn't a bad thing, in fact it was incredible. What he'd been doing for the last twelve years was noble and so worthy of praise, but he clearly didn't want it. This was a secret he'd tried very hard to protect. Kate wasn't sure how he would react to her knowing. She jumped right in.

"So, I had our research department look into you a couple of months ago."

Grady laughed. "Okay, and did they find out about those three illegitimate children, because I can explain." He grabbed another piece of chicken and then looked up when Kate was silent.

She was looking at him. "No, but they did find out that you have, well you pretty much are, The Roads Foundation."

Grady held steady. Perhaps he'd been asked this before? "Um, not sure who your research guy is, but he's got that wrong. I'm not part of the, what did you call it again?"

"The Roads Foundation. Grady, I know you know what it is. The children's hospital, you were supposed to be there when your dad was at the dedication? You never showed up."

She could see him exhale, his energy change.

"Well, there you go. If I was, as you say, this foundation's leader, wouldn't I show up?" He wiped his hands with a napkin.

"Not if you've spent the last twelve years funneling money through a multi-layered trust structure to fund a foundation run by three of your friends from college."

Grady's smile fell, and Kate knew her research guy was spot on. "Peter, your best friend, sits on the board," she added gently. Grady said nothing.

"Grady," she touched his hand, "what's going on? Talk to me."

"Who did you tell?"

"No one. I saw the report when I got home and I called you."

"Was anyone copied on the report?"

"No. The only reason it was noted is they were looking at potential exposure with taxes. My background check guy noticed the sums, dug deeper, and then noted there was nothing illegal and no exposure. He had no idea what he was uncovering."

"Shit."

"What? Grady we just spent all weekend together. Why are you doing this? Why is this all a secret? Christ, people bend over backwards to make sure they get press for their good deeds. Why can't you let—"

"You don't understand. You and I, we live in different worlds."

"I'm clear on that, but you are a public figure—"

"My father is a public figure."

"Right, but you, by association, are in the public eye and the public thinks you are something quite different than you are. I don't understand why someone would want people to think less of him than the reality."

"Leave it alone, Kate."

"I can't. I'm sorry you don't see value in this, but your father hired me to do a job and that's exactly what I'm trying to do. You would be celebrated. The work your foundation does is amazing and honorable. Why would you—"

"It's best to not let anyone in."

"Grady, what does that mean?" Kate said, dropping her fork, no longer interested in eating.

"In my world there are a handful of people I let in. The rest are kept at a safe distance by the image and persona I feed them. I don't care if people think I'm an idiot."

"But—"

"Kate, let me finish. I don't let people in because that's what works for me. It's easier and it keeps the parts of me that make me my mother's son safe. I don't need to share who I am with the world. It only brings grief and pain. I can't, I won't allow it."

"Then why do these things?"

"Because it's who I am, it's where I find my worth, my value. These people, these shelters, or homes, or kitchens, these are real and I *feel* when I'm there."

Kate's breath caught at the reference to feeling. She'd felt for the first time in a long time when she was around him and his foundation did the same thing for him. *God, they were both messed up.*

"If I let the rest of the world into this, if I give that piece of myself to the vultures that hunt me and my family for a sport, if I do that, then they'll find me and ruin me."

"But you don't even let your family in."

"They wouldn't understand. They can't help themselves, they're part of the machine. The Roads Foundation would become a vehicle for them, a way to jump in the polls."

"Information like this would win the election for your father. I know that's not what you want to hear, but it's the truth."

"If you share this, it will destroy the foundation, our work will be tainted. Don't you understand? The only real way to give is giving without credit or awards. Otherwise, it's just bullshit."

"First, I disagree. Not all philanthropists are anonymous and they still do great work. Bill and Melinda Gates, hello? You're hiding behind a persona that is completely fabricated and I don't understand why. It's as if you think you're not good enough to be the face of what you are doing. Is that it?"

Grady stood up and started clearing the plates.

"Grady?"

He turned to her with a youthful, lonely look on his face. "I'm asking you not to share this. My father will win this election without the foundation. I need this kept private. It is my right, damn it, to have something private."

Kate stood up. Grady moved toward the door and grabbed his jacket.

"Can you tell me why? Why you're not the chairman of the board? Why you are hiding?"

Grady ran his hand over his face and laughed. "Oh, well that's the million dollar question. I don't have any answers, Kate. This is what I do, it's what works for me, and I don't give a rat's ass what people think of me as long as I continue to keep this foundation moving on my own terms. Are we done here?"

Kate didn't know what to say, so she nodded. He held her eyes for a moment and in them was a plea. He looked down and walked out.

Chapter Twenty-One

*T*hree days later, Kate's oldest brother, Neil, was turning thirty-six. She was still somewhat relaxed from her weekend away, but Grady's secret, and her promise to keep it, was causing her some angst. Kate was pretty sure an evening spent with her family would finish her off and her time at Santuario del Corazón would be a distant memory. Carrying Neil's gift, a salad bowl she had asked Reagan to make, and the bag of ice her mother had called and asked her to bring, Kate knocked, and then walked through the front door of her parents' house. They'd sold the home she and her brothers grew up in and downsized, in anticipation of her father's retirement. That was almost eight years ago. Kate was beginning to think her father was never going to retire. Her mother kept hinting, but Kate and her brothers agreed that their Dad needed to work. "He would go nuts without the job," Ethan had said the last time they met for lunch.

Kate heard voices out in the backyard. Sliding the back door open, she braced herself for the full Flanagan family onslaught.

"Katie!" she heard her father and brothers chant. It was a welcome greeting that always made her feel loved.

"You're late, honey. Just put that ice in the cooler and take a seat. We're about to say grace for my very first baby boy." And then there was her mother, Kate thought, as she dropped the ice into the cooler and grabbed a soda.

"Hey, Katie grab me a beer on your way over," Neil called out.

Kate kissed cheeks around the table and handed her brother a beer.

"Happy birthday, biggest brother," Kate said as she took her place at the table. She had called Neil her biggest brother since she was a little girl born to two big brothers. As long as she could remember, Ethan was her big brother, or "other brother" as he was often called, and Neil was her biggest brother.

"Thanks, Sis," Neil said, before the Flanagan family bowed their heads and listened to their mother's long-winded grace.

"Amen," they all said in unison, and then the food made its way around to all of them, Kate's father, both her brothers, her mother and Ethan's wife, Faith. Ethan and Faith got a babysitter for her niece, Chloe, because at Neil's request tonight's dinner would be followed by a family poker game. That was met with some reluctance because the only person who ever left a family poker game with money was Neil, but he was the birthday boy, so Kate's father broke out his coveted poker chips from Atlantic City, circa 1987.

"How's work, Katie?" her father asked. "Your mother tells me you were working last Saturday?"

"It was only for a few hours," Kate said, looking at her mother, who was always looking to stir things up. "I finished a proof review for Mark. He needed a break."

"Sounds like you need one too, sweetheart. Don't let those suits run you ragged."

The potato salad finally reached Kate and she helped herself to a spoonful. "I'm not ragged. It's just been busy lately with the campaign. Things will settle down after the election."

"I sure hope so," her mother couldn't resist chiming in.

"Neil, does thirty-six feel any different?" Kate asked, trying to change the subject.

"Nah, I still feel twenty-six." He smiled.

"Still act like it too," Ethan piped up.

"True," her mother said, pinching Neil on the arm. "Thirty-six and still no grandchildren for me."

Kate took a deep breath and let it out very slowly, because she could feel it coming. She could almost recite her mother's speech word for word. She looked up and shook her head at Neil as her mother delivered.

"I mean isn't it ridiculous, my son is thirty-six, unmarried and no babies. And then you, Katie. Thirty-two, failed marriage and no babies either. I'll tell you, I'm not sure what I did to deserve such self-centered children."

By this point Ethan was smiling and all three of the siblings said the last line of the speech in unison with their mother, "Thank God for Ethan and Faith."

Kate's mother huffed and the rest of the table laughed.

Kate got up to get more potato salad off the side table when she heard Ethan say, "Ma, don't count Katie out just yet, she's awfully friendly with a certain Mr. Fancy Pants." Kate turned back to the table just in time to hear Ethan mumble, "I mean, he's not Nick or anything."

"What?" she said in a tone that silenced the table, not an easy thing to do in their house.

"Nothing. I'm just joking. He's definitely different, you know, not like your ex."

"First of all, I'm not dating anyone, so I'm not sure where you're getting your information, and secondly," she tried to clamp down on her anger, but it had been brewing for some time. "Secondly, you are so right. Grady Malendar is nothing like Nick."

The entire Flanagan family looked up as Kate leaned on the table like some television prosecutor. "He's better. He's a better man."

Neil scoffed for a single beat and Kate lost it.

"Nick cheated on me. Hello? I feel like I'm screaming and no one can hear me."

"Honey, you are sort of screaming."

"Yeah, thanks Mom. I'm serious, what is with all of you? He's a cheater. Nick slept with another woman while we were married.

Did it multiple times with someone on the job."

"Katie, I don't think we need to rehash all of that right now. It's your brother's birthday," her mother said, reaching for her arm.

"Right. Sorry Neil, but since you all brought it up as part of your usual smart-ass banter, I'm going to finish it."

Kate could hear her father clear his throat.

She didn't care. "He cheated, destroyed our marriage. Why is that just brushed under the carpet? What, what does the guy have to do before you take my side on this? He's a cop, I get it. Who gives a crap? Seriously, there's more to life than the damn badge."

Kate felt the punch of that last part reverberate around the entire table and finish with an actual gasp from her mother. Kate was sick of the Grady comments and really, over the Prince Nick routine. She must have hit her mark because the table was silent. Her father cleared his throat again and carefully put his napkin on the table. Kate recognized the gesture as him trying to control his temper.

"Katherine," her father began, using her full name, another sure sign he was boiling under the surface. "I think we're just trying to say that you have to look at the company you keep. Whether you respect it or not." *Oh Christ, here we go,* she thought. "The fact is you come from a real family, we are cops and we don't live in the penthouse. You're the genuine article, we raised you that way." He looked at Kate. "He's just ... not ... and I, I think we all worry that you're getting into something you can't handle. That's all." Her father was breathing normally now. "And one more thing. I know that Nick broke your heart. I see it every day and he is not, should not be," he looked at her mother and her brothers, "an idol in this house. You're right, he is a cheater, and my family comes well before my badge. If we've made you feel any different than that, then I'm sorry."

"Dad, I'm just trying to—"

"Katie, you're a grown woman and we respect that. If this guy is someone you want to associate yourself with, then we trust you."

"It's my job. Why can't you guys see this? He's a client. I deal with these types of people all the time. I don't get why you're homing in on Grady."

Her father smiled at her brothers and they all turned to her.

"What?"

"Whatever you say, honey. Just watch yourself. That's all we're saying. You can never really trust a politician."

"Amen to that!" Kate's mother chimed in again.

"Yeah, well whatever you've got going on with him, the guy wears pastels and that's just . . . it's not right," Neil said. The whole table, including Kate, started to laugh, and she threw her napkin at Neil's face. His eyes warmed and he smiled at Kate. It was an oldest brother "I'm sorry" smile, and she loved him for it. They were stubborn on a good day, downright cruel on the worst of days, but they were her family. She loved them all and tonight's conversation was a start. Maybe all it took was speaking up, setting them straight. She was learning.

Chapter Twenty-Two

"We're all here. Okay, great," Stanley said, closing the conference room door and looking entirely too pressed and shiny for a Saturday morning. "Thanks for coming down on such short notice, Grady."

Grady smiled and held up his large paper coffee cup in a toast. It was as much of a gesture as he could muster considering it was five o'clock in the morning. He looked over at Kate, who apparently wore her sexy secretary glasses this early in the morning. His mind replayed other images of Kate, as Grady tried to replace Stanley's endless droning with something more appealing. Kate climbing up onto the table at the hotel, willingly playing his cereal game. Kate with cotton candy and mustard on her mouth. Kate vigilantly defending him and his character. All the many lovely sides of Katherine Galloway flitted in and out of his consciousness. As the caffeine from his coffee began to hum, Grady tuned back in just as Stanley was asking him a question.

"Grady, I know you've done some events with your father in the past, but when was the last time you did any charity, community-type work?"

Kate nearly spit her coffee across the table. Grady patted her on the back.

"It's been a while. Why? What do you need?"

Kate looked at him. He winked at her and played his part.

"Well, your father was going to speak down at the homeless shelter, The Mission I think it's called, this afternoon and maybe help them serve dinner, but he's had a last minute opening with the animal rights conservation crazies, so I'd really rather see him at that." Stanley had no shame and everyone was fair game. Sure, why not call people who dedicated their lives to protecting those who could not protect themselves "crazies," why not? As long as the cameras weren't pointed on him, Stanley pretty much thought everyone was nuts and, dare Grady say, beneath him.

"Happy to do it. Just let me know when and where?" Grady said.

"Okay, can you say a few words while you're there?"

"I think I can manage that." Grady smiled and finished up his coffee.

"Kate," Stanley moved on, "I'll give you a copy of the senator's original speech. Make sure Grady covers at least some of the topics. If they're over his head, just leave them out rather than making it awkward. Got it?"

"Yes, I'm guessing there's not going to be anything in that speech that's over Grady's —"

"Okay," Grady interrupted, "well, we've got to meet with our canvassing group and hit the pavement, so I will be there, Stan."

"—ley. Stanley, Grady," Stanley bellowed after them as he and Kate were leaving.

"I don't give a shit," Grady said under his breath as they rounded into the hallway on their way to their assigned group of volunteers.

"My God, how do you deal with him?" Kate asked.

"Are you kidding me? You deal with assholes like Stanley every day. Appease, it's all about appeasing the stupid. It's all they know."

Kate laughed. God, he would stand on his head just to hear her laugh. "Can I quote you on that, Mr. Malendar?"

"Probably best not to. It's anyone's race at this point, Kate, anyone's race," Grady said, giving her his very best impression of his father.

"You realize he could be right around the corner. That if he heard you, he would know you were mocking him."

"Kate, it's before six in the morning. I can guarantee my father is not in this building." He held the door open for her and they met with a group of people so committed to his father and his father's policies that they were willing to get out early and spend the morning going door to door drumming up votes. The impact his father had on other people's lives always amazed Grady. He saw politics as a jumbled mess that accomplished little if anything at all, but when he listened to his father speak, even he believed things were possible. It was a gift, Grady supposed, and as they all loaded into a campaign bus, for the first time in a while, Grady was happy to help.

Kate sat in the bus as Grady and a few older people set out to knock on doors. He really didn't mind this part, talking with people. Most people were quite fascinating. He walked next to a woman wearing a flowered dress and a big straw hat. Her toes were painted with tiny flags, and she wore the same white comfort sandals his Nana used to wear. She hooked her arm in Grady's and he shortened his stride to accommodate.

"You look awfully handsome, young man, with your navy slacks and this white shirt. Patriotic, I like it. Is this linen?" she asked, feeling the sleeve of his shirt.

Grady nodded and said, "It is. Good eye. I love your hat, by the way, and speaking of patriotic, did you paint those toenails yourself?"

At his question, she laughed and swatted him. Mavis, that was her name, introduced herself to Grady, and in between knocking on doors and selling his father's message on community involvement, she told him about her seven grandchildren and her youngest daughter who taught dance in Pasadena. A couple of hours passed, mostly in pleasant conversation with his fellow volunteers, or the residents of Whittier who were kind enough to open their doors.

There were a few crazy moments, there always were on the door-to-door circuit, but all in all, Grady had a good time. As they climbed back on the bus, he walked Mavis back to her seat and managed to narrowly escape agreeing to take her daughter for drinks. Grady pulled his sunglasses off his face and plopped down in the seat next to Kate. She looked up and handed him a bottle of water.

"I'm sorry you missed that," he said.

Kate closed her laptop. "I'm sure. Glad you're back in one piece. Door to door is never easy."

"It actually wasn't that bad. I met some friends."

"I saw that," Kate said, smiling and waving back at Mavis, who had turned around and was waiving at Grady.

"I'm trying to think of a highlight for you. Let's see . . . " Grady took a sip of water and then put the plastic cap back on. "I think I'm going to have to go with the small round gentleman that came to his door sporting a turtleneck, running shorts and boots."

Kate looked at him through her glasses and started to laugh. He wanted to throw the glasses off and take her right then and there on the bus, but then he remembered Mavis was watching and well, people just didn't do that on a campaign bus, so he continued.

"Yeah, he's my pick. I introduced myself and started to do the spiel about community centers and involvement. About three sentences in, he stops me and tells me Senator Malendar is a servant of the devil and if I'm his son then I will rot in hell too."

They both broke out laughing. Mavis turned around again, but this time she seemed a little bit like a bus driver hushing rowdy children.

"Seriously, at that point what am I supposed to say, 'Okay, well, thanks for your time, sir. Have a great weekend?'"

Kate's sides hurt from laughing.

"My God. What did you say?"

"I just backed away and eventually he stopped giving me the death stare and slammed his door."

"Oh, wow. I can see why that was a highlight."

They were both hysterical, actually crying at this point, and then Grady's hand dropped into the hand resting in Kate's lap and they both stopped laughing. Her hand was cold, small, and before he knew what he was doing, he had taken her hand in his. She didn't pull back, but instead looked up to the front of the bus and then rested her head back and closed her eyes. They were just there, sitting on a bus holding hands. Grady put his head back too and squeezed her hand just a little, to make sure she was really there.

As promised, the next stop was The Mission homeless shelter, where Grady gave a speech on perseverance. After reading the speech Stanley had given to Kate, he couldn't stomach it, so Grady improvised. Pulled in some of his favorite quotes from writers and historians. People who actually knew a thing or two about hanging on in the absence of hope. When he was finished, he and Kate agreed to help serve dinner. There were reporters covering his appearance, but he made his best efforts to point them toward the people staying in the shelter. He asked that the reporters listen to their stories rather than worrying about his ridiculous life. Most of them would ignore him, he knew, but he had to try.

When the bus pulled up to the campaign headquarters, everyone had left for the night. Grady and Kate said goodnight to the volunteers. Kate needed to grab some letterhead for Mark, so she ran into the office. Grady tipped the bus driver and followed her in.

"That was a great speech today," Kate said, putting a stack of letterhead and some envelopes into a box. "I'm not sure I will ever figure you out."

"What's that supposed to mean?" He stood behind her.

"It's not a big deal. It was a terrific speech, it's just hard to tell sometimes when you are faking it and when someone, something means . . . something." He was standing right at her back, so Kate naturally turned around, quickly placing the box between them.

"Christ Grady, no one knows who you are, the important parts of you are hidden away and then you pull out a speech like that, off the cuff? Does that make you a pro?"

"Peter knows me, Sam knows me, and so do you. You know me, Kate. Probably because I've lost the ability to fake it with you."

"Oh, please. Just stop. You sound like a bad country song."

Grady laughed. "Call it what you want, but it's the truth. I couldn't fake it with you if I tried. There's no need. You care about me, have feelings, so we are both in." Grady took the box from her hands and set it down on the table.

He felt her tense and then waited for her to shut him down. "I have feelings all right, but at the moment, they aren't friendly. I want you to stop playing around."

Grady took two steps and he was right in front of her. Kate backed up as far as she could, but stopped at the counter. The neon campaign sign glowed from outside of the small building. Grady moved closer, put one hand on either side of her, and Kate kept her eyes on him, she really had the most bewitching eyes. He could see her chest inflate and then a slow breath escaped her lips. Those lips, his eyes stayed on her moist, incredibly kissable lips.

"What are you doing?" barely escaped her mouth as he touched the side of her neck. Her eyes drifted and her skin was so soft that for a minute he almost thought he was imagining the touch.

"You can be mad at me tomorrow, but I'm going to kiss you. It's past time, Kate."

"Oh God, this is going to hurt," she said, stiffening.

Grady laughed, he couldn't help it. The look on her face sent a rush of warmth, a need to hold and protect, and when she placed her hands on his chest, he was pretty sure his heart jumped. Grady held her face, gently brushed her lips. When Kate's eyes fluttered closed, he relaxed into the moment, this one moment, he had a feeling would only leave him wanting more.

"I'll try to take it easy on you." He smiled and noticed how her hands felt on his chest, how beautiful she was with her eyes closed cradled in his hands. And then he kissed her. His lips molded to hers, the scent of her Chapstick, the hum as her mouth opened to him. He was gone. His hands moved through her hair and down her back. Kate's hands threaded under his arms and she pulled him closer. Her touch. He knew this was not going to be easy, that he did hide and give people something so fake it almost nauseated him sometimes, but in her arms, kissing her, he felt everything shift. He would need to find a way, find room in his life for this, for her. If she ever let him in, he would need to be ready. Kate moaned, tilted her head, giving him better access, and he took it. Everything she was willing to give in that moment, he took.

And then the moment was gone. Kate's phone vibrated. She pulled away and looked around as if the empty office would somehow come to life and shake its finger at her. She cleared her throat, quickly touched the screen of her phone, and Kate Galloway was back on.

"Hello, Mark. Is everything all right?"

"Senator Malendar needs to go to Washington, D. C. for a function he committed to in exchange for campaign funding. Stanley just called and they need to leave the day after tomorrow. They anticipate the trip will take two days. I think we should use this opportunity for some photo ops and shoot our run-up to election commercial. Grady will need to be there for the last day, so you can fly over with us, or come a day later, up to you," Mark's voice said across the speaker phone. In her just-kissed fluster, Kate must have hit the wrong button. Grady smiled and could hear the rustling of papers, which meant Mark was still at his office at eight o'clock. Kate rubbed her tender lips together and Grady could actually see the sting of guilt that she was clearly not working.

"Will there be a press announcement discussing the senator's trip? Anything we want to highlight that may help the strategy at this point?" Kate asked.

"Ernesto put together a statement. It's fine, he copied you on it. It's short and sweet. There are a lot of high-dollar donors at this thing, so it's not really something we want to highlight. Sort of counter-productive to the whole 'regular guy' thing we're pushing right now, but Washington is always good for publicity shots," Mark said. "Listen, I need to get home before my family disowns me. We can talk more tomorrow, but I wanted to give you a heads up."

"Okay, I'll let you go. I got that letterhead you wanted, so I'll bring that in tomorrow too. Have a good night."

"You too." As Kate was about to hang up, she heard Mark say, "Hey, how'd your stuff go today? I heard The Mission was a hit. Nice job. Is he driving you crazy yet?"

Grady smiled and wiggled his eyebrows. Kate hit a button and put the phone to her ear. "No, not yet." *Who was she kidding?* Grady thought. They were driving each other crazy. "Yes, it was a good day. Grady was great." Kate said her goodbyes again and hung up.

They stood in the neon-lit office space. Grady said nothing. There was nothing to say. That kiss said it all for both of them. Kate grabbed her box and turned to him. She took her bottom lip into her mouth as if he needed reminding of what just happened. He could still feel her lips on him and the look on her face said she wanted more. So did he, and because neither of them had any idea how much more, they turned, mumbled a goodbye to each other, and ran to their cars.

Chapter Twenty-Three

*K*ate had avoided Grady for as long as she could, but she had a job to do and Mark asked her to check in at a volunteer dinner the following night. Kate had plans with Reagan, but she stopped by The Yard on her way home. The senator had invited all of his current volunteers hoping they would bring friends to expand his outreach force. He was shaking hands and talking to the restaurant staff when Kate arrived. Grady walked over to her and just as they were finished with awkward niceties that follow after you kiss someone you're not supposed to be kissing, Grady's sister, Kara, approached like a bad storm.

"Kate, it is Kate isn't it?"

Kate looked at Grady as if she were asking if Kara bit, and then nodded.

"Great, well I just wanted to say that my father is running for re-election to the United States Senate, not some county seat in the backwoods."

Kate wasn't sure what to say.

"Kara, what's this about?" Grady asked.

She flipped her hair and put her plate down on the table next to them.

"I'm saying, who picked this place? I mean, this venue, this place, is not exactly up to standards. We're not playing in the farm league for Christ sake."

Kate was about to mention that this was a neighborhood restaurant and exactly what they were going for, but a tall good-looking man with glasses and a white apron, all in contrast to his full-arm tattoo, approached from the kitchen and stopped behind Kara. Wiping his hands on a towel, he smiled at them. Oh that's a deadly combination, Kate thought.

"Aw, Kara. You say the sweetest things."

Kara flinched just a bit, clearly recognizing the voice, then she turned and rolled her eyes.

"Shouldn't you be back behind the counter, in the kitchen sweating or something?"

Kate and Grady both looked at each other. Kara was never exactly nice, but even her attempts at tactful had gone out the window tonight.

"Well, you would know all about sweating in the kitchen, wouldn't you?" he said. Kate could tell Kara was thrown, and she wondered who the hell this guy was. If he kept putting Kara in her place, she might have to buy him a drink. Kara seemed to hide behind her best snobby purpose, and if looks could kill this guy would be a dead man.

"You're good on the counter too, if memory serves," Mr. Sexy Chef said.

Kate almost choked on her drink and turned away, so Kara did not see her laugh, not that she was looking at Kate. Kara appeared frozen and speechless. Two things not often in her Gucci bag of tricks.

Just when things were getting off-the-charts awkward, Mystery Hottie extended his hand to Grady. "Logan. Nice to meet you, finally. It's a pleasure hosting your dad at my place."

Kara huffed and turned her back, grabbing another drink off a passing tray.

"Grady. Great to meet you. This is your place? It's fantastic."

Logan smiled the pride only hard work can put on a man's face. "Thanks. It's a real labor of love."

Kara snorted this time.

"Been open just two months tomorrow," Logan said.

"Well done, man. This used to be something didn't it? Was it a garage?"

"Hardware store and a lumber yard."

"Right, I see it now. Incredible building. I love what you've done. And the name, The Yard. Perfect."

Logan beamed. "Thanks. Can I get you guys anything?"

Kara spun around as if on cue. "This food is atrocious."

Grady was about to hold her off, but it seemed his new friend was perfectly comfortable. Logan stepped into her, shaking his head slowly. "No it's not."

She stepped back.

"I mean, seriously what were you going for here? The spices are all wrong, flat even."

"Nope, the flavors are right on and you know it."

"Maybe this just isn't my speed. My pallet is a bit more sophisticated than backyard barbecue."

Logan raised his eyebrow, held her gaze, and looked like he was waiting for a final blow. He must know Kara, Kate thought.

"That is what you're going for, right?" She looked around his restaurant. "Barefoot backyard meat grillin'? You pairin' this with some bathtub gin from the bar there, Logan?" she finished, mocking the casual comfort of the restaurant.

Logan shook his head slowly, stepped into her again and tilted, just a bit. Kara's sarcasm fell to the floor as he reached forward, brushed past her body, and ran his thumb along the plate Kara had set down before she started her tirade.

This guy was in no need of rescuing; he could clearly take care of himself, and Kara too for that matter. Kara looked like she'd stopped breathing. One touch from Logan and it seemed her entire body was inoperable.

"Looks like you managed to get some of this atrocious food

down after all. Empty plates don't lie." Logan said, then brought his thumb to his mouth and sucked. "Damn near perfect spice, I'd say," he smirked and then walked away. "Great seeing you again, Kara. Be sure to stop by anytime."

Kate and Grady both turned and moved to the bar as Kara stomped off toward the bathroom.

"Oh, Logan, whoever you are, I want you on my team," Kate said, with a smile that made Grady's heart race.

He was getting used to that, racing heart and Kate seemed to go hand and hand. It had only gotten worse now that he knew her taste, the sound she made when she let go. Even if it was for just a moment.

"Right? I'm not sure who the hell he is, but he knows my sister," Grady said.

"And she clearly knows him," Kate added, wondering how those two would ever be in the same circles. A server in a short skirt came by and practically melted into a puddle right in front of Grady.

"Can I get you anything, anything at all, Grady?" she asked in a smoky voice. Kate turned to Grady to see if he registered that this woman was clearly trying to climb him with her eyes. He did, of course, and smiled.

"I'm great, um," he looked at her nametag, "Amanda. Just fine for now, thank you."

"You certainly are," smoldered Amanda.

"Kate, did you want—" Grady had turned to ask, but Amanda was gone.

"Good God, women of all shapes and sizes just swooning over you all the time. It must be exhausting," Kate joked, as Grady grabbed some nuts off the tall table.

"Not all women swoon, Kate. Lately I'm encountering runners." He smiled and she skipped right past swoon and on to complete paralysis. He leaned in, "You're not swooning, are you, Kate?" The bar was packed and they were pressed together. Kate tried to breathe. She took another sip of the club soda in her hand, wishing it were tequila. Tequila would know what to say, how to put him in his place.

"Is that supposed to be some kind of turn on? You know, the whole lean in when I'm not expecting it thing?"

Oh, that was clearly not the right thing to say, club soda, because Grady leaned in more and Kate looked for an exit.

"Do I turn you on, Kate?"

Exit, where was that exit? In another second, she would be allowed to use the fire exit.

"I mean forget the swooning," he continued, with hooded eyes and some sort of spicy sauce on his breath. "Since you brought it up, do I turn you on?"

Holy shit. His eyes were locked on her and . . . *was he kidding with this?* This had to be some kind of joke, a test, and she was about to implode.

"Okay, well as fun as this is, I need to get going," Kate said after she was able to close her mouth and miraculously keep from drooling.

"What? Things are just getting started. Aren't you staying for the whole thing?"

"Nope. Just stopped by to make sure everything was up and running. Looks good and now I'll make my exit with the rest of the entertainment."

Grady took her arm and Kate looked around.

"What are you doing?" she asked.

"I was going to ask you the same thing? What's wrong?"

Kate tugged and Grady released her arm. "Nothing. I'm doing my job. This isn't my world, Grady. I have a life outside of this little story we are putting on here and it's time I returned to it. Besides, I still need to pack for D.C. tomorrow. Last minute trips are not my favorite, I'm a little off schedule. We meet at the airport tomorrow night at five."

"I'm sorry if I made you uncomfortable, it's just that since I, since we kissed, it's been hard." Grady smiled at the innuendo, but Kate didn't. "It's been, err, difficult to go back to whatever this is."

"Right. I understand and I apologize."

"Oh, please don't do that."

"No, I do. I should have never let that happen. I've just lost my balance a little, that's all."

"Me too," Grady said. Their eyes held and amid the noise, Kate found herself lingering again. A glass broke behind the bar.

"Okay," Kate pulled back, "so nothing is wrong. Everything is fine. Enjoy your evening."

"Okay." Grady reluctantly let her go. "I hope I don't get in trouble tonight, Ms. Galloway," Grady said, falling back on the game they played.

Kate laughed. "Behave, Grady," she said as she walked toward the exit.

"Doing my best, ma'am. Doing my best."

Kate walked out and called Reagan to see if she needed to bring anything. Tonight was Wedding Favor Assembly Night, and Kate would probably have to bribe Reagan with pizza.

When Kate arrived, Reagan came to the door in what looked like a kimono, hair at the nape of her neck, and the strange plastic clogs she'd taken to wearing lately. Reagan swore they increased her circulation, and Kate was not going to argue. She looked frazzled, like she'd had two much wedding already, and it was still a month and a half away. When Kate put down the pizza and got a little closer, she could tell Reagan had been crying.

"Hey, what's going on?"

At her question, Reagan stopped buzzing around and looked at Kate. She started to cry.

Kate pulled her into a hug. "Hey, hey, it's okay. What is it, honey?"

Reagan wiped her eyes with the sleeve of her kimono and took a seat on the big green overstuffed chair in her tiny living room.

"Nothing. I'm fine. I just—" She started to tear up again.

Kate sat next to her. "Please tell me what's going on. You're making me nervous."

Reagan took a deep breath and tried to explain. "I don't know what I'm doing."

Kate attempted to step in, but Reagan held up her hand and continued. "Normally I'm okay with that, I sort of like my nutty way."

"Me too," Kate said with a smile.

"But this wedding is coming and I'm going to have to marry this man and what if I don't know what I'm doing and I end up messing this up or he wakes up one morning and wonders what the hell he ever saw in me?" Reagan put her hands to her face and leaned on her knees. "I know it's stupid, but for some reason I'm a mess tonight. I think it's all this damn tulle."

They both laughed, and Kate handed Reagan a paper plate with two slices of pizza.

"Everything you're saying, all of those feelings and all the other ones you will have until your wedding day are normal, honey." Kate took her own pizza and sat on the yellow paisley couch next to Reagan's chair. "It's a big deal, getting married, Rea. I kind of think the people who don't have a bit of a meltdown are the weird ones. Ya know?"

Reagan folded her pizza, took a bite, and moaned up at the ceiling. "Nona's?" she asked, with her mouth still full.

Kate smiled. "Nothing but the best for you, Mrs. Frazier." Reagan almost choked at the sound of her married name.

"Holy shit. That's right. I mean I'm keeping my maiden name professionally, but legally I will be Reagan Frazier." She took another bite of pizza and then added, "Eh, it's not that bad. Has a nice ring, don't you think?"

Kate hugged her dearest friend and said, "It sounds perfect, Rea."

She smiled at Kate like a hesitant child waiting for parental approval before jumping in the pool. Nerves were normal. Kate remembered not being nervous at all the weeks leading up to and the day she married Nick. Like she told Reagan, those people, the calm oblivious ones, were the ones to watch out for.

"Okay. I'm going to get us some caffeine and we are going to beat this tulle into submission," Kate said, heading into the kitchen.

"Oh God. Please, no more tulle. Can't we just give all of these people a damn gift card and a pat on the back?" Reagan laughed from the living room.

"We could do that, but I'm guessing these hand-made bowls from the super successful artsy bride would probably be a nicer gesture."

Reagan sighed and started on her second piece of pizza as Kate set the drinks on the steamer trunk that acted as Reagan's coffee table.

"Well, if we must. It's all right there." Reagan gestured to her overflowing dining area. "Let's finish eating first. Maybe you could tell me a story while we work." Reagan batted her eyelashes and Kate laughed.

"Well, I could tell you a story about the campaign I'm working on and a certain someone who kissed me in the dark campaign headquarters. Sounds sort of slutty and totally unprofessional, because it really was."

"Oh hell, yeah he did! Tongues, tell me about the tongues." Reagan jumped up and sat next to Kate on the couch.

"There were tongues, and his knows what it's doing."

"Sweet Baby Jesus, should we open a window?"

Kate laughed so hard her sides hurt as Reagan grilled her for every detail. By the time they both fell asleep in Reagan's living room, the pizza was gone and the wedding favors were finished.

Chapter Twenty-Four

The next evening, most of the senator's staff and a few people from Bracknell flew to Washington, D.C. on a private jet. Kate had been in first class once, but she had never been on a private plane. She felt awkward as her heels clinked up the metal stairs and she tried not to look down. Taking a deep breath, she entered the leather-smelling, neutral beauty of a plane that was nicer than most apartments, her apartment in fact. It looked nothing like a commercial airline, and as she set her bags down on the seat, she pretended not to notice. A model-like blonde touched her shoulder and quietly asked if she could get Kate a drink.

"Yes, um, I'd like sparkling water. With a lime?"

The supermodel nodded and walked away.

Kate sunk into the soft beige leather seat. It was high-backed and swiveled. Kate tried not to act like a five-year-old, but she really wanted to spin around despite it being late and her eyes feeling scratchy. There were blankets draped over each seat, luxurious navy blankets. Kate reached up and pulled one across her lap. Cashmere, of course they were cashmere. Kate was getting situated for a long flight when the woman returned with her drink. She smiled and notified Kate when dinner would be served and where the assortment of snacks were located, should she need anything. Kate thanked her, turned on the light just over her shoulder, sipped her water that was served in a crystal glass, and felt . . . calm. It had been a long time since she felt relaxed, calm, and she wondered, not for the first time in her life, if the wealthy and privileged always felt this way. Was calm for sale?

Kate was raised believing that hard work was the key to success, a fulfilling life. She'd worked hard, shunned excess as frivolous, and made her father proud. Kate could change her own tire in record time and never called roadside assistance. Roadside assistance was for weak or silly girls. Certainly not the only daughter of the Flanagan clan. Kate had always painted her own apartment walls, hauled her own groceries up the stairs, Christ, she even licked her own envelopes. Self-stick was for sissies. Most of the time she appreciated, felt good about her abilities, but there were times she was tired. Tired of proving herself, standing on her own for the sake of saying she stood on her own. Sometimes she thought she overdid it. Worked too hard to show everyone. *Who exactly was everyone?* She wondered now trying to read over Grady's speech for tomorrow. No one cared if she changed her own tire. It's not like there was a gold star for that type of thing, and AAA was only $29 for the year. Why didn't she have AAA? God help her, maybe Grady was right. People ask for help and lean on each other all of the time. That hadn't been her experience. She made a couple of notes in pencil on the speech, flipped to the next page, and let out another deep breath as Grady took the seat across from her. He looked good in the rich leather and the soft cabin light. He fit right in.

"Kate," he said in a whisper that made her smile. In the dim light of the cabin it seemed like they were children sharing secrets by flashlight.

She looked up. "Yes, Grady."

"Favorite part of Washington, D.C.? I assume you've been?"

"I have, a few times. Although never like this," she smoothed her hands over the cashmere blanket across her lap. "Not even close to this actually."

Grady moved to the seat next her and took some pretzels from the dish the flight attendant had placed in the center of the table.

"Favorite part?" he repeated.

Kate thought for a moment. She already knew her favorite part, but was hesitant to share. She decided it wasn't a big deal, so she told him.

"The cherry blossoms."

Grady nodded. "Flowers are always a hit. They are beautiful."

"It's not just their beauty. That is lovely, but I like that they bloom in such an otherwise cold town. To me, they feel like the pink of Washington's cheeks, you know? Everything else is so upright, neat. The blossoms mess that up and give it life, a pulse. I like that they bloom where they probably shouldn't."

Grady was quiet, looking at her.

"Eh, I guess that's silly, childish, but you asked, so that's my favorite part," Kate said, feeling awkward.

"I know exactly what you're saying," Grady finally said.

When she looked up at him his eyes practically glowed in the dim cabin light. The man was really more than she could take sometimes. He was effortlessly sexy.

"I mean, I can't say I've ever thought of cherry blossoms that way, but I like the way you see things," Grady continued.

"Thanks," she said quickly, and then returned to reading. When she looked up again, Grady was asleep. With the blanket up around his shoulder, he looked so calm and vulnerable. There was a part of Kate that wanted to protect him. Even though she was certain he could take care of himself, she wanted to help, keep him safe. That was her last thought before she clicked the light off and tried to get some rest.

They checked into the hotel just after midnight and Kate fell into bed. Grady had helped with her bag and she pushed him out the door before she did something stupid and asked him to stay. Kate was tossing and turning; she could never sleep after a long flight. Her body was sensitive to everything, the blue glow of the alarm clock, the streetlights peeking through the heavy drawn curtain of her room.

She finally resolved that she was awake and grabbed her laptop. Her phone vibrated. It was Grady.

"What's wrong?" she asked quickly.

"I was hoping to hear your sleepy sexy voice, Kate, but clearly you are always on alert," he said in a sleepy sexy voice all his own.

"Grady, it's two in the morning."

"I know. My room has a clock too, Kate. I'm done trying to sleep, so I thought, if you were up for it, I'd take you somewhere?"

"Not much is open right now," Kate said, closing her laptop and enjoying the sound of his voice. Her stomach fluttered.

"Yeah, well I've got some connections."

Kate smiled and could think of nothing she would rather do than drive through the city at two in the morning with Grady. *Christ, you have it bad.*

"Okay. I'll meet you in the lobby in ten minutes."

They sat in the back of a Lincoln Town Car as they passed by most of the monuments, lit and ethereal against the night sky. When they got to the gate at Arlington, they were met by a guard. Grady got out of the car, spoke with the man for a few minutes, and got back in the car. The gates opened and they were ushered in.

Kate shook her head. "Do I even want to know how that just happened?"

Grady smiled and looked out the window.

"I'm not sure who gets into Arlington National Cemetery in the middle of the night," she said.

"Rich and I go way back. He's been the night guard since before I was born." Grady looked at Kate. "It's a favor."

"That's some favor," she said, and then they were both silent as the car wound through the white headstones.

Generations of fallen men and women, alone and inexplicably breath-taking.

A few minutes later, Grady and Kate were standing in the viewing section at the Tomb of the Unknown Soldier.

"I've always been fascinated with this place," he said, sitting down like a kid on a field trip.

"Arlington?"

"Yes. Well, actually this spot, these guys. The times I was allowed to come to D. C. with my dad, our driver would take me here and I'd sit and watch the changing of the guard over and over again," Grady said softly. He looked straight ahead at the impeccably dressed guard pacing the Tomb. There was not a trace of charm or charisma, just fascination, serious and genuine fascination.

"I remember memorizing the steps, you know, counting all twenty-one, and then the twenty-one-second pause before the about face. It's really a dance they do every hour, well, I guess it's every thirty minutes during this time. It's always crowded in the summer."

Kate nodded.

"I prefer winter," Grady confessed.

"Why?"

"Because that's when it really counts, winter. Not that it's ever easy, but these guys are here doing their routine 365 days a year. Summer may get a little hot, but winter is cold and lonely and they are still here, even when no one is watching. They are at their best, pushing their limits and no one is watching. That's important."

He looked at Kate and she couldn't have looked away from him if her life depended on it. She was mesmerized. Kate thought she was done being mesmerized by anything.

"These guys, the sentinels, they commit for two years. Did you know that?" Grady asked.

Kate shook her head.

"They spend the first six months studying. No outside contact, no television. It's an honor, really." Grady turned toward her and continued quietly. "During Hurricane Isabel, they were told to stand down for safety reasons and they disobeyed, didn't want to leave the Tomb. Isn't that incredible? I mean in a town with so much bullshit, that kind of genuine commitment . . ."

Kate would look back on this moment in the glow of her nation's capital, the summer air, a place, at a time most people never get to experience it, as the very moment she knew she loved him, as in, was in love with him. She would never have been able to admit it then, but that was the moment.

"Alone?" slipped off her lips.

"What?" He turned back to watch the guard.

"When you were young, you watched alone?"

"Sometimes Ray, our driver at the time, would get bored and come out to sit with me, but I was usually alone. I liked being alone. Still do." He turned and looked at her again.

"Well, that's interesting, because you never seem to be alone."

"That's all just a game, Kate. The summer months, ya know?"

Yes, she thought she did. Standing there with Grady as the second guard made his approach, Kate began to truly understand him for the first time. She turned to watch the iconic ceremony. Grady was fine sharing his summer months with the world, but he was determined to keep the hard-fought winter months for himself.

The benefit was a success and the campaign raised the money they needed to get them through election night. Grady's speech went off without a hitch. He brought youth and humor into a room that desperately needed it. He sat with his father on the plane ride home. It was the first time Kate had seen the senator smile since they left California. He clearly loved his son, but there seemed to be a complicated relationship between the two. Kate wasn't sure why theirs should be any different from the rest of the world. She supposed money didn't change family.

Chapter Twenty-Five

*K*ate was not anxious to attend the Carousel of Hope Ball this year, for obvious reasons, but a few days after returning from Washington, D. C., there she was. Her mother had already commented that Kate's dress was cut too low in the back, but she also added that Senator Malendar's speech was informative and moving. She approved, that's what she said. As if the whole of the Malendar family was waiting for Mary Flanagan's stamp of approval.

Kate found Grady with her father. Police Chief Flanagan was looking dapper in his tuxedo, a "penguin suit," as he referred to it once every two years when he broke it out for just this event. Her father was a handsome man. Dark hair cut very short and balding in the back. His mustache was perfectly trimmed for the evening and for some reason, Kate remembered that when she was a little girl he went through a stage where he curled his mustache up just a little at the corners. Her mother had hated it, but Kate recalled fondly now, standing at a distance watching her dad, that she loved sitting in his lap and twirling his big dark mustache. Her father was a good man, a hard-working man. In that moment, she realized her father and Grady had a lot more in common than most people would think. They were already talking as she approached.

"Not very many people are fans of the LAPD these days. Are you blowing smoke up my ass to get to my daughter? Because that's not going to work."

Grady looked at Kate, seemingly not shocked one bit by her father's candor. In fact, he almost looked like he enjoyed it.

"Sir, I'm not really looking to 'get to' your daughter. I'm guessing you've already formed an opinion of me, and probably one well-deserved, so no, I'm not blowing smoke up your ass. I'm genuinely impressed with the changes you've implemented over the past few years. The police department is just one spoke in the wheel. With all due respect, you guys aren't responsible for all of the city's success, nor are you to blame for all its faults. Communities, governments, non-profits, are all part of the problem and the solution. I do think you should rotate your vice and narcotics cops out, promote them even, as it seems like some of them stay too long at the party and end up lost."

"Is that so? And how exactly would you know that?" her dad asked, standing a little taller. Kate recognized his shoulders thrown back a bit as his defensive stance. She had seen him do it with her brothers. He was preparing to put Grady in his place, but she could have told him there was no need. A few more words and he would not only respect Grady, he would actually like him, but that was for her father to figure out.

"Just my opinion, sir. I watch the news, read the papers, just like everyone else."

"From your gilded cage?"

Kate began to interrupt, explain to her father that he had no idea what Grady did, but she felt Grady's hand at the base of her back. She stopped, unable to move because his hand was on her skin. Her mother had said the dress was cut too low, maybe she was right. Kate steadied her breath.

Grady glanced at her quickly and smiled. "Sure, if that's what you want to call it. From my cage, that's what I see. Some of those officers are good men and women who seem like they're pushed too long, too thin. At the same time, I'm sure you train the hell out of them and it's hard to move them along, but . . . " Grady took a pull of his beer, "hell, I don't know. *You* manage the third largest police department in the country, I don't. None of the work you do is simple."

Kate's father seemed speechless. "You get this from your dad?" he asked.

"My opinions?"

"Yeah."

"No, they're all mine." Grady looked Chief Flanagan square in the eye and it was Kate's turn to smile. Not many men, people in general, could take on her father, but Grady had found a way to discuss the job without sounding like he was trying to fit in. He was still himself, even acknowledged his gilded cage, but got his point across. He would probably make a great politician, but then Kate realized he was far too good a person for that game. Her father and Grady launched into another discussion, and Kate excused herself to go talk with her brothers. As she turned away, she ran right into the one man she could have gone the entire evening without seeing. Her heart immediately shifted into overdrive with a mix of nerves and something else far too complicated to figure out.

"Nick."

"Kate. You look beautiful," he said, steadying her by her shoulders. Kate immediately found her balance and stepped back.

She looked down and ran her hand along the eggplant-colored silk of her dress and willed herself to relax. She had felt fantastic tonight when she had left her apartment, sexy even, and she was not about to let Nick "change her energy," as Reagan would say.

"You do too," she said, finally making eye contact.

Nick laughed. His dark brown hair looked like it was starting to gray a bit at his temples. His tux was modified. He wore a black straight tie instead of a bowtie; it was much more Nick's style. Kate found herself wondering if that was the same tux she'd helped him pick out the summer before they were married. It must be, how many tuxes did a man own?

"Would you like to dance?" Nick asked as if it was the most normal thing. This snapped Kate out of her memory.

"I would not," she said quickly. She saw the shock in his eyes and laughed a little out of sheer nerves. "I just don't think that's a good idea, do you? I was pretty sure I would see you here tonight, and it's fine. I'm just not sure we're ever going to be buddies, you know? Does that make sense?"

"Yeah, sure, Katie."

"Don't."

"What?"

"You know what. Don't do that easy, 'We're just hanging out at my parents' house' banter. We don't do that anymore, we're not those people. I don't sit on your lap and laugh at your jokes."

"Kate."

"No, it's fine. Really, I just want to make that clear. Lay out what we are and what, on the occasional awkward moments we have to see each other, we are not. So much of our marriage was about what you wanted, what made you comfortable. So, in our divorced life, I'll let you know what is acceptable for me."

"Okay." Nick rubbed the back of his neck.

Kate watched as his face seemed to pinch together and he tugged on his tie, trying to loosen it.

"It was good to see you, Nick," she said as she turned to leave, and then changed her mind. She felt better, stronger, and she wasn't going to let that feeling leave just yet. "Actually, it wasn't nice to see you. Expected, inevitable given the event, but not nice. I'm pretty sure it's never going to be nice. Anyway, enjoy the evening." She turned to leave again, the back of her dress swishing against her legs, but once again turned back. One last jab. "Oh, and congratulations, by the way. I noticed you're getting married."

"Kate." He reached for her, and she retreated, stepping backward, as if he was a rattlesnake.

Nick sighed. "I was going to let you know before, give you a heads up, but—"

"But you didn't, right?"

The look on Nick's face was the same one she had seen thousands of times. It was the same pathetic, poor-me face she used to rush to remedy. "You didn't give me a heads up because, well it's not about me, is it? Never really was." Kate's eyes flashed with anger she didn't let out very often anymore.

Both Ethan and Neil approached and stood next to Nick. They smiled. She was not sure where they came from, but she was fully prepared to now watch her brothers launch into shoptalk with her ex-husband. They were all cops, it was what cops did.

"You look great, Katie," Neil said. "I'm pretty sure Grady was finally able to roll his tongue up before he started talking with Dad."

"Yeah, those two seem pretty tight already," Ethan added looking out toward the dance floor.

Both brothers, decked out in tuxes too, although Neil's tie was already pulled free, took a pull of their beers and looked at Nick as if they had just noticed him standing there.

"Nick," they said in unison.

"Hey, guys. I was trying to get your sister here to dance with me, but I've just managed to piss her off." Nick smiled his normal "you know women" smile, but neither of her brothers replied. Nick seemed a little uncomfortable, and then asked, "Wait, who the hell is Grady?"

Neil smiled, taking another sip of beer. Kate watched the whole thing play out like a scene from some Irish version of *The Godfather*.

"Kate's new man," Ethan said.

Nick looked at Kate. She was smiling.

"He is not my new man. What's gotten into you two?"

Neil looked at Nick and said, "He's totally her new man. Loaded too. Private plane, the whole shebang."

Nick grew increasingly uncomfortable. This was not the way her brothers normally acted around him. Something had changed, and while she started to laugh at their tough-guy routine being turned on one of their own, she could have cried too. Touched, she leaned in to kiss them each on the cheek.

A moment later, Grady and Kate's father came up next to her. Her father took his place next to Neil and Ethan and Grady's hand was again at the base of her back. Grady seemed restless, maybe even a little nervous. Another first, Kate had never seen Grady Malendar nervous.

"Kate," Grady said close to her ear, "dance with me."

Nick piped up. "Ah hey, we were talking here, Buddy."

"Yeah, that conversation seems to have run its course, Buddy. I mean really, what more could such a captivating, vibrant woman like this actually have to say to you?" Grady answered.

Nick looked like he was going to punch him. Her father, Neil, and Ethan smiled and held their beers up to toast Grady.

"Yes, I would love to dance." Kate said.

Grady took her hand and she said, "Goodbye Nick," over her shoulder, just as she saw Nick's newly-minted fiancé part through the crowd.

Kate smiled and glanced at the woman now standing with her ex-husband, the woman he'd slept with during their marriage, and she realized that she felt fine, silly even. She looked back at Nick and said, "Good luck with that," and then turned toward the dance floor with Grady.

He spun her into his arms and she rested against his chest for a moment, breathed him in. "Thank you," she whispered.

"Anytime, gorgeous. Have you ever been jealous, Kate?" She looked at him and didn't know what to say. "Can't say I've ever felt that particular emotion until tonight." Kate laughed and he spun her out in a grand Fred Astaire move.

Her head fell back and she laughed some more as he pulled her in again. "I thought you said you were an awful dancer?"

Grady twirled her around the dance floor like a pro. "I lied." He smiled a devilish grin. "Now keep up sweetheart, because we definitely have an audience," he said, and then he dipped her back right there in front of everyone she knew and some of the people she worked with. Kate should have been embarrassed, this wasn't professional, but instead she was filled with such pride for the men in her life, the good ones. They allowed her to shine and stood by her when that became a little difficult. Grady spun her again and Kate remembered what Reagan had said as she was leaving for the ball. "Screw them all, honey. It's a party. Get your freak on." And that's exactly what Kate did. Well, within reason.

Chapter Twenty-Six

Two weeks later, Kate walked toward the back of the hotel lobby where Senator Malendar was holding his final big event of the campaign. They had driven the campaign buses up to San Francisco and arrived yesterday. Grady of course arrived late, had some things to take care of, Kate now knew what that meant, but she kept it to herself and made excuses for his delay. He arrived in his recently repaired Porsche only an hour before cocktails, which was now in full swing.

The St. Regis was an incredible place. Kate had been to a few functions there, for work of course, and it was still stunning. The way some people lived, just their day-to-day life, continued to blow her mind. The elevator dinged and she walked out into the Overlook Terrace Room. Everyone was positioned in the open air. Intimate and casual. Kate stood back and observed. The senator looked flawless at the podium reviewing his speech. An older, distinguished hometown guy with his sophisticated wife standing just slightly behind him—it didn't get much better. A light breeze tussled his salt and pepper hair. This was what voters wanted, this was the image, and part of Kate's job was to make sure they got it. The election was four weeks away and Senator Malendar was up four points in the polls, almost two full points ahead of Driggs, his opponent. He was a little weak in San Francisco, still ahead, but they needed this last push. The senator would be addressing local business owners and the heads of several conservancy groups. God, Kate loved this job, especially when she believed in what they were selling. Her father still teased her that she was a glorified snake oil salesman, but he was wrong. She presented people in their very best light.

Kate did a quick check to make sure the press seating was adequate; all the microphones were angled to combat a gust of wind interrupting the speech. Javier would do a live webcast and blog entries were ready to go for both the senator's website and his wife's. The lighting was perfect, not sunset yet, but soft. People began taking their seats and Kate spotted Grady. Did he look good everywhere? His hands were casually in his pockets as he stood talking to his father. They both laughed that laid back laugh that Kate swore only money could buy. As much as Grady drove his father to insanity, his father's eyes warmed when he looked at him. There was a bond there and Grady made the senator laugh like none other. The breeze brushed over Grady's face, and his cheeks were flushed by the warm summer air. His eyes were even bluer, if that was possible. *Kate, please try to focus. Wait a minute . . . Navy dress, dark hair, great shoes, and touching Grady's shoulder.* Who was she and why didn't Kate know about her?

"Max," Kate called over her shoulder, still looking at the two of them like they were in some damn catalogue shoot.

"Right here."

"Who's that?"

"Little more specific please. Lots of people," he said looking up from his laptop.

"I'm not going to point. Over by Grady, navy dress."

"Oh, not sure. I'd like to find out, damn she's . . . "

"Thank you. Yes, she is. I need to know who she is."

"Kate, it's time to take the prelims. Everyone's here," Elaine, the photographer said on her way toward the group, followed by her minions carrying tripods and strange things that looked like they could summon alien space ships.

"Right. Max, find out who she is later. Make sure you get Elaine's best shots to Javier, so he can get the photos on the website before the speech begins."

"Got it."

Kate walked behind Elaine's crew. Grady looked up and smiled. Most of the crowd took their seats, as it was clear that the senator, his family, and some key people were going to take photographs. Navy dress stood there, whispered something in Grady's ear and then . . . then she brushed the shoulder of his jacket. *Who was this woman?* More importantly, did everyone talk about people the way Kate did? *Navy dress at three o'clock.* No wonder she couldn't seem to connect anymore. She'd turned into a machine, for crying out loud.

Cameras began to flash. The senator and his wife, the senator shaking hands with the president of some society, the senator and his children. Perfect, it really was perfect. Last shot, a group shot, the senator in the center flanked by his wife, his daughter, two or three small business owners and . . . "

"Wait." Kate walked in front of the cameras and looked right at Navy Dress. "I'm sorry, you are?" she said, pretending to adjust the tablecloth that was blowing free.

"Excuse me?"

Hmm, Navy Dress was either dumb or a snob. Great. "Your name?" Kate asked undeterred.

She looked at Grady and smiled. "Avery. Are you . . . "

"Kate. I'm with Bracknell and Stevens. We're the PR firm that represents the senator and . . . " Kate brushed Grady's shoulder to prove a point. *What the hell is wrong with me? Kate, don't overdo it.* " . . . Mr. Malendar." She smiled her best country-club smile. "Anyway, he should stand next to the senator, so you, you can stand at the end, but we'd like Grady next to his father."

"Kate," Grady said, looking at her like she was just a little nuts.

"You know what, it's been a long day. Please, just stand by your father."

"Does it really matter?"

"How about you let me do my job, okay?"

He said nothing, but of course Navy Dress piped up. "Grady, it's fine. I'll just . . . " she smiled and moved to the side.

Was she snickering? Kate turned and walked back behind the cameras. Her face must have been five shades of red and she felt like a fool. That was ridiculous, she didn't need to do that. Kate didn't look at Grady again. She didn't even see the final shot. It hadn't mattered by that point. He probably thought she'd lost her mind and he'd be right. Kate just couldn't stand there and watch Navy Dress toss her hair one more time. *Oh, God.* What was happening to her? Suddenly, this whole thing needed to be over so she could tuck herself in to the quiet sanctuary of her hotel room.

The senator's speech was fantastic, even with the left microphone dropping out for just a second. The crowd began to mingle and the feel was casual and sophisticated—just as planned. Candles were lit on each small table. Kate was the only thing that was neither casual, nor sophisticated. She had done her job, stupidly crossed a line, and now it was time to be where she belonged. Alone.

Kate congratulated the crew and started packing her things. Cocktails and little sandwiches came out on trays as the sun began to set. She looked up as Grady approached. A gentleman stopped him and they spoke for a minute. She hurried to finish packing, hoping she could get out before he . . . too late. Grady touched her shoulder and when she looked up he was smiling. It was the charming, boy-with-a-secret smile, she really hated that smile. He stepped closer, too close. Kate tried to maintain her professional face, but his eyes were soft and warm. He touched the side of her face and she thought she was going to go up in flames right there in front of him.

"Kate."

She knocked his hand away. "Don't patronize me."

"I'm not, but you can't continue to pick at me like we're in grade school."

"What? I'm not. You should've been next to your father for that picture. There's no question. Everyone agreed."

"She's a family friend."

"I don't care."

"Yes, you do."

"I, I can't . . . "

"What?"

"I don't care. I mean, I care because it's my job. You can . . . "

"I can what? Do whatever I want? Nope, sorry that doesn't work anymore." He leaned into her ear. "I think about you all the time, wondering when I'll see you again. If I'll get a chance to brush past you, smell your hair, kiss you again. So you see, I can't do whatever I want, Kate. Pathetic maybe, but that's where I'm at."

Kate couldn't breathe. She kept packing and repacking the same papers into her bag. "You see me practically every day," she said, as if what he just said meant nothing.

"It's not enough." He wasn't going to let up.

She found the strength and looked at him. "Grady, this—"

"I know, it's incredibly inconvenient for you. I can see that, but I don't think I'm alone here. I realize this puts a real kink in your 'pissed off at the world' period, but there's something here, Kate. Now, we can ignore it, but I wouldn't bet the farm on that strategy."

"Bet the farm?" She looked up at him. "You realize no one under sixty-five still says that, right?"

"Nice try. You're changing the subject."

"Fine. Well, ignore is exactly what we are going to do." Kate grabbed her briefcase and reached for her coat. Grady put his hand over hers and just like that, her heart began pounding up to her ears.

"Feel nothing there?"

Why was everything so easy for him? He wasn't going to do this to her. Her job, she was here to do a job.

Kate took a deep breath. "Stop. I didn't say I felt nothing, but unlike you, I'm not a child. I can control my emotions. I don't lose control anymore."

Grady raised an eyebrow and she knew he was referring to her scene. True, she was not in control merely twenty minutes ago, but she was not going to let him have the upper hand.

"There's a spark," Kate continued. " Okay, so what? We're not in high school for crying out loud." Kate turned and walked as quickly as she could into the hotel. *That was good, Kate, really good.* Now if she could just get to her room before her heart jumped right out of her chest.

Chapter Twenty-Seven

*H*er shoes were off before she closed the door to her hotel room. Kate threw herself into the very plush chair. She had to admit it was nice to live among actual furniture. She thought of the new couch and chair she'd ordered. They would be delivered when she arrived home. Furniture was good. Removing the clip, Kate shook her hair loose. *Did he say he couldn't wait to see her? Almost every day isn't enough? Christ, Kate, how many times do you think he's used that line? Don't kid yourself, the man is a legend.* Her logical mind knew, but there was something genuine in his eyes, almost like it was hard for him to say.

There was a knock at the door. Her heart picked back up. A man in a black suit introduced himself as the concierge.

"Ms. Galloway?"

"Yes," Kate said.

He smiled and extended a small silver tray. "Message from Mr. Malendar, ma'am." She took the envelope and turned for her purse. Placing a few dollars in his palm, Kate thanked the concierge and slowly closed the door. Grady had precise handwriting. She had never noticed before. A note—he'd written her a note. *Open the damn thing, Kate.*

She pulled out a single white card:

Kate –

I'm in the bar just off the lobby. There are several eligible-looking, as you call them, bimbos, and a rather large sculpture just begging to be climbed. If you do not meet me down here in 15 minutes, I'll be left to my own devices. It'd be a pity to have a scandal this close to the election. I know you'll make the right decision.
Grady

Kate smiled. She looked up and saw herself through the entry-way mirror. It was a stupid "girl with butterflies" smile. She thought about the note's content and the smile dropped as quickly as it appeared. *He couldn't be serious. He wouldn't . . . damn.* Kate needed to get to the lobby. Oh, who was she kidding? She was smiling again. Clearly a glutton for punishment, Kate ran her fingers through her long auburn hair, threw on some jeans, a little lip-gloss, and she was in the elevator.

She stepped off the elevator and walked toward the jazz spilling from the bar. Grady was standing with his back to the crowd, his jacket in his hand and his collar open. He did a visible double take when he saw her. It was probably because not many people dared to enter the bar at the St. Regis in jeans. Maybe it was his turn to be embarrassed.

"You just made it. I was about to have a drink and start climbing."

Kate smiled. He was funny, but he scared the crap out of her.

"Grady . . ."

"Nope, before you start in on me let's get out of here."

"What?"

"My car is right through those doors."

"Grady, you really need to lay low. Where are you going?"

He gently took her arm. "We . . . are going for a drive. No reporters, no work, just a drive."

Kate quietly asked her stupid heart to cut it out. "And if I don't go for a drive?"

He gave a faux-longing look up at the sculpture above the bar.

"Christ, fine," she caved.

"It's a good thing your hair's down," he said, opening the door to his sleek grey convertible Porsche glistening under the lights of the hotel. "You're gorgeous, by the way." He closed the door and walked around the other side without looking at her. This guy was really good. In spite of everything she knew, in spite of all the lessons she had learned, she was simply happy to be sitting with Grady Malendar. Deep analysis would come later; right now she rested her head. They drove in silence for a moment. Her hair blew wildly in her face, she left it, didn't tuck it, allowed the disarray. Kate leaned over and asked where they were going.

"Over the bridge," he said, keeping his eyes on the road.

"I can see that. Sausalito?"

"We'll stop there on the way back, but I'm taking you to one of the most reporter, PR, politico-free areas I know."

Sounded great. The winding road took them past the Pelican Inn with its small streetlight. The moon was large enough to cast its own glow, and Kate could see Grady smiling as he parked.

"Muir Beach," she said.

"Yup, Muir Beach." Grady got out and popped the trunk.

Kate opened her door. He grabbed a blanket and her hand. It was silent except for the low rumble of the waves in the distance. She felt like they were the only two people on the planet. This was not a good idea, so she stopped.

"Grady, this is really surreal, and you're right, it's a great place to get away, but I . . . "

"You can't?"

She nodded.

"It's too good, too much fun?"

"It's just not appropriate for me to be here."

He laughed, Kate knew he would. "Not appropriate? Kate, this is probably the most appropriate thing I've done in a long time. I just want to sit with you, just you, for an hour. That's it."

"On romantic Muir Beach in the moonlight?"

"Is this romantic? You know, it is quite romantic now that you mention it, but that's just a coincidence."

He took her arm again and this time she followed.

"Just an hour, and then I really need to get back," she said in vain, as they crossed the small wooden bridge and the beach came into view. It was breathtaking. That word is used far too often because this . . . this really was breathtaking. Grady kicked off his shoes and left them in the sand. He rolled up his pants, and suddenly what Kate was sure was thousands of dollars worth of suit looked like casual beach wear. She stepped out of her shoes and he took her hand again. A group of people were sitting on pieces of wood around a bonfire farther up the beach. Grady spread the blanket and sat down. Kate looked out at the ocean, took a deep breath, and joined him.

"So, you've been here before?" he asked her.

"I have, well only once at night. Greg Parson's graduation party. We were dating . . . yeah, the beach is romantic." Kate laughed. "So weird, I haven't had that memory in a long time. Anyway," she said, smoothing some sand off the blanket, "I was in high school. I haven't seen High School Kate for a very long time." She let out an awkward, sort of insecure laugh that she did not recognize. "Not sure where that came from. Yes, it is incredible here at night."

"It is." Grady looked at her, and his gaze was so warm that she moved away. He laughed. "So, what is it about me that completely turns you off?"

Was he kidding? That would be a big nothing; there wasn't one thing about him that turned her off.

"What?" she tried to laugh. "It's not you."

"Oh, please don't give me the 'It's not you, it's me' line. I used to use that one in college."

It was quiet. "Grady, I'll admit you're a surprise, not what I thought you would be, but this," she gestured to the both of them, "this is just because I'm boosting your image, you feel beholden and grateful for the attention. It's normal. It's very flattering, but . . . "

His face became serious. Not something she'd seen much of since meeting Grady.

"I don't want you to be flattered and I'm not beholden. I'm talking about you as a woman, not part of some PR team. When I'm with you I feel like we . . . I see you. You're still there."

"You see what you want to be there."

"No, she's still there. The girl you described that night at whoever's graduation party. She's buried way in the back, but she's there. Those luscious lips and haunting blue eyes . . . he was a lucky bastard." He leaned forward and she pulled back.

Her heart was racing, almost like it was running to save its own life. This had to stop. "Grady, I want you to listen to me, carefully. There's a really good chance I've lived my best love, given the most I'll ever give to a man. I'm damaged, and you need to know that. Don't make this into something it's not or fill it with some romantic notion of who I am. You've seen enough of my personal life to know it's pretty screwed up. I'm not what you think I am, believe me, there are newer models out there. We both know you've test-driven plenty. Whatever you're feeling, it'll pass. Let's keep this professional and not . . . let's just not go there."

"Wow, do you have a rote answer for everything? That was great how you just wrapped me up and sent me on my way. Here's what you don't understand, I can't stop this, won't leave, and whether you know it or not, you can't either. You make me . . . ah, I don't know. Everything is clear and I'm enough when you look at me. I feel. That in and of itself is a big deal, but . . ."

She started to interrupt, her mouth halfway open, the words stopping on her lips.

Grady's eyes pleaded with her. "Please, let me finish." He took her hand. "Kate, look at me. I don't need to love you or have sex with you to pump myself up or mend my ego. I need . . . *want* to be around you. To hold you, laugh with you, and even fight with you. And you're right, you do make me better, that's true, but I can offer you something too. I have things you need. You need me, I can feel it and believe me, no one has ever needed me. They've needed my money or my family connections, but never me. You need me, Kate, and God, over the last couple of months I've needed you." His voice softened as he rubbed a circle into her hand. "You're not damaged." He moved closer and touched her face.

Kate didn't know what to say. She stared into his welcoming eyes, frozen. This was not good. This had to be the whole "you make me a better man" complex. He needs someone to mother him and keep him in line. She'd filled that role over the last couple of months, and now that his life was looking up again he transferred that good feeling to her. *Jesus, Kate! Maybe he just thinks you're hot and wants to take you home!*

"Grady, I appreciate your feelings and you are, it turns out, a really great guy, but I'm not the right woman for you. I'm not the right woman for anyone, I'm afraid. All I really want is to just be left alone."

He wasn't listening. His crystal blue eyes fell to her mouth. His breath was warm and she couldn't move.

"No one really wants to be alone," he whispered as he leaned closer, looking straight through her.

"When we were in D.C. you said you liked being alone. Remember, you said you still like being alone." She was babbling and he moved in closer. The moonlight pooling in those eyes was not helping Kate find her words.

"I lied." He gently kissed her, just a passing of lips, breath.

"I'm afraid," she said as he brushed her lips again.

"I know." He touched the side of her face.

"This isn't going to work," she said softly.

Grady smiled and traced her lips with his thumb. "It seems to be going along nicely so far."

"You don't understand . . . " She was struggling to order her brain to pull back, but he kissed her. He gently took the back of her neck, bringing them closer together, and she melted. Lost in a kiss so tender and filled with so many things she had buried deep inside and locked away. All at once she felt. She was no longer numb, but even wrapped in all of his warmth, Kate's brain yelled to her heart that this too would end in pain.

Grady couldn't stop kissing her, touching her. He knew she would be different, he could feel it the closer he got to her, but the softness, the sheer vulnerability that peeked out of her for just a moment was more than he was prepared for. She was undone and dazzling, laying on a blanket with him in the moonlight. She was the most exquisite sight he'd ever seen, and he knew he wanted her and would want her for the rest of his life. The thought didn't scare him. It should have, but he felt nothing but belonging and a deep need to protect the softness in her.

Kate stared up at the stars as Grady touched her hair. He was lying on his side propped up on one arm. He took a deep breath.

"That wasn't so bad. I don't think there was any damage."

Kate laughed. "None that you can see, anyway," she said turning to him.

"All that I see is so beautiful."

They were quiet, looking into each other.

"I think about you." Kate said softly, as she looked up at the stars.

"Excuse me?"

"You heard me, all right, I think about you."

Grady smiled.

"I mean not every day, well maybe every day, but it's not an every minute thing. Some of it, most of it, has to do with work. I just . . . I'm human, a human being."

"I know."

"Well, I wanted to get that out. I do in fact recognize that you're a person and I think about you from time to time."

"That's good to know. I mean with me being the client and all. It's good that you think about me. Kate?"

"Yes."

"Most of it has to do with work, that's what you said. What do the other thoughts have to do with? Just curious." Kate flushed and his smile deepened.

"I . . ."

"Yes?"

Grady could actually see her trying to order her thoughts. "I think about why you won't let me . . ."

"Let you what? Don't hold back, I mean whatever it is you'd like to do."

"Why you won't let me use all of the great service you do in the campaign. That's what I wonder."

"Nice try, that's work. You specifically said, most of your thoughts."

"You're pretty relentless," Kate said, looking up at the stars.

"I'll have to add that to my list of character traits right next to abnormally curious," he replied.

He pulled her under him for another kiss. Dear Lord, she surrounded him. He couldn't get close enough.

They heard laughter from the group down the beach and Grady could see reality smash right into Kate. He could practically hear her start to question her choices, see her looking around for reporters or whatever else she constantly worried about. She squirmed out of his arms and stood brushing the sand off her jeans.

"We should go," Kate said.

Grady moaned and rolled onto his back. "And she's back, ladies and gentlemen."

"What's that supposed to mean?"

"Nothing," he said, as he stood up to fold the blanket.

"We do need to get back. We can't just—"

"Sit out here on the beach in the moonlight and kiss each other senseless? I know it's so . . . what was I thinking?" He actually put his hands on his hips in an attempt to impersonate her. It was kind of funny, but Grady could tell Kate was not amused so he dropped it.

"Grady. You may not need to live in reality, but I do. It's all I know."

"Please, let's just go to the car," he answered. "Don't dissect it and chart it out. Just leave it at this; I'm falling in love with you,

Kate. In reality, standing right here and even back in the conference room at your office, at the grocery store, pumping gas, you name the place in your 'real world,' and I'm falling there too." He finished folding the blanket and brushed the sand off his pants. "And you, sooner or later, and God please let it be sooner, you're going to let me in. Believe me Kate, I get it. I've never felt this way. I know I scare the hell out of you, but I'm not going away. I'm not going to fly off in my Lear jet with my silver spoon in my mouth. This isn't a joke or a game for me." He started walking toward his shoes.

"This was . . . nice," she managed.

He whipped around and took her by the shoulders.

"Nice? Well that's a first."

Kate looked down at the sand. "What do you want me to say?"

Grady let her go and ran his fingers through his hair. He was laughing, frustrated . . . hell, he wasn't sure what he was. Kate looked like she was just trying to breathe.

"What do I want you to say? I want you to tell me you have feelings, any feelings at all. I want you to say that when I look into your eyes and feel alive, that I'm not alone."

"Grady, I'm sorry. I can't be what you need me to be."

"Don't you get it? You already are everything, everything I need and damn it of course you won't have me. Figures, typical, really. I spend most of my life trying to avoid women who want any type of conversation, much less commitment, and here you are pushing me away. Karma!" he laughed, and they continued walking.

When they got to the car, Grady put the blanket in the trunk. Kate stood looking back at the beach. He was beside her, quiet. Then she turned to him, looked at him for a little more than a beat and he knew it, she was falling too, but not enjoying the ride. Kate dropped her head to his chest and breathed a sigh.

"Don't." He lifted her chin. "Don't stop looking at me like that."

Kate didn't say anything. Grady kissed her lightly and then opened the car door for her.

They drove back to the hotel in silence and Grady realized the look in Kate's eyes, the glistening of the moonlight along the water as he kissed her, would have to be enough. For now, anyway.

Chapter Twenty-Eight

"Stanford University opened in 1891," the perky brunette tour guide in the tan shorts and snug polo with the Stanford seal said, as she masterfully led the group while walking backwards.

A woman with short dark hair asked about the church looming ahead, and Mrs. Malendar asked Brandy, the tour guide, about the different columns.

"Great question. The columns are all sandstone, but each is unique because they were all hand-carved. Now, if I can get everyone to look down as we walk this way. You'll notice each graduating class gets a class plaque in the main quad." She stopped at the class of 2006 and looked at Grady. "Since we have an alumnus in our group, Mr. Malendar, could you tell the group what lies under each plaque?"

Grady smiled. "Sure, each class puts together a time capsule before graduation. Those capsules are held below each plaque."

"That's right. Thank you, sir."

Kate looked around at the great quad, in awe of the history, the beauty. The group moved on to get a better look at the columns and then on to Hoover Tower.

"Did she just call me *sir?*" Grady fell back in step with Kate and asked in genuine shock.

"Sure did." Kate laughed. "How's that making you feel there, old timer?"

"It's only been seven damn years since I was a senior here. She's what? Twenty-two? I could date her."

"You could. Not sure she's into you, sir, but you could sure try."

"You're enjoying this, aren't you?" Grady hit the brim of her baseball cap.

"Hey, cut it out. Don't damage the Columbia Blue." Kate fixed her hat. "What was the question? Am I enjoying watching our young adorable tour guide refer to you as *sir* rather than, *Wow, he's so hot*? Yes, yes, it's refreshing. Smart girl."

"Did you have to wear your damn Columbia cap to my alma mater?" Grady asked as they caught up with the group.

"Um, sure did. Are you crazy? I have to represent the Ivy."

"Oh Christ. Stanford is just as Ivy."

"Eh, but not quite, not officially, now is it?"

"It's better than Ivy. Better weather, better school, minus that pompous East Coast snobbery."

Kate laughed. "Whatever you need to tell yourself. There's definitely not a bit of snobbery on this campus. I wonder if that's why Stanford has that green tree in their logo. Trying to push something green. Ivy envy. You think?" Kate was enjoying toying with Grady, who was still shocked that he could even remotely resemble a *sir*.

"You're insane. Stanford lets in just slightly over 5 percent of applicants. We don't need green. Look around, Ms. Galloway. We're the shit. The wind of freedom blows!"

Kate shook her head. "It blows all right." Kate laughed so hard, the rest of the group turned around. Senator Malendar and Mrs. Malendar made their way to the back of the group.

Grady leaned in. "Oh shit. You're in trouble now, lioness. Dad's a Bruins man."

Kate tried to look as professional as she could in shorts and a baseball hat.

"Kate, I love those sandals," Mrs. Malendar said as they approached.

"Oh, thank you. On sale, Nordstrom Rack."

Grady smiled, leaned into Kate and whispered, "If I wasn't already falling desperately in love with you, that comment just sealed it." Kate shot him her best "be quiet" look, and Grady fell back a little, in step with the senator, and anxiously awaited his mother's response.

"Really? Well I didn't know Nordstrom had a sister store."

"It's fantastic really. Everything that doesn't sell, or is out of season in the regular Nordstrom eventually moves to The Rack."

"I'll bet there are some great deals there. I'll have to check that out."

Grady and his father both looked at each other, amused that his mother was trying to relate. She'd never been to an outlet store in her life.

"So, Kate. I gather you went to Columbia," the senator prompted.

"I did, sir. Go Lions!"

"Actually, I'm pretty sure Grady is the *sir* today." He nudged Grady, who was shaking his head while Kate laughed.

"Indeed he is," Kate said. "That's a smart girl, our tour guide."

"Glad to see you're giving him grief about that."

"Oh, yes. It's all part of the service at Bracknell and Stevens."

The senator laughed as they caught up with the tour group at White Plaza just in time to hear the tour guide ask if anyone would like to explain or participate in the tradition of fountain hopping. The entire group looked expectantly at Grady.

"Right. Fountain hopping is a tradition dating back long before my time," he started.

Kate laughed as Grady still tried to validate his youth.

"It is where students basically fall into the fountain. It's fun. Yes, I've done it. No, I will not demonstrate."

The group laughed and they moved on toward the Cantor Arts Center.

"So, Kate," the senator said, "I wanted to thank you for agreeing to be the point person for Bracknell today. I know Mark was supposed to be here, but it's nice having you."

"You are very welcome. I've never been to Stanford's campus, so this is a treat for me too. It's beautiful."

"We've actually never been on the campus either," Grady's mother added. "I mean we've been to the stadium, when Grady graduated, but it is nice to see the campus now that my husband is speaking here."

Grady flashed Kate his big cheesy grin, the one normally saved for jokes or people he could barely tolerate, and she felt as if she should tread lightly.

"Oh, I . . . well I thought Grady went to Stanford," she said.

"He did," Bindi confirmed, taking the senator's sunglasses from him and cleaning the lenses with a cloth she pulled from her purse.

"So, being senator, I'm sure you just never had the time," Kate continued carefully.

"We had the time." Senator Malendar chimed in, putting his glasses back on. "Grady was supposed to go UCLA. He was accepted into their honors program, but he decided to go to Stanford instead. I went to UCLA, and my father before me and his father before him. Malendars are UCLA men."

"Except for me," Grady said, putting his arm around his father. Something he clearly didn't do much of these days. Kate wasn't sure what to say.

"Except for you, that's right. So in protest, I never set foot on this campus until he graduated," the senator finished.

"With honors," Grady added.

"Right, with honors, but a damn history degree."

"You know what they say. How can we ever lead into the future—"

"Oh, Grady. Stop harassing your father. He's here now," Bindi spoke up.

Grady shook his head, looking around and forward. Kate suddenly felt desperately uncomfortable and prayed no one asked her for her opinion, because she was pretty sure it wouldn't be welcomed. Thankfully, they had reached the end of the tour. The senator shook hands, took pictures, and Stanley arrived to take him to the law school for his speech. Senator Malendar was gracious and the crowd loved him. Kate felt good about that. Grady had bowed out of watching or participating in his father's speech. He kissed his mother and agreed to meet back at the hotel for dinner.

"Kate, could you please finish answering any questions the tour group or the press may have about the senator or Mr. Malendar, and then stay back with Mr. Malendar until this evening?" Stanley asked, and of course Kate obliged.

She was working after all. Just when things with Grady started to feel like life, part of her life, she was reminded that she was at work. Not that she didn't like her job, it was just sometimes confusing.

Kate did as she was asked, and fielded a few more questions about the senator's plans after leaving the Bay Area. Grady answered some questions about his time at Stanford. It was all pleasantly wrapped up, and Kate found herself walking through the Rodin Sculpture Garden with Grady. A much quieter Grady than she was enjoying earlier.

"Did you mean what you said back there?" Kate asked as they found a bench to sit down.

"About?"

"Your time here. When that woman asked you if you enjoyed your time at Stanford, you said they were some of the best years of your life. True, or the right answer for the good senator's son?"

"True," he said without hesitation. "I grew up here, learned who I was and for the most part what I wanted."

"Can't be easy living under the shadow your father casts."

Grady shook his head. "There are far worse things in this world than being a senator's son, Kate. I was fine, but it was nice to get away. Find my own way." Their eyes met and as the sun began to set, all Kate could think about was kissing him on the beach, the things he had said to her.

That he was falling in love with her.

She could see it now when he looked at her and she wondered, wondered if he knew she loved him too? Kate took a deep breath.

Dear God, how did I let this in? The election was in two months and then what? There was still a part of her that believed this whole thing was simply a product of being together all of the time. Really, would they have ever met, gotten to know each other, any other way? The whole thing was ridiculous actually. Hadn't her brothers both said she was out of her league with him? Maybe she should have listened to them. It was too late now.

"I can hear the gears turning in your mind, Kate," Grady said, standing up and offering her his hand.

"What's with you and the hand holding in public? Do you ever follow directions?" she asked.

"I was never really into that."

Kate laughed and then grew serious when she remembered what she wanted to ask him.

"So, your parents never came to Stanford? I mean, your mom didn't drive you up to school, bring you cookies, move you in?"

It was Grady's turn to laugh. "Kate, my life up until I left for college wasn't exactly family dinners and game nights. My father has been a senator since before I was born. This show, the dance, is really all I know family to be, at least my family. I had a driver bring me to college. A moving company brought my stuff to my dorm. My father was pissed and he spent four years proving his point."

Kate took his hand. She needed to touch him.

"So now you hold my hand. Huh, it's the sympathy card that works with you." He smiled and then pulled her behind a tree and kissed her. Urgent, his hands racing up her body, as if he craved the human contact. Kate felt the tree against her back as her hands went into his hair and she was lost in the spin of him. Photographers could have been anywhere, but he needed her, and somehow, in that moment, nothing was more important. When they came up for air, Grady took her hand and continued walking.

"My life was fine, Kate. Just different. I'm okay with that. This school allowed me the freedom to figure things out, it gave me my purpose. I have no complaints."

Chapter Twenty-Nine

They arrived back to Los Angeles the following morning, and Kate had a mountain of work waiting on her desk when she got to work. She caught Mark up on the key moments during the senator's trip and went over the new reports showing him easily leading his opponent. Mark seemed relieved, at least momentarily, and thanked Kate for handling things while he was at his daughter's high school graduation. When she got back to her desk, Sabrina brought in a huge arrangement of flowers. Blue hydrangeas and white roses, Kate's school colors. She smiled, and Sabrina was smart enough to say nothing, but she sighed on the way back to her desk.

Kate opened the tiny card that came with the flowers. It read simply – *For you, Kate.* How could three words mean so much? Kate touched the card to her chest and leaned over to smell the gorgeous blooms.

She knew Grady was speaking with a neighborhood watch group this morning, so she texted him:

Thank you. I suppose your Stanford trees aren't so bad after all.

She plugged her phone into the charger on her desk and got to work tackling everything that had piled up while she was playing fairytale.

Kate was exhausted by the time she got home. It was raining for the first time in weeks, and she'd just been on the phone listening to both her mother and her father telling her that Ethan's wife, Faith, just found out she was pregnant with their second child. Kate already knew because Faith had texted her a picture of the positive test stick. She sent back happy faces and kisses, but hadn't had a chance to talk with them yet. Her parents were thrilled, of course, and then instead of leaving it there, had to launch into when she was going to start a family. That of course led to why she was working so hard and never dated. By the time she reached her front door, she was soaking wet and about as far from a fairytale as she could get. She needed her slippers and her new couch immediately.

She had just settled in when her phone vibrated.

"Hey," Grady said when she answered. "How was your Friday back?"

"Well, after your flowers arrived, it went down hill from there. Where are you?" Kate asked, kicking her slippers off and pulling her feet onto the couch.

"Oh, you know, the bar, pounding back a few."

"Not funny. Seriously where are you?"

"All right, someone is grumpy. Anything I can do to help?"

"You can tell me that you're safe and sound in your bed. That you have no plans to blow off steam, and that getting back at your father for trotting you around a school he never cared about until it was determined it could help his election, is not on your agenda at all. I've just had to deal with my parents, I can't handle any fall-out from yours right now," she said, realizing her stomach was growling.

"Wow, that was a mouthful. I'm pretty sure I've dealt with those feelings in a positive way. I'm down here at Golden Phoenix, thinking of buying some Chinese and showing up at your door. But now I'm thinking you're not in the mood for me or my egg rolls," Grady said.

"I— well I was going to just sit here feeling sorry for myself, so why not. Don't forget the hot mustard and come on over."

"Be there in about thirty minutes. Sit tight. Don't start the pity-party without me."

Kate gave a half-hearted laugh and hung up the phone.

They sat on the couch with white paper boxes and chopsticks, watching the first *Mission Impossible*. As the credits rolled, Kate hit the mute button and leaned back, resting her head on the back of the couch.

"Not a whole lot of tabloid fodder here," she said, turning to look at him. "People might start to think you're just an average guy if you keep this up."

"True. Maybe someday they'll realize my life is none of their business. Are you okay? You seem stressed, angry, I'm not sure."

"See, normally I would agree with you, but you are not just laying low, living a quiet man's life, are you? With the exception of the last few months, you are a different guy. It's hard to keep track sometimes." Kate chose to ignore his questions because she found she was angry, confused.

"Wait, what are we talking about here, the campaign or our relationship?"

"What relationship? There isn't a relationship," Kate scoffed and got up to clear the food.

Grady followed.

"Because you're not sure who the hell I am? Is that what you're telling yourself now? There would be a relationship, you'd admit you have feelings for me, but oh this just in, you're not sure who I am?" Grady said, stepping into the kitchen.

"I'm talking in generalities here. I'm saying that you should figure out who you are. Just some friendly advice. Only here to help, Mr. Malendar."

She had pissed him off, she could tell these things about him now, and he moved into her space. "I know exactly who I am.

Since it's clear that we are now talking about our relationship, or lack thereof, I need to say that you, Kate, you are the one who needs to figure things out."

"What? We're not talking about me. This isn't about me. Stop twisting things around because you can't just be true to who you really are." She pushed past him and walked back into the living room.

"Oh, I get it now, you're not sure which man you're in love with." He stepped in front of her again. "If it's the guy all the women make goo goo eyes at, the one who acts like an idiot, well then you've repeated the same mistake."

Kate looked into his eyes. Anger hung between them, but Grady kept pushing.

"If it's the guy who's warm and fuzzy, the guy who helps sick people and children, then you want to parade him out like a trick pony so your client will win another damn election? Is that it, Kate? Either way, I lose, and do you want to know why?" He was inches from her now. "Because you are the one hiding. You're scared shitless, so don't turn this on me. Don't make this about me, because this conversation has nothing to do with me, or your job that you conveniently hide behind. This has to do with your heart, all caged up in there." Frustration spilled off him. He held her shoulders. "Let me in, God damn it," he pleaded.

"Get out," she said on a shallow breath.

Grady's hands dropped, he sighed, grabbed his coat and went out into the rain. When the door slammed, Kate sank to her couch. She was shaking, as if an intruder had just left her house. She *was* hiding, and she was dangerously close to being found.

Thirty minutes later there was a knock at the door. It was loud, frantic. Heart pounding, Kate knew who it was. She didn't have to look. She tried to collect herself, but it wasn't doing much good. She needed to buy some time before Grady was in front of her again.

"Who is it?"

No answer, just more knocking.

"Yes, who is it?"

"Kate, you know who it is."

"Grady? We don't have anything to discuss unless something is wrong? Why are you—" "Open the door, Kate," he said, his voice unsteady and breathy.

Kate slid the chain across the track and unlocked the door. Her shaking hand turned the knob and even though she knew why Grady had come back, she didn't expect what happened next. He gently pushed the door open and closed it behind him. He stared at her, water dripping from his lovely face, and turned the lock. His eyes were intense, almost like he was trying to figure out a puzzle. Dropping his coat at the door, Grady slowly came toward her, wet and still attempting to get his breath. He said nothing, not one word. Kate backed away as he kept coming until her back hit the wall of the entryway. He stood inches from her. She could feel his breath. Hands trembling, he brought them to her face, brushed them along her hair, sculpted gently, looking at Kate like . . . Christ, like no man had ever looked at her before.

She could not look away or come up with some clever, biting thing to say. She was putting all effort into getting oxygen as his hands settled along the back of her neck. He was cradling her face and still he said nothing. Kate couldn't breathe, so words were impossible. They stood listening to each other's breath. Grady was soaking wet. Water dripped from his gorgeous flushed face. Kate lifted her hand and moved the wet hair off his forehead. His eyes were so clear and his chest pulsed under his now nearly-transparent white shirt. It shot through her so fast, she didn't have time to think, process or analyze. All she knew was she wanted him. Just as he was, rich, poor, smart-ass, gentle warmth, she wanted it all. It didn't matter how long she had him or what the rules were. She wanted for the first time in a very long time, and that was enough. Kate touched his chest, unbuttoned his shirt, and peeled it off his shoulders. Grady's eyes followed her hands moving across his body. She waited for him to say something, but still nothing. He moved his hands to her sides, trying to free his arms from the wet shirt now buttoned at his wrists. He flicked one wrist free as the shirt, still attached to the other wrist, whipped up and across Kate's face. His eyes went wide and she broke with laughter.

"That . . . shit, are you okay?" He pulled her to him with his free arm. They were both laughing now. "That never happens."

Kate could not stop laughing. Here they were in this very passionate moment and Grady, Mr. Smooth, couldn't even get out of his shirt.

"Seriously, I'm usually pretty good at this. I really saw that going differently in my mind."

She reached down and undid the last button at his wrist. The shirt dropped to the floor.

"I mean can you believe that? I actually have moves. It's just you. It's when you—"

"Grady?"

His arms crossed in front of a most wonderful chest. He was still rambling about the shirt slap and Kate had moved on to the chest, the arms, and the wet linen pants. All of that mixed with fumbling, laughter and his flushed cheeks. She was gone.

"Yeah."

"Come here."

He stood in front of her.

"Closer."

He smiled, unfolded his arms and stood almost nose-to-nose, staring into her eyes. *Jesus Christ!*

"Grady?"

"Yes, Kate?" he said, putting his hands up on the wall and boxing her in. He hovered, skimmed her body with his eyes and met her breathless stare.

"Touch me."

He slowly brought his lips to hers, arms still extended on the wall. His lips brushed, continued along her jaw and down her neck. It was soft, he was barely there, but her entire body felt him. She unraveled one tiny nerve at a time. Kate brushed her fingers along his collarbone, over the caps of his shoulders, and then touched her lips to his neck. Grady's arms wrapped around her and his mouth was on her. She melted into him and was filled with the warmth of the very best spring rain. She could feel his breath change as her hands traveled along his back. What began as soft, quickly turned urgent as they both slipped past the line Kate had clung to in a desperate attempt to save herself from feeling what was now racing through her entire body. Her thoughts suddenly reminded her it had been a long time. They tried to fill her with insecurity and doubt, but with each touch, all thought was muffled and Kate let go.

After, they lay at the base of her new couch tangled in each other, listening to the rain dance on the windows. It was dark except for the glow from what was left of the candle Kate had lit when she got home. Grady ran his fingers along her spine. His breath rhythmic, soft. Kate began sliding off to the side, but he held her in place.

"Just, could I just have one more minute wrapped in you?" he asked.

She smiled into his chest and stayed right where she was, listening to his heart and feeling peaceful, surrounded. Kate tilted her head up to peek at him. He kept one arm around her and put the other behind his head. *Sweet Jesus, he was even comfortable with himself naked.*

"I don't want to let go," he said, tracing a finger through her hair.

"Well, at some point we'll need to . . . "

"I don't need anything. I'm all set."

She touched his face. "You have bushy eyebrows."

"Hmm, not sure I've gotten that one before," he said raising an eyebrow dramatically.

"You do, they're bushier now that I'm close and . . . "

"Naked on top of me?"

She laughed. "Yes, that too. I like them and," her fingers moved down his cheek, "what's the story with this?"

"I need to shave?"

"I know that, but did you shave this morning? I mean that's an awful lot of stubble for the end of the day." Kate was being playful and he smiled.

"I sort of shaved this morning. It's not my favorite thing to do. I had pretty bad skin growing up, mostly on my cheeks and chin. When I was younger it was hard to shave and now I kind of use the stubble to cover up my not so smooth skin. It's all about covering up the less appealing parts, right?"

Kate smiled.

"Also, I suppose I'm a hairy guy?"

"Nice hairy. I like your hair." She touched his lips. "And I love these . . . these lips. I've secretly always loved them."

He kissed the tip of her fingers. "I like you this way."

"What way is that?" She touched his chin.

"Warm, relaxed and basking."

"Basking, huh?"

"Yes, I think so. Let me get a closer look." In one move Grady was over her, surveying. For a moment she was self-conscious, but the way he looked at her was something unreal, and then he made her laugh. "Well, you are definitely not hairy, so that's good." He ran his finger along her face and she closed her eyes. "Oh no, don't close those. I could look into them forever. There's so much in there, it's endless."

Kate opened her eyes.

"This nose is pretty cute, but right back at you with these," he gently touched her lips. "Who knew these luscious lips would be so . . . " He kissed her and she felt desired and wanted. The comfort and ease of touching each other's face, so simple, but intimate. She looked at Grady, into the blue of his eyes that turned down a little at the ends. His eyes were mischievous, intelligent, and at that moment the look in them made her feel something she had never felt before—cherished. Tears pooled in her eyes and one slipped down the side of her face.

Grady wiped the tear away. "You are breath-taking, and I am—I'm so in love with you."

She melted and tears continued. "Where did you come from?"

"Technically? Well in the biblical sense, I came from a very nice woman named Bindi, but . . . "

She could tell he was trying to make her smile, stop the tears. She loved him for it. She loved him. She knew it, maybe she had always known it. "Grady," she said.

"Kate."

"I'm in love with you too, all of you. I don't know how I got here, but you are here," she touched her hand to her chest, "and I can't get you out."

Grady took her hand and kissed it.

"I've heard some great lines in my life, but those words," he shook his head and took a long breath, "I've been waiting for something from your elusive heart." His lips closed over hers and then she stood, leading him to the bathroom.

She smiled over her shoulder. "Absolutely no comments about the size of my shower. We can't all have a bathroom the size of a small apartment."

"If this is leading where I think it is, I doubt I'll even notice the bathroom."

They lathered, laughed some more, kissed, caressed, and made love on the other two pieces of her new furniture before sliding off to sleep. Kate couldn't remember being so satisfied or so whole. She hadn't felt whole in a long time; she may have never felt what she was feeling now. The pain that was buried beneath the surface when Nick chose to be with another woman had left her a while ago, replaced by indifference and a driving need to survive. As part of her survival Kate had shut down, but Grady was right, she was still in there—the happy, whole part of her—and she was an incredible woman. She had just forgotten.

Chapter Thirty

They were eating Fruit Loops on her thoroughly christened couch and watching *Law and Order* as the sun came up and washed Kate's apartment with a light she swore was different. It was pink, warm, fuzzy sweater pink, and she hoped that it never went away because everything was magical in this light. Especially Grady's rumpled morning body, sitting next to her in nothing but boxer shorts. They had put his clothes in the dryer at some point, but she was presently happy he had forgotten about them. His hair was off in different directions, his stubble, his eyes, the whole package together with the "Loops" was a deadly combination. Kate let out a slow breath of appreciation for early morning Grady.

He had helped her unpack a few more boxes at some ungodly hour of the night. Her books, her frames . . . she had forgotten all about the frames. Forgotten about most of the things, her things, that she had packed away.

Kate jumped up to get more milk. She was in nothing but a T-shirt and Grady was clearly no longer interested in law *or* order. He pulled her into his lap and kissed her.

She smiled up at him. "It's early, let's hit some estate sales."

"Not exactly what I had in mind, but sounds good. I've actually never been to an estate sale," Grady said, in between kissing her again.

"Of course you haven't. Probably because you grew up in an estate," Kate laughed.

"Doesn't someone have to die to prompt an estate sale?"

"I've never really thought about it, but probably. Or maybe they're downsizing," she said, finally getting up and grabbing the milk from the kitchen.

"Eh, not sure that really happens. Can't say my mom ever had an estate sale. I however had an award-wining lemonade stand in the second grade. No big deal."

"Did you serve organic, homemade lemonade in crystal glasses?" she asked, sitting beside him.

"No. I think they were champagne flutes."

Kate gave him a quick "Really?" look, and Grady laughed.

"Nope, sorry to disappoint, just clear Solo cups like everyone else. Did you ever have a lemonade stand over there in the hard working real world? Probably grew the lemons yourself?" he teased.

Kate pushed him back on the couch, straddled his lap. Grady pulled her up and carried her back to her new bed. They didn't make it to the estate sales until later in the day, much later.

Grady left that evening to feed Bo and get some work done. Kate met Reagan at Hana's, as planned, for her last weekly dinner as a single woman. Reagan's wedding was the following weekend. The drink of the night was an Aviation. Kate loved them because they were light, crisp. Reagan loved them because they were purple and served in dainty glasses. Their food arrived and after going over the final wedding checklist one last time, Kate relaxed into the booth and confided in her friend.

"Doesn't it bother you, Ben's money?"

"Kate, you're not exactly poor. I know you live a simple life, but your father is the Chief of Police. You have great shoes and a Louis Vuitton bag. You're not loaded, but you are certainly not living check to check."

"I never said I was, but Ben makes a hell of a lot more money than I do and I just wonder if it gets to you."

"I honestly don't think about it. He's not extravagant, so it's not at the forefront of our relationship. It's money. We can take some nice trips, but he still books us at the Best Westerns because they are always the best locations."

They laughed.

"Now, Ben is certainly not as wealthy as Grady, because that's what we are actually talking about here, right?" Kate said nothing, smelled the sweet violet of her drink. "That kind of wealth is a different level, but it's all just money and you can't really hold it against the guy because he's not poor."

"I slept with him. I mean, we slept, actually there wasn't a whole lot of sleeping. Christ." Kate downed the rest of her drink.

Reagan took her hand, smiled, and quietly started bouncing in the booth.

"Okay, well that's an interesting plot twist. You're not smiling, so should I assume it was . . . not a good experience?"

Kate looked up from her empty glass, swallowed, and Reagan knew.

"That good, huh?" Reagan said.

Kate just nodded. She didn't know what to say. It had been a while since she had anything sexy to discuss.

"Of course it was, have you looked at the man? Well, sure, you've looked at all of him now and I'm guessing, even though I'm almost a married woman, that the view was pretty sensational. Kate? Are you going to say something?"

Kate closed her eyes. Allowed the buzz of expensive gin to wash over her, and then she opened them and said, "I love him."

"Of course you do, honey. You would have never slept with him, or not gotten much sleep with him, if you didn't."

"I told him. I said those words."

Reagan said nothing, waited for her to continue.

"I'm just not sure where to go from here, you know. He knows now, he has me and I . . . well, I don't have a safety net anymore. I have furniture now and yesterday I unpacked my books, took out some pictures."

Reagan's eyes began to tear. She quickly wiped them away and took her friend's hand. "He's not going to drop you, honey. He's loved you for a while now, and I'm guessing that's not something he takes lightly. Is the money the problem, or the safety net?"

"Both. I mean you're right that he doesn't really flaunt it, relatively speaking. I suppose if I had a plane, we'd use it too."

"Yeah, we would!"

The both of them laughed together, and Reagan signaled for dessert.

Monday morning, Grady was back in Kate's bed watching her spin around the room in all her just-had-a-weekend-of-incredible-sex glory. She ran around brushing her teeth and getting ready for work. Most of her boxes were now put away, but he found she still navigated around the room as if they were there, as if she might trip over something. She was so stunning his chest hurt, and when she kissed him and sent him on his way before getting in her car for work, Grady knew how he wanted to begin every day for the rest of his life. He got into his car and drove home. Bo had been with his neighbor and deserved a very long walk.

Kate and Grady continued on in much the same passionately in love and laughing way while they were either at her house, or his. But in public, they agreed, they had a little over a month before the election, and it was best to keep things professional. Which was extremely difficult because every time Grady saw Kate, let alone touched her, he wanted to gather her in his arms and go back to her couch. As the real world started to seep into their lives again, Grady couldn't help but worry.

It was one thing that he had been subjected to the fishbowl and reports his whole life, but now he was in love, he was loved, and he wanted to protect that more than anything. So, if they went hiking, it was on off hours, and they mostly ate at home. On the rare occasion they were approached by reporters, Grady stood in front of Kate and politely answered questions. They were very much a couple, but trying to not be a couple. Grady felt alive for maybe the first time in his life and was starting to actually resent the hiding. But he had Kate and only forty-three days to go.

Chapter Thirty-One

Reagan and Ben were married on the rooftop patio of the Oviatt Penthouse in Los Angeles. Reagan wore a simple strapless blush dress with a crystal and beaded overlay made from her mother's wedding dress. No veil. She was incandescent—subtle makeup she did herself and blonde mermaid-hair piled in a loose bun. There were dragonflies and one crystal frog, compliments of her nieces and nephew, pinned into her bun. Ben wore a bow tie, a vest under his dark navy blazer, and dark tan pants. He decided to shave for the wedding, but wore his glasses, and when everyone stood and Reagan walked toward him, he had to take them off to wipe his eyes.

Reagan made a silly face, as they had agreed she would do if he started to cry, and Ben shared the most brilliant smile Kate had seen in a very long time. Ben's teeth were a little crooked, so his smile was like a very cool professor, Tom Cruise. When Reagan's father passed her hand to Ben, she turned toward him and Ben took both of her hands in his, brought them to his lips and kissed her as if they were already alone, on some magical street in Venice. A breeze tousled Ben's hair and Reagan reached up to push it out of his face. Kate looked at the two of them, the wonderful warmth played out in front of her, and she saw a different kind of love. A comfortable, cozy, imperfect, and yet so-perfect love. Kate's heart opened, softened, that her friend was so clearly happy. Many would say that Ben was good for Reagan, that he gave structure to her crazy artist life, that she finally had to clean the clay out from under her nails when she met Ben, but they would be wrong. Ben loved her clay, even when it ended up splattered on his briefcase, or dried onto her nose when he bent for a goodbye kiss in the morning on his way into the office. Reagan was his "lampshade," he had once said.

"Before I found you, I was just a bare bulb. You're my flowery, doily ball, grandma shade, Reagan. You cover me, surround me and defuse my harsh light into something so beautiful," he added, as he now spoke his vows to her. There wasn't a dry eye on that rooftop as Ben kissed the bride.

Reagan was a potter. Her work was now pretty famous, she even had one piece in the Guggenheim. She and Ben opened a small gallery of her work last year. Ben was an investment associate at Capital Group. They met at a Forte Foundation community event. Reagan volunteered for the foundation, which promoted opportunities for women through art education and creative healing. Ben was there handing out water bottles when she asked if Capital Group owned stock in water bottles, and shouldn't they be promoting reusable bottles and less waste? Ben said he was hooked from that moment on. He asked for her number and Reagan opened his hand and wrote her number inside with a Sharpie. Reagan was skeptical when she called to tell Kate she'd met someone. Reagan was always skeptical, until she met Ben.

"He'll probably never call and then say he washed the number off."

"He will not. Is that what you were hoping when you wrote your number in a grown man's hand? Are you self-sabotaging again?"

"No, annoying shrink person, I am not screwing myself. I don't do that anymore, I simply live alone and avoid things that will send my heart through a meat grinder."

"That sounds incredibly healthy."

"Said the kettle. Do you really want to get into healthy?"

Kate had looked around at her new empty apartment and said, "No. But, we aren't talking about me. So, how did, what's his name again? Get through your mental security?"

"Ben, his name is Ben, and I don't know. His eyes are brown. They are sort of big for a guy, and he has a crooked smile. Nice strong hands, chewed nails, which was refreshing for a suit type." Kate could hear Reagan let out a slow breath. "His shorts had a crease."

"Wait, you mean like they were ironed?"

"Yeah."

"Why is this important?"

"He looked so neat, so tidy. I sort of want to mess him up. Maybe tie him to the bed and see what he looks like when he's—"

"Okay, we can stop there."

Reagan laughed. "Isn't that weird? I haven't had those thoughts in a long time. He was so different, sort of like I'd been drifting around in a sea of people who barely saw me, and then there he was, looking at me, seeing me, and I saw him too. Does that make sense?" Kate nodded and Reagan shook her head. "But, mainly it was the ironed shorts that did it. I want those suckers in a ball on my bedroom floor."

"Wow. Down girl. Take it easy on the poor guy."

"Anyway, it doesn't matter. He's not going to call. I had that really bad skirt on. The one you call my Janis Joplin skirt. I look thick through the middle in that one, so he's not calling."

Kate laughed and mentally agreed that the Joplin skirt was not Reagan's best look, but she was gypsy beautiful, with long tangly curly blonde hair, and eyes that seemed to only be given out to creative people. Reagan really saw people, looked into them. Kate was sure this poor corporate guy took one look at her and she could have been in a potato sack. Reagan intrigued men, but very few bothered to step close enough and take a chance. Like she said, she was an expert at avoiding. The next day, Ben called and kept calling. They were engaged a year later.

After the ceremony, Kate was talking to Reagan's Aunt Gwen

about her recipe for apple cake when she saw Grady approaching. She excused herself and walked toward him. He wasn't smiling.

"Grady," Kate looked around, for what, she wasn't sure anymore. "I didn't realize you were—"

"Invited? Yeah, well that's the thing. The woman I'm—what would we call it?—with, the woman I'm with," he leaned into her and whispered, "sleeping with, that kind of with—Kate. She was the maid of honor at this wedding, it's her best friend's wedding." Grady searched for a place to talk privately and took her arm. "You'd think I'd be her plus-one, right?" His face was playful, but there was an undercurrent of annoyance, but it was still a pretty attractive face. He wore a tweed jacket, white shirt, and dark pants, open collar. He blended perfectly with the wedding theme. How the hell did he do this, Kate thought, coordinate with his surroundings? It's like he called ahead. "But, for some reason, I haven't heard from my girlfriend, my lover."

Kate looked around and shhhed him.

Grady kept her moving and gently pushed through a door that led to a sitting area inside the penthouse, maybe a private dressing area, Kate wasn't sure, but they were alone. "I haven't heard from you in three days, Kate. What's going on?"

"What? What are you talking about? I've seen you, has it been three days?"

"You know exactly how long it's been. You've been counting the hours right along with me. Don't lie. Why are you at this wedding alone? When you're with someone, with me? Do you not want to be seen with me?"

"Oh, yeah, that's it. You're a real embarrassment. Cut it out. I just didn't think it was appropriate with the campaign, we agreed, it's best if we lay low and this is private. Most of what we do can pass as work-related, so I didn't know."

Grady stepped into her space. "Work-related? I'm not sure I'd call what we do, work-related anymore."

Kate stepped back. "You know what I mean. We're not exactly defined. I—hell, I don't know, I just didn't invite you. I had a lot on my mind helping Reagan and I didn't think about it. And yet, you're here anyway." Kate laughed, hoped he believed her, tried to convince herself.

"This isn't going to work."

Kate's face fell.

"I'm not just going to crawl back into my place. I can't just go back on your color-coded schedule, I know how it feels now."

"What?"

"This push-away thing you're doing. That's what this is, right?"

She said nothing so he approached her again.

"It won't work. I know now what it's like to breathe in your space, to wake up next to you. I know your real laugh, I've had your feet in my lap on Sunday morning. Behind the curtain. I'm way behind the curtain here, Kate."

"Grady."

"No, don't. Just close your eyes." He turned her toward the window and Kate could feel the chill of the unoccupied room and then the penetrating warmth of his body as it closed around her without even touching. "Can you see me? Can you feel my hands on your body, my stubble scraping over your . . . ," he whispered in her ear and Kate gasped.

Her entire body came alive.

"Can you see it? Do you see my eyes when I look at you, Kate?"

She swayed and found her back leaning just slightly against his chest. She stayed there, eyes still closed, hoping she could clear her mind, wash away every detail of what he was saying, but it was useless.

"Can you see it, feel me?"

"Yes," she said, on the softest whisper.

"It never goes away, it's not supposed to. I've waited for you, Kate and I'll keep waiting. The election is less than a month away. I just need to know I'm not here alone."

Kate was petrified. A dramatic word, she knew, but appropriate. She was drowning in him, and she needed him. She had promised herself she would never need, get lost, again. She opened her eyes and turned to face Grady. His face was serious. He needed too, but at the moment he seemed more comfortable in the knowledge. Kate touched the side of his wonderful face and his eyes closed. She leaned in to kiss him on the cheek and spoke into his ear.

"You are not alone, I'm here."

His eyes opened and she pulled back.

"I'm scared. I don't know if I can do this," she said.

"You're doing just fine."

"Oh really, because I'm shaking and as appealing as the feeling is, I'm not sure I can function for the long term."

"Why are you scared to be with me?"

"I'm not scared of being with you." She leaned forward again and softly spoke into his chest what she couldn't bear to admit to his face. "I'm scared of what it will be like, what I will be like, when you're gone. When it falls apart and I . . . "

Grady gently lifted her chin, met her eyes, and gave her a gentle kiss and without one word, reminded her that he had her, he wasn't going to let go.

Chatter and clinking glasses could be heard on the other side of the door, but it didn't matter. He did that to her, cleared away the noise. Kate took his face in her hands and kissed him again. This time there was nothing gentle about it. She wanted him. She honestly couldn't get enough. Grady returned the kiss and they were tangled, touching. Kate's head fell back, as Grady kissed her neck, and then someone knocked on the door. Kate pulled away, instinctively fixing her dress, as Grady smiled and moved toward the door. The knock came again.

"I know you're in there," Reagan's voice said from the other side. "That's why I knocked. I didn't want to see anything I couldn't unsee." She laughed. It was an intoxicatingly happy bride-giggle laced with some very expensive champagne.

Kate laughed quietly and joined Grady by the door.

"Unless of course Grady has his shirt off, that might be worth a look," Reagan said, sounding like she was actually leaning on the door at that point.

"Ooops, sorry that was not appropriate, I'm a married woman now."

"Reagan?" Grady said.

"Ah ha! I knew you guys were in there. Sneaky make-out session at my romantic wedding. If that's what's going on in there, I have to say, Mr. Senator's Son Love of My Best Friend's Life, I approve,"

Grady looked back at Kate who shook her head in joking denial.

"Reagan, sweetheart, I'm going to open the door. I need to make sure you're not leaning on it. Ben will kick my ass if I let you face plant on your wedding night, so step back, okay?"

They could hear the ruffle of material and what sounded like Reagan kicking a glass across the floor.

"Okay. I'm off the door. Get out here, you two love birds." Grady opened the door and Reagan was standing in all her bride beauty. She'd let her hair down, or more likely it had fallen down, because Reagan knew how to have a party. Her hands on her hips, an open bottle of champagne tucked into a few fingers. Kate smiled and walked out of the room followed by Grady.

"You two," Reagan said, swerving a bit and putting one arm around Grady's waist and the other around Kate's shoulders, "my best friend in the world, and you." She looked at Grady. "You're just a good guy, Grady. Kate tells me everything, and I mean everything." She wriggled her eyebrows. "I have to tell you that—"

"All right, that's about enough of that," Kate gently guided her away from Grady. "I think we need to find Ben," Kate said looking around for the happy groom.

"Okay, okay." Reagan leaned in and whispered toward Grady. "She totally sleeps in your shirt. The one she took from your house. She's never slept in anyone's shirt."

Grady laughed and Kate continued in vain to pull her away.

"Right? That's huge," Reagan continued. "She's totally upside down for you, Grady, my friend."

Kate couldn't help it, she started laughing too, as the three of them made their way past the dance floor and over to Ben. He spotted them and was looking at Reagan the way he always did, with complete adoration.

Reagan kept talking and was now bopping to the Bruno Mars

song the DJ had just started playing. She leaned into Grady one last time and kissed him on the cheek. "Thank you," she said, capturing him with her glittering eyes. "Thank you for finding her, my precious friend, and helping her to . . . " Reagan's eyes teared up and she held a hand to her chest.

They had reached Ben by this point, and Kate could only stand there and watch Reagan as she finished sharing her heart.

"Not that she wouldn't have found her way out anyway, but I love you for helping her see, see herself the way the rest of us do again." She hugged Grady and he hugged her back, his own eyes watering by this point, Kate could see. Not that he'd ever admit to it.

Ben shook Grady's hand as his wife still hung onto their hug.

"She gets a little emotional when she drinks," Ben said smiling.

"Nothing wrong with that. Congratulations, man."

Reagan let go and moved to hugging Kate, who probably should have been embarrassed, but her friend was so beautiful in her honesty that Kate didn't care. She was practicing not caring about stupid things lately. It felt good. The four of them hit the dance floor and closed down the party celebrating what Kate was certain would be the everlasting love story of Reagan and Ben.

Chapter Thirty-Two

Kate's eyes drifted closed on the way back to Grady's house. He wanted her in his bed even more now that he knew she stole his shirts. Grady looked at the clock on the car dash. It was just after one in the morning. Having an inspired idea, he turned on Wall Street and headed toward the flower district. The parking lot was packed with grower trucks all unloading and setting up for tomorrow's market. Grady undid his seatbelt, leaned over, and kissed Kate. She smiled, still sleepy, and then opened her eyes slowly, surprised to see they were not at his house. Kate pushed her hair off her face and leaned toward the car window to get a closer look. Grady got out of the car and walked around to open her door.

"Where are we?" Kate asked, still groggy as she accepted Grady's hand out of the car. "Wait, is this the flower market? We ... this isn't open. How—? Who are all of these people?" Grady guided her toward the back door.

"They're growers loading in for tomorrow's market." They reached the door and were greeted by a short balding man wearing a Bazooka Gum T-shirt and chewing on a cigar.

"Hey, hey, sorry guys, but this is loading time. The market don't open to the public until five. Less of course you're florists and then we . . . wait, Grady?"

Grady smiled. "Hey, Leo. I know it's loading, but I was hoping to impress my girl here with some of my big-time connections. It's all who you know in this town, you know?"

Leo transferred the cigar in his mouth to his two chubby fingers and laughed like it wasn't the middle of the night. He gave Grady a hug complete with a hearty slap on the back. "How you been, brat? It's been a while."

"I'm good," Grady said, taking Kate's hand. She must have been tired, because she didn't pull away. "We're just coming home from a wedding and I was hoping to give Kate a behind-the-scenes tour."

"Kate." Leo stuck his cigar in the beanbag ashtray sitting on a metal stool next to the door. He brushed his hands on his jeans and then offered one up to Kate. "It's a pleasure to meet you. Welcome to our market."

Kate shook his hand and smiled. "Thank you, Leo. It's my pleasure as well. I've never been here at night."

Leo ushered them in and stopped Grady.

"This one's a keeper, eh?" he asked.

Grady laughed and nodded. "That she is. Have I ever brought anyone around to meet you?"

"Nope," he said, picking up his cigar and taking a big puff.

"Then you've got it right. She's the one. I love her something sick, Leo." Kate turned from her spot up ahead and watched the two of them still talking.

"It was bound to happen to you, my boy," Leo said laughing and patting Grady on the back. "Well, then, get in there and show her a good time. Rick has already arrived, so start with the orchids. Those are always a show."

Grady nodded. "Will do. Thanks for making me look cool. How's Marie?"

Leo tilted his head back and forth in a so-so motion.

"She has her moments. Pretty much kicked the cancer's ass again. Doc says she's in remission, but those meds, all that poking and prodding at her . . . " Leo's eyes got a little glassy. "Eh, you know what? I got no complaints. She's a fighter and still as gorgeous as the day I met her."

"She is a beauty," Grady said, smiling and trying to ease some of the pain in Leo's eyes. "Grandkids are good?"

"Terrors, all three of them, but they keep us young." Leo looked at Kate, who was standing in the center of an aisle, eyes closed, smelling the flowers. "Speaking of young, looks like your lady already appreciates our market. Now get going before she changes her mind about you." Grady turned to look at Kate in all of her inhibition-abandonment, and his heart pulled not for the first time that evening.

"Good idea. Thanks, again. We'll catch you on the way out."

"Sounds good." Leo waved him off, picked up his clipboard, and got back to work.

Grady came up behind Kate and wrapped his arms around her, and again Kate let him.

"Are you falling asleep on your feet, or imagining you are in a sea of the most beautiful flowers?"

Kate smiled, eyes still closed.

"Both."

Kate opened her eyes.

"This is incredible. So different at night. The sounds and the lighting, it's . . . " Kate couldn't seem to find the words, and then she pulled him behind the masking of an empty stall and kissed him. It looked for a minute like she might have kissed him right there in the middle of the aisle, but the election was a month away and Grady knew that Kate's PR-self never really slept. Kate pulled back from the kiss and released Grady's shirtfront she'd been gripping in what felt like desperation. He knew all about needing Kate, but it was nice to see he was not alone.

Grady's face eased into a deep smile. "Okay, well, note to self, flower markets in the middle of the night are worth it." Grady snaked his arm around her waist and kissed her again. This time was slow, as if they had all the time in the world. When he pulled back, her eyes were still closed. He brushed her cheek, kissed her cold nose.

"Mmm . . . the smell is amazing. Why have I never noticed the smell before? I've been to this market dozens of times and somehow it's different, it's different with you. Everything is." Kate opened her eyes and looked into his. For a brief moment she looked like one of those teenage girls strapped into a roller coaster about to depart. Excited, but still not sure. Grady had seen that look before, but less frequently these days. He took her hand and led her back to the main stalls.

"You haven't seen anything yet. Let's start with orchids and then move on to roses. There are over three dozen different kinds of roses at this market on any given day." Grady handed her a map that outlined each stall.

"Did you know that technically George Washington wasn't just our fist president, but also the first rose breeder in the United States?" Grady felt like a child on a field trip with a pretty girl he was trying to impress.

"I did not know that very interesting fact. Money probably, I mean who else could afford roses at that time?" Kate said, picking up the aroma of coffee in the air.

"Always comes back to money doesn't it? Maybe he was the only one willing to till the soil, create the right chemistry. Maybe he worked harder," Grady said, leading her toward another entrance.

Kate laughed. "Maybe, Mr. Malendar, maybe that's exactly what it was. And I'm sure he took care of all that gardening by himself, right? I mean being the president and all, I'm sure there was no staff," she said, rolling her eyes.

"Actually, the presidency was nothing like it is now. Things were different—"

"One word, Grady, one word, *slaves*." Kate moved past him and toward the coffee booth. "I mean that's all I have to say. Sure things were different, different worse, for everyone but white wealthy men."

"Christ, we are talking about five different things now. How do you do that? Turn one comment into a full-on discussion. Monumental issues all because the man grew roses."

Kate turned to face him, still walking backwards.

She smiled. "It's a gift."

They both laughed.

"Yeah well, this isn't a win," he said. "We will resume this discussion once I've had at least three or four hours of sleep."

They both agreed, and stopped at the coffee booth just inside the main entrance.

"Bless your soul. I will have the largest coffee you have," Kate said.

Grady laughed and so did the woman now pouring the coffee.

"I'll have what she's having," he said, and reached for his wallet.

Warm coffee in hand, they set out to explore the stalls. Dodging carts and vendors buzzing in and out.

"So, Leo is a friend of yours?" Kate asked.

"He is. I've known him and his wife, Marie, for almost eighteen years now."

"Huh," Kate said, touching the greenery as they passed one of the stalls. "Do you know him from here, or . . ."

"He used to be our family florist. Owned a little shop in Pasadena when I was growing up. I worked summers at his place, cleaning up, riding with him on deliveries. He taught me pretty much everything I know about flowers and a big chunk of what I know about life. His wife got cancer when I was in high school."

"Oh, I'm sorry."

"Yeah, well, she's a fighter, but the expense of her treatment almost crippled them. He was a small business with small-business benefits. He also had crazy taxes. When I was in college, I'd help him with his returns over winter break. It's where I really learned about the middle-class squeeze." Grady picked up a huge coral rose and handed it to Kate. "I mean, have you ever seen anything so extraordinary?" he asked, changing the subject.

"No," she said, moving to him, but careful to keep her distance, "I've never seen a more extraordinary rose or a more extraordinary man."

Kate looked at him and there it was. He wanted to be that man in her eyes more than anything else. That thought, he would admit, was a little scary.

"So, what happened to the flower shop?" Kate asked, putting the rose back.

"She was in remission for a while with the first bout, but it came back around the time I graduated. Leo couldn't hold it together any more. They needed benefits and cash, so he sold the business and came to work here." Grady sipped his coffee. "He said she was all that mattered in his life, so if he had to have a job, he'd get a job."

Kate sighed. "That's a very sad story. For him and the state of our country, but he seems happy."

"He is happy." Grady smiled and pointed out sunflowers bursting out of newspaper cones. "He has two kids, three grandkids, and Marie is in remission again. They were married fifty years this past January."

Kate raised her eyebrows. "Wow, that is something I can't imagine."

Kate yawned and Grady could easily imagine that many years, as long as they were with her.

"Getting tired?" He asked.

"Nah, just ignore that. The coffee should kick in any minute."

"Well before you start fading, let's hit the tulips. We should probably get out of here anyway before the florist buyers show up. It's a zoo in here by three."

They continued walking and Grady commented, sort of like one of those home gardening television hosts, that "tulips were from the lily family." Kate followed that with the fact that "they were also related to a family that included onions." They were quite a pair, the two of them, delirious flower nerds. Grady bought a huge bunch of tulips and picked up another bunch of daffodils while the woman in a green apron wrapped the tulips in newspaper. Grady threw out his empty coffee cup and put his free arm around Kate. She quickly moved it and looked around. Grady laughed.

"Oh yes, this will be a scandal if anyone catches us here at the Los Angeles Flower Market, drinking coffee and geeking out over flowers. That is a scandal from which my father will not recover." He tried to hold her again and Kate grew serious.

"It's not that we are here, it's that people don't need to know we are here together. I mean . . . damn it. I'm usually articulate when I'm not around you."

"I know, I've seen you bullshit with the best to them."

"Shut up. You know what I mean. We can't be seen," she said, holding up finger quotes, 'together.' It doesn't look right for either of us."

"Fine," Grady said as they approached the exit and Leo.

"Ah, looks like you found something for your pretty lady there, Grady."

Kate blushed and looked around again.

Grady smiled and handed Leo the daffodils. "For Marie."

Leo nodded his head. "Her favorite. I'll get them to her this morning. Brighten her day. Thank you." He hugged Grady and then kissed Kate's hand. Kate should have continued to be on guard, should have corrected Leo that she was not Grady's lady, but looking in the man's weathered brown eyes, it didn't seem important. In the whole context, as Grady had put it, who cared?

"Good night, Leo. It was a pleasure meeting you," was all she said.

Kate and Grady walked into the ink-colored evening, alight only by dim street lamps. The fragrance of thousands of blooms lingered all the way to the car. Kate would remember this night forever. She would replay the evening hundreds of times, and mark it as the magical start of her very best friend's married life. She would also remember that she had never felt more in love or more off balance in her entire life. When they got to the car, in the shadow of the parking lot, Kate took Grady's face in her hands and gently kissed him.

"What was that for?" he asked.

"For showing me things."

Grady touched the back of his hand to her cheek.

"For turning things upside down, surprising me, making me feel cherished, and giving me the most wonderful view." She kissed him again.

Chapter Thirty-Three

The following Tuesday, Kate walked into her office to find Mark and a stack of tabloid magazines. Internally she gasped at the headlines, her heart was racing, but she let nothing show. On the outside, she was the same as always. Ready to work. Within an hour, her staff was working on gathering the facts and coming up with a damage control strategy. Kate filled her mug with coffee from the office kitchen and went behind closed doors. She needed a minute. She was only halfway through her much-needed minute when Grady knocked and then walked right into her office.

"Kate, I wanted to get to you before this crap broke."

"Why?" she asked on a whisper, holding her mug with both hands. She stared out the window, and did not turn to face him. She couldn't.

"Um." She could tell by his voice that he was suddenly uneasy. "Because . . . I thought we could have a good laugh. Kate, I know—"

She spun around and the look on her face silenced him. It wasn't anger, she was simply struggling to say in one piece.

"It's fine. Did you really think this was ever going to work? Were you delusional enough to think that I believed you loved me forever, Grady?" Kate said batting her eyelashes and holding her hands up to her face like an innocent schoolgirl. "I get it. I'm a big girl and believe me. I've done this before. We had a good time, things happen."

"What?" Grady was stunned.

Kate turned aloof and finished him off. "I'm just pissed that this is going to hurt the campaign and that you managed this on my watch." She looked down at her desk and despite the look in his eyes, she willed herself to stay together. *Survive, Kate, at all costs.*

Grady actually stumbled back a step as if he'd been physically hit. "Am I really supposed to stand here and . . . ? Do I have to explain to you that I didn't . . . oh, Kate, are you kidding me?"

She looked up at him, her jaw clenched, and broke his heart. Kate could see it in his face, but she couldn't stop the flood of doubt and suspicion. It didn't register with her that it might be just another stupid rumor. She immediately believed he was a scumbag that slept with a hooker. Part of her felt awful now that he was finally in front of her, dumbfounded, but most of her began putting on the armor. She'd spent the last hour pacing Mark's office, listening to the sordid details, and closing her heart off like one of those medieval drawbridges. Above everything, she could not let the pain in. If there was any chance, any chance at all, that he would, that he . . . she just couldn't let any of it in. She wouldn't survive. Grady took her arm and she pulled away. He took a deep breath and his eyes were angry now.

"First, first of all, I don't pay for sex. I don't have to." *Touché, nice opening and probably very true.* "Second, when I'm with a woman—"

Kate turned away and he took her face gently.

"When I'm in love with a woman, I don't . . . I can't even believe I need to say this to you." His hand dropped and he moved around her office like a prowling cat, frustration simmering. "I'm not Nick, god damn it! In fact, screw him for doing this, making you into this." He flailed his hands up and down. "I thought . . . Jesus, we haven't . . . we're right here aren't we? You, your first thought was that someone that . . . even though my heart literally jumps to be near you, that I'd throw that all away. I'd pick up this hooker and take her to the Wilshire. What'd she say?" He ran his hands over his face. "Oh, yeah, 'Just like in *Pretty Woman*,'—really? That's not even the best lie anyone's ever told about me. This wasn't even a really good one, Kate."

She turned away.

"Shit, what am I doing? I've had just about enough of this fucking campaign screwing with my life. Not being able to be with you." He seemed to laugh in pain. "You know what? This probably works perfectly for you. You're never going to let me all the way in anyway, are you? Believe whatever you want. I've done nothing."

Kate continued to look at the wall. She thought he was going to leave. This was almost over, but he turned and walked behind her. "I'm not perfect, but I did not do this. You know I'm yours Kate, and you're mine. You of all people know that I did not do this. I love you. Can't you just let me . . . " He touched her shoulder and she went back behind the safety of her desk.

Kate never looked up, never looked at him.

"Love me back, all the way. I'm worth it, I promise."

A tear fell on to the folder Kate kept moving from one side of her desk to the other. She said nothing, and began going through papers.

She heard him exhale. "Goodbye, Kate." He walked out of her office and they were done. *Tested and failed, Kate. Nice work!*

The glow of the neon above the bar washed over a heavily-pierced bartender. This was a dive bar, even for Grady. He didn't care. He needed somewhere to hide, some place no one would recognize him getting shit-faced a week before his father's election. Peter walked in and took the barstool next to Grady.

"What are we drinking?"

Grady looked up, no sparkle, no charm. He was sick to death of all of it. "Heineken." Grady tilted his bottle toward Peter.

"Okay, still foreign, but mainstream. Aw man, that's your 'I no longer give a shit' beer."

"It is?"

"Yeah, domestic is usually kicked back, having a good time. Craft is my favorite, Grady. Craft beer is your thinking, plotting beer. I love that one. Foreign dark, like a Hefeweizen, is international travel, pensive, sometimes moody Grady. Foreign light, usually obscure, is dressed up formal, probably should be drinking wine, but no way, Grady."

Grady had finished his beer at this point and was staring at Peter, who, pissing the bartender off, had ordered water.

"Anyway, foreign, mainstream, that's the 'I don't care, throw something at me' Grady. What happened?"

"You know you're not normal, right?" Grady asked.

"Yes, that's a given. Spill it. Why are you at this—" Peter turned on his barstool to take in the entire little roadside shack bar— "lovely establishment?"

"Because I'm a damn hamster on a wheel and I wanted a drink."

"Nice try. You've been a hamster all your life. This isn't poor Grady, senator's son. We'd be well into the scotch by now and you'd be at my house. Never in public."

"Jesus, you should probably write a book about me, or how about a play, asshole?"

Peter smiled and then put his hand on Grady's shoulder. "You know I'm going to drag it out of you, or I'll have to call Sam and she'll definitely get you to fess up, so let's make this easy. What happened?"

Grady ran his hand over his face and ordered another beer. "Well, I'm not sure if you heard, but I apparently bought myself a hooker and took her to the Wilshire. As you can imagine, she's a real looker, so you can see why I would drop my completely-stunning, sexy, smart, woman and decide to spend, and I quote, the most wild, hot, erotic night of my life with a woman in a glitter bra and fake-leather skirt."

Peter laughed a little at Grady's delivery, but could see he was in pain.

"No way. We all know you can't abide fake leather."

Grady smiled just a little before bringing the beer to his lips again.

"She believed it," Grady said, putting the bottle down on the damp cardboard coaster.

Peter took a sip of his water and let a few bars of Ronny Milsap's "Smokey Mountain Rain" wander out of the corner jukebox before he replied, "No, she didn't."

"She did. You didn't see her. She was all starched shirt, thank you, but fuck you if you thought for one minute that I loved you. She was so damn quick to just fall in line with everyone else."

"Quick. That's the word. It was just her initial reaction and you probably walked in on it."

"How the hell do you know?"

"Because she loves you and you're not easy to love. Your family, what you appear to be on the outside, all the damn attention, it's not easy, man, and you know it. Plus you add in all of her baggage and it's just— it was a fight, that's all."

"I'm not so sure about that. It looked pretty clear that she's one of them now."

"Why is everything so *us* or *them*? I've done things that have pissed you off, I haven't always been a good friend."

"True."

Peter laughed. "You haven't given up on me. You never give up on your family or your friends, even though they often deserve it. So, give her a minute. Let her calm down."

"What if this never goes away, all this crap, what if she can't handle it?"

"Are we talking about the same Kate here? She's more than capable of dealing with all of the shit in your storm. It's her damn job. She's probably just a little tender when it comes to this particular topic."

"Screwing hookers?"

"Yeah, that tends to piss all women off." They both laughed.

"Shouldn't you be home, cuddled up with our best friend?" Grady prompted.

"I'm on my way. She's probably already asleep surrounded by wedding magazines."

"Six more months, man, and you'll be married. So weird, right?"

Peter shook his head and got that dreamy look he always had when he talked about Samantha Cathner. "Nah, it's not weird at all. Seems like I've been waiting forever."

They looked at each other for a beat.

"Jesus," Grady said, and pushed at Peter's shoulder, "get the hell out of here. We're starting to sound like girls, and this is a very manly, chest-hair kind of a bar. I'm not looking to get my ass kicked. Go home, Shakespeare. I'm fine."

Peter stood, hesitated. "You sure?"

"Yeah, I'm heading out too."

Peter turned to leave.

"Hey," Grady said over his shoulder.

Peter turned back around.

"Thanks."

Peter smiled.

"Any time."

And with that, he left and Grady put a twenty on the bar.

Grady was in bed, almost asleep. He was not in the mood for anything other than Kate, and she now thought he was some slimy hooker trawler. The first knock on the door was soft. He almost missed it, and then a second more forceful one followed. He squinted at the clock, saw that it was one in the morning, and clicked on his bedside lamp. The knock came again. Grady slipped into his jeans. Buttoning them and walking from his bedroom, he called out, "Hang on. I'm coming." Turning on the entry light, he could see Kate through one of the two floor-to-ceiling windows beside the front door. He opened the door.

"You see, the thing is—" Kate stepped past him into the foyer, put a box she was carrying down, and turned to him. "I don't want this." She gestured to him, his body, with her crazy hands. "The looks, all the women with their dreamy-eyed 'I'd be better for you than she is' looks. I don't want any of it."

"Kate." Grady closed the door and locked it.

"No. I want average, maybe even boring. No planes or great suits, and absolutely no charm." She noticed his chest. "See, like this. Can't you put a shirt on?"

Grady was leaning up against the door now, with his arms crossed. "Kate."

"What?"

"Why are you at my house with a box of—" he peered at the box she'd set down, "—doughnuts and a gallon of chocolate milk at one in the morning?" He couldn't help but smile. She looked at the milk, still in her hand, and set it next to the doughnuts. She was standing in front of him now with messed-up hair and wearing a big sweatshirt over what looked like silky pajamas, multi-colored striped socks, and clogs. Her cheeks were pink. She was beautiful and he wanted her almost to desperation.

Kate dropped her keys on the table and looked down as if she were trying to find her words. Grady was still waiting for an answer. He walked to her. "Kate?" She looked up. "Doughnuts, Nesquik? What's going on?"

"It's time to fatten you up."

Grady laughed.

She went on, "You'll need to dress differently too. You could start by dressing period, more clothes maybe, and dear God, change that cologne or body wash, whatever the hell it is, that has to go too. You need to average-up, Grady Malendar, because I'm not doing smart, charming and sexy this time around. My heart needs to stay focused. If it's ever going to think about pairing up again, it needs to find a simple, decent guy, and you," she poked his chest as he came into her space, "you are distracting it. You are distracting my heart."

"Is that so?" He smiled and forgot that only hours before she was enraged and insulting. She believed the vultures and had shot him several looks he didn't deserve. He forgot all of that as she looked up at him with her ridiculous plan.

"Yes, it most certainly is so." Her hands opened to lay flat on his shoulders. They were face to face. Kate dropped her head to his bare chest. "I'm sorry," she whispered.

Grady let out a breath and kissed the top of her head.

"It's just . . . I don't want to feel like this, stupid like this, questioning like this. I was never that person, and I don't want to be her now, but sometimes I wonder if I should have known."

"Known what?" He put his arms around her.

"Known I was being cheated on, known . . . you know?" She looked up at him and Grady's heart hurt a little for her. "I think that's where this is coming from, it must be, because I'm not this woman. I don't believe this kind of crap, but when I saw her on the news, I don't know, I . . . my mind told me that I was being stupid again, opening myself up again. I'm not making sense. I can't stand women like this, clingy, questioning, but then I wonder if you have to be that way?"

"Not with me. You don't ever have to be that way with me. Kate, I'll walk away before I will ever cheat on you. It's not my thing. It's a shitty thing to do to someone, let alone someone you love. If I ever fall out of love with you, I'll tell you, straight up."

"How can you say that? You can't know."

"Sure I can, can't you? It's a character thing, Kate. You know that as well as I do. Some people have it and some people don't. I have all sorts of crap on my 'to fix' list, but infidelity is not one of them. When I'm with a woman, I mean . . . "

Kate looked at him.

"When I'm with a woman exclusively."

She laughed. "And how often does that happen?"

He smiled and wiped what looked like icing off of her cheek. "Well, I haven't always been a settle-down guy. Never found the right person."

Kate started to pull away and Grady held her arms.

"Until now. Now, what's happened now is that I . . . well, I can't see anything else. Anyone else. I'm not exactly familiar with what's going on right now, but I can tell you that I never lied to any of the women I was with in my past. I didn't see a need. I like honesty. I prize it over most things, so I give it to the people in my life."

Kate seemed tired, and Grady imagined he often wore her out. She rested her head on him, and it felt like she was finally opening, giving herself in spite of everything.

"Me too," she said, closing her eyes.

Grady lifted her face with both hands. "You too?"

"Me too. The honesty part. I'm that way. I don't really know how to be any other way, but I think sometimes people think they're honest, and then things happen and they find themselves in situations. Hell, I don't know."

"No. That's not true. We all have certain . . . non-negotiables. Things that no matter what, we hold on to. You don't falter on the non-negotiables."

"You don't. You're right." Kate looked into his eyes and he knew she believed him.

"Now about fattening me up." Grady leaned toward the dough-nut box and lifted the lid.

Kate came behind him, wrapped her arms under his arms and around his warm chest.

"This might be a strategy I can get behind," he said.

Grady removed a long-john from the box, bit almost half way through, and looked over his shoulder at Kate.

"I think it has merit, but maybe not the clothes and the smell," Kate said, as she moved to his neck. It sent jolts of heat through Grady's entire body. He turned to face her, offering a bite of his doughnut.

Kate took a small bite, closed her eyes and moaned, "This place really knows how to make a doughnut."

Grady was still hanging on her moan as he popped the last bit of doughnut into his mouth. "They are good. Kate," he said, put-ting his arms around her waist and pulling her close. "What about the Porsche? Please say we can keep the Porsche?" He gently kissed her neck and Kate's head fell to the side allowing him in. "We could . . . ," he trailed kisses along her collar bone, "maybe limit it to weekends?" Kate mumbled a few inaudible words as he moved to her ear while his hands found her hair. "Was that a *yes* to the Porsche, Kate?" He could feel her smile against his jaw.

"Fine," her breath was coming in fast now. "The Porsche stays, but we are going to have lots and lots of doughnuts." Grady pulled the sweatshirt over her head, tossed it aside, and kissed her. Her lips opened on a sigh and he took more, needed more. They bumped into the entryway table, knocking the doughnuts over.

Kate turned and they both laughed. "You need to eat those," she said and started to crouch and pick them up, but Grady lifted her into his arms.

"Later. I'll eat them all, every last one, but first I need to build up an appetite." He carried her to his bed and found out that her pajamas were in fact silk, and so was everything underneath.

Chapter Thirty-Four

*W*hen Kate entered Bracknell and Stevens the next morning, Mark was already talking on his phone and pacing outside his office. He at least looked showered, which was a step up from yesterday's fiasco. As Kate walked past him, toward her office, he gestured with his free hand that she needed to go into his office. She set her things on the chair just inside her own office, and returned to Mark as he was finishing his conversation.

"Yes, yes, I've got that, but I'm not sure what else we can do at this point, Stanley. We are, yes. This the eleventh hour and you mentioned that things are looking good. I'm just wondering if you are being a little—right, no of course not. Already done. Yes, it's . . ." Mark leaned over his desk, searching, and then grabbed a piece of paper.

Kate felt like she should do something to help, but she was afraid to move. He was like a one-man band.

"Here it is, yes, the ad was already proofed. It's fantastic. I sent you a copy. Okay, I will send it again. Listen, Kate just got in and we need to go over some things. Right, yes, I will talk with you at one o'clock. Great, thank you." Mark hung up the phone and leaned both hands on his desk, head hung low while he regained what Kate was sure would be his last shred of composure.

"That was Stanley?" Kate asked, hoping Mark would clarify the whole conversation.

He nodded, still maintaining his brace on the desk.

"And . . . things are good?" she asked.

Mark looked up. The circles under his eyes had gotten darker. Kate wasn't sure how that was possible. Mark finally stood, ran a hand over his face, and took a sip of coffee.

"Things are good, but Stanley is panicking. Hookergate really threw everything into a tailspin."

Kate made a move to speak, but Mark continued. "I know it was bogus crap, not even a good smear attempt, but to hear Stanley tell it, it still got media time. It still left a mark."

Kate didn't bother arguing. She was trying to stay neutral. Sleeping with the client, or son of the client, was a bad idea all the way around. Mark still thought Kate was barely tolerating Grady, and she wanted to keep it that way, at least until Election Day.

"I didn't see anything in my reports this morning. Has it affected the polling numbers?" she asked carefully.

Mark shook his head and took a seat at his desk. "Like not even half a point. It was a blip. They know it was a blip, but Stanley enjoys riding my ass. I'm really starting to feel like a trained dog on this one, Kate. They're killing me."

"I know. Anything I can do?"

Mark clicked his mouse and looked at his computer screen.

"No. You've been great. The last two stops you have with Grady, any issues? Please say there are no issues because I'm not sure I can take it at this point."

"Not one. I've confirmed the addresses, transportation, and the details. We even have the dress code. It will go off without a hitch. Grady was just saying this morning that we are in the home stretch." Kate froze. *Shit, that was too familiar. This morning, Kate? Why not just say after the two of you got out of the shower?* She looked out the window to avoid eye contact.

"Good, good." Mark wasn't even looking at her. He was engrossed in his computer screen.

Kate took the opportunity and stood to leave. She made it to the door.

"Wait, this morning? It's eight o'clock and you've already spoken to Grady?"

Kate nodded, her pulse picked up.

"Great work, Kate. I mean, to think you were pulling your hair out just a few months ago. Things have certainly improved, right?"

Kate smiled. "They really have. I've learned to work well with Mr. Malendar." This was super awkward.

Just as Kate's mind told her everyone knew, Mark laughed. "Lighten up. I'm sure you call him Grady by now."

Kate's face warmed as she remembered panting his name just a couple of hours ago when he woke her up early before she had to leave for work. Things were certainly going well this morning, but there was no way in hell Mark needed to know that.

"Okay, well, I'm going to get started on my day. Let me know if you need anything else," Kate said, backing toward the door.

Mark nodded, still looking at his computer, as if she'd taken his lunch order. Kate slipped out just as his phone rang again. She quietly closed the glass door and prayed Sabrina, the gourmet baker wasting her time as Kate's assistant, had made some kind of yummy breakfast bread. Kate had not bought Toaster Strudel for weeks, and she was starving.

Grady woke up in his bed alone. His body still humming and the smell of her still wafting out of his bathroom. She had showered and gone. Off to work. He texted her: *Go away with me this weekend.* A few seconds later she responded: *Who is this?* Grady laughed, rolled out of bed and called to remind her exactly who he was. By the time he hung up they had plans to drive up north and look at the fall colors. Grady called ahead and reserved a bed and breakfast. They could be alone and away from the madness that was growing every second as Election Day approached. Grady agreed to pick her up after work.

They succeeded in getting away. No one at Big Bear Lake cared who Grady was. They took pictures and walked hand in hand without a single glance. Kate even relaxed and Grady never wanted to leave. They found a little restaurant-bar for dinner, ate steak, and shared some obscene brownie skillet for dessert. Kate's hair was wild around her face and they both wore jeans the entire weekend. It was normal, and God how they both needed some normal. Kate reminded him that escape was not real life, but all he cared about was having time with her. They finished their dinner just as the band was starting up.

"Dance with me?" Grady stood and extended his hand. Kate was surprised.

"Are you telling me you know the two-step too?"

"I am." He urged her to take his hand again.

"How do you know that I know the two-step?" she asked.

"Oh come on. Cop's daughter, beer from a bottle drinker, someone taught you the two-step along the way. Neil and Ethan don't exactly look like the ballroom types."

Kate took his hand and followed him to the dance floor. "Well, you are in luck because I happen to be a pretty fierce two-stepper."

"I knew it."

They found a place among the spinning couples.

"Let me lead, Galloway," Grady said, as he pulled Kate around another couple.

Kate tried to concentrate, but she started to laugh. "Who taught you your moves, cowboy?"

"That would be my Nana. Right before junior assembly," Grady said, turning Kate under his arm. "She told me that my ballroom was weak and she was going to teach me a real man's dance."

"Just like that?" Kate asked. The song ended and everyone clapped.

"Yup, Nana was a straight shooter."

Kate laughed and as they took their seats, she asked, "Do you get all your quirky sayings from her?"

Grady raised an eyebrow. "Quirky?"

"Yes, like *straight-shooter*, no one says that anymore. It's similar to the hairy eyeball comment you made last week and shenanigans the week before that."

"Wow, I had no idea I was so . . . odd."

"It's not odd, you're just, well, you're you." She kissed him. "Now, don't be such a Nervous Nancy and—"

"Nelly," Grady said, putting some money on the table and grabbing her around the waist. He wanted her alone.

"Nelly, who's Nelly?" Kate asked as Grady moved them toward the swinging saloon doors.

"Nelly, it's Nervous Nelly, not Nancy. Nancy's not nervous." He was at her ear, behind her, by the time they stepped out into the cool night air.

"Well, Nancy would work, they're both 'N' names, and so it would work."

"Nope." He moved along her jaw line and turned Kate to face him. "Has to be Nelly. That's the phrase. This is coming from the corny Nana phrases expert."

"Oh well, in that case, Nelly it is." Kate smiled and the wind brushed her hair into her face. She laughed and he knew she was his person. His out-of-the-spotlight, winter months person. He kissed her and the last piece fell into place.

Chapter Thirty-Five

*W*hile Grady and Kate were finishing breakfast and packing for the drive back into LA, Mark was pulling what was left of his hair out. It was Sunday, but Stanley had called at seven. He and the senator wanted to meet and discuss any Hail Mary strategy he might have. Things were too close going into Election Day. They'd increased the senator's likability among younger voters, but he was only 2 points in front of Jeff Driggs. It had been a tough project, but Mark felt good about the work they had done. Sure the hooker thing had made things a little shaky, but the numbers were solid, close, but solid. Mark took a sip of his Starbucks. He didn't have anything left to give these guys and he had a feeling that's not what they wanted to hear. They would arrive any minute, entourage intact, expecting he would have answers. He scratched the back of his head, closed his tired eyes, and waited. Ten minutes later the doors of Mark's office swung open. Show time.

"Senator," he said, standing and extending his hand. "Stanley."

All three men shook and took a seat at the all-too-familiar conference room table.

"Thanks for coming in on a Sunday, Mark," Senator Malendar said, taking his coffee out of the carrier on the table.

"Not a problem. What's up?"

Stanley put a piece of paper in front of him.

"This is what's up. It's still too narrow a lead, margin of error. It's tight, and we both feel like we need one last push." Mark had been in this job too long, he could actually predict the future, he thought.

"Okay. What kind of push did you have in mind? We put together that spot about Drigg's alleged affair and you didn't want to run it. We agreed to run clean and even in the eleventh hour, it seems we've stayed that line. Are you thinking of pushing back after the hooker thing? Do you want to run that?"

"No," Senator Malendar said, standing up and walking to the window. "I'm a sitting senator, for Christ sake. I'm not some amateur and I don't plan on acting like one now. What that little shit did to Grady, quite frankly, shocked even me."

"Sir, the college thing and the hooker were both bogus and the voters know that now. It may still be hurting you a little with on-the-fence conservatives, perception and all, but I think considering everything, things are looking good. Stanley, what exactly is it that you're looking for me to bring to the table at this point? The election is in three days." Mark rubbed his eyes.

Stanley put his hand on Mark's shoulder. "Listen, I appreciate—the senator and his family appreciate everything Bracknell has contributed, it's been outstanding work. I just want to make sure we've looked under every stone. Turned them all over. If we can't go negative—" the senator shot Stanley a warning, "—*won't*, we *won't* go negative, then maybe we look at playing up something new." He looked to Mark.

"Well, we have the photos from last weekend. Grady worked on a house for Habitat for Humanity. We haven't used any of that footage. We could probably put something together."

"Yeah, okay, that was a great feel-good project. Maybe playing that up is that little extra we need," Stanley said.

"Let me see if I can get ahold of Dillon in research. He can get us that footage, names and any quotes."

Mark dialed Dillon and started telling him what they were looking for.

"What? What about The Roads Foundation? No, I'm talking about last weekend when he was working with Habitat for Humanity. I need the names and some images if we are going to put a spot together." Mark listened, and his eyes widened as the senator and Stanley looked on. "Yeah, hang on, I'm going to put you on speaker." He held the receiver in his hand. "You are both going to want to hear this." Mark hit the button on the phone console.

"You there, Dillon?"

"Yes," a voice crackled over the speaker.

"I'm here with Senator Malendar and Stanley. Could you please repeat the question you just asked me?"

"Good morning, sirs. I'm sorry for the confusion, I just thought when you were asking about Mr. Malendar that you wanted more information on his Roads Foundation connection."

Stanley held the back of the soft leather chair, looking like he was bracing for bad news. None of them needed bad news at this point.

"And what connection is that, Dillon?" Mark asked.

"I'm sorry. I gave the report to Kate. Maybe she's the person to discuss this with. She asked that I delete the report, said it wasn't relevant."

Both Stanley and the senator were anxious now.

"What did the report say? Spill it, Dillon," Mark said. He was tired.

"Um, well I had to do some digging. There was a flag on Mr. Malendar's tax returns. It was brilliantly disguised, but my guys are good, so . . . "

"Dillon!" Mark barked.

"Right, sorry. Mr. Malendar is The Roads Foundation. I mean he and his three friends, but he's the money. On the surface it looks like he's funneling money to a trust, but that trust is then accessed through three separate accounts for The Roads Foundation projects."

The room was silent as all three men looked at each other. Stanley leaned into the speaker in the center of the table.

"Let me get this straight. You're telling us that Grady Malendar is the funding, the mind behind one of the largest philanthropic organizations in California, possibly the country?"

"Yes, that's what I'm saying, sir. But, I'm pretty sure he doesn't want anyone to know. I mean he's been doing this since he was eighteen."

"Eighteen?" The senator asked, shocked. "That's impossible. He's my son. I would know if he was running a foundation, or funding, whatever. This makes no sense."

"Dillon, thanks. Do you have access to the report you sent Kate?" Mark asked.

"Is Kate there? Can you get it from her?" Dillon's voice grew shaky.

"She's out of town this weekend. Forward me the report."

"Sure, yeah."

"Thank you." Mark disconnected and looked up to something he hadn't seen since the senator became a client. Stanley was smiling. A big, teeth and all, smile.

"Well, well, if this pans out, senator, the little shit just won you another term. Probably a few more after this one."

"Stan, I've asked you not to call him that." The senator looked at Mark. "I'm stunned, I mean Grady's a great kid, but I'm— maybe I'm a little hurt I didn't know. A father should probably know these things about his son."

"Sounds like he didn't want anyone to know, sir," Mark said.

"Right, maybe we shouldn't—" Senator Malendar started to say.

"Don't do it, don't even think it." Stanley interrupted. "I can't use your opponent's affair, or his daughter's suspicious visit to Planned Parenthood. We are using this. Your son's a damn hero, assuming this is true."

The senator said nothing, and as he had always done, let his machine work.

Mark received the report within a half hour. He made a few phone calls and there was no denying The Roads Foundation was the brainchild of Grady Malendar. There was a great picture of

Grady and the three Roads executives when they were back in school. It would be online in less than two hours and in tomorrow's paper. Stanley was right, Senator Malendar had just sealed his re-election. It might be on the back of his son's hard work, but that was the nature of the political beast, Mark told himself.

When he arrived home that night, it felt yucky, even a bit wrong, but he'd found his Hail Mary, and all Mark wanted was a decent night's sleep.

Chapter Thirty-Six

The next morning, Grady's phone was dancing across his nightstand. He had dropped Kate off and fell into bed happier than he had ever thought possible. That all changed the moment he picked up his phone.

"Grady! Shit, man, where have you been?" he heard Bryce say, and instantly he knew. He could feel the walls, the same ones he had tried so hard to open to let Kate in, closing around him.

"The press is everywhere," Bryce went on. "Outside the office, our homes. I managed to escape this morning, but Eric still can't get out. They know, I'm sorry, but it's everywhere, Grady. None of us have said anything yet, but we need to say something. This looks like we have something to hide and Christ, Grady, we don't."

Grady looked around the corner through his glass front door and sure enough there were press vans and reporters outside his home. His sanctuary. The tree house he built was being invaded and he knew exactly why. He had broken the one rule he swore to uphold when he was seven years old. No girls allowed in the tree house.

"I'll send a car for Eric. Is Jason there yet?"

"Yeah. What are you going to do?"

Grady moved toward his closet to get dressed. "Not sure yet."

He cradled the phone on his shoulder while he flipped through his suits. He would need to wear a suit.

"What do you want me to do?" Bryce asked.

"Just sit tight. Don't say anything. I'm stopping by Bracknell and Stevens on my way in. Plan on a press conference in an hour or two. As Nana would say, Bryce, 'The jig is up!'"

Grady hung up and ignored the rest of the calls flashing on his phone. Stanley, his father, several reporters he recognized from the LA Times, and Kate. Grady swallowed back what felt like betrayal and got into the shower.

Grady reached Bracknell and Stevens less than thirty minutes after Kate gave up trying to call him. He walked straight past Sabrina and into Kate's office. She was sitting at her desk with her face in her hands. She looked up when he closed the door behind him and braced herself for the blow. At least this time, when her heart shattered, she could say she saw it coming.

Grady was in a suit and wringing his hands at his sides. She knew better than to ask him to sit.

"Where is he?"

"Who?"

"My father."

"Grady, I'm not sure. It apparently broke in this morning's paper."

"How?"

"I'm not actually sure." She could see him trying to take deep breaths as his eyes jutted back and forth, sort of like an animal under attack.

"I asked Mark this morning and he said they got the information from research. He asked why hadn't I shared this with him earlier? I told him I didn't think it was that big of a deal."

"Let me guess. He and my father and Stan thought it was."

"They did," Kate replied, standing up. "Grady, listen, I told them to delete the report, I took it off my computer. I guess they wanted some footage on the Habitat for Humanity thing you were doing and it came out—"

"Don't. Just stop explaining. You ran the report. You poked around in my life, got into my life and that—that Kate, is why this is happening. That is why the foundation offices are flooded with vultures and the men that have done more for Los Angeles than this office, or my father, could even imagine, can't get out of their homes. You, Kate. I let you in. My mistake."

Kate sat back down and confirmed that even seeing the pain coming didn't lessen the impact. He was angry and he had every right to be. If he needed to blame this all on her, if that helped him, then she would take it. She did order the report. She did pull up his secret for the world to see and yes, because of what she did, his father would win another election. He had already jumped three more points. All of those things were true and because she loved him, she would take it.

Until he said, "You used me."

"Excuse me?" Kate stood up.

"You and this place. Your bullshit business. You used me and my work to get what you wanted. Oh, I'll bet there's a big bonus in there for you too, Ms. Galloway, when the senator wins re-election."

"Now wait a minute." Kate raised her voice and Grady stepped into her. She didn't back down.

"No, you wait a minute." With that, Grady dropped into a laugh and stepped back from her. "This is stupid. I have to go to a press conference now." Grady shook his head. "This is actually my fault, Kate. I know better. I don't live in the real world, isn't that what you said?"

Kate tried to reach him, but he held his hand up.

"You're right. I don't, and I'm heading back to my world now. You see, I like it there. We work there and while I appreciate your taking me on a tour of reality, I think I'll pass. Goodbye, Kate."

Before she could say a word, he was gone. Kate slowly sat behind her desk, bowed her head, and did something she had not done in a while. She cried.

Grady had the media relations director for The Roads Foundation issue a statement outside of their offices confirming that Grady Malendar was in fact a founder and, as of this morning, president of The Roads Foundation. The statement also said that Mr. Malendar would be at the official opening of the Robert Everoad Law Enforcement Resource Center later today, in his official capacity.

Grady met with the guys, and Jason was happy to step into the vice president position. Grady knew they were all secretly thrilled everything was out in the open and there was a part of him that was happy to relieve their stress. It had not been easy sneaking around for the past thirteen years, but Grady had thought it was what was best for the work they did. He still thought that, but he had no choice now. They had yet to feel the pressure his name and his father's connections would bring down on The Foundation, but all Grady could do at this point was face it head on. Three hours later he did just that.

"Ladies and Gentlemen, thank you for coming out today. My name is Grady Malendar, and when we started The Roads Foundation out of our college dorm room almost thirteen years ago, the goal was to enrich communities without destroying their essence. Money tends to think it has all the answers and money without knowledge, history, listening, can be destructive. It was never our intention to tell people what they needed. We have always wanted, preferred, to be listeners. We are a complement, a student, and a helper for the great people of Los Angeles today. Behind me is the new Robert Everoad Law Enforcement Resource Center. It's the first of its kind in California. This center will employ retired police officers, so their experience is not lost, it will be repackaged and available as a valuable resource for current officers. This center will provide a historical context to the work our men and women do today. This building will house counseling, education, guidance, and a positive support structure for our officers. Being a police officer in a large city is a difficult job on a good day. Chief Flanagan felt the best way to support his officers was to use the resources of retirees, as well as returning veterans. There is a brotherhood among officers and soldiers that often gets a bad rap, and he would like to see that bond used in a positive way."

There was a grumbling among reporters and Grady smiled. "Yes, I know there are females in the military and law enforcement, but I like the word brotherhood. It worked in the speech, you all know what I mean, so if you want to turn this into something it's not, I've learned I certainly can't stop you."

The crowd laughed, but Grady knew, some of them at least, would be sure to mention "Mr. Malendar's sexist remarks."

"The Roads Foundation heard Chief Flanagan, and we have helped the city of Los Angeles make it happen." Grady finished up his speech and then introduced Kate's father, who looked imposing in his uniform. Chief Flanagan said a few surprisingly warm words, shook Grady's hand, and then the statue of Peter's father was unveiled by Mrs. Everoad. There was applause and a few tears. Grady and his father, the soon to be newly re-elected Senator Malendar, cut the ribbon.

From a PR standpoint, Kate's work mind told her it was a resounding success. Not only because it made for good print—family affair, working class, upper class, all the key triggers were there—but also because it was genuinely good and progressive for a city she loved. Her personal mind, her heart, was a very different story. She was proud of her father and her brothers, she always was, but she had never been more proud of anyone in her life than she was of Grady at that moment.

He was so brave. He'd come out of the shadows, and allowed people to see him outside of his father or his wealth. She watched him shake hands and talk with people as they entered the new building and she wondered if this was the way he had to do it. Maybe he had to start in the background and slowly work his way into ownership, adulthood. Maybe that's how everyone came of age, in his or her own way, at his or her own pace. She was certainly no expert, but in her own life she had learned to take her time, that all things arrived when they were supposed to.

Everyone had entered and was now touring the building. Kate stood from the bench she was sitting on just across the street. Her job was done, Mark had texted her his thanks and that he would see her on Tuesday, Election Day. Kate was free to leave, she felt good about her work.

Grady had not looked at her once during his speech, she hadn't expected him to. There had been no phone calls, no texts even. The reveal of things he wanted kept private was too much for him, too much for their relationship. She knew that and her heart broke. Not along the same scar as it had when her marriage fell apart. This wound was different, deeper, because she thought she had known love with Nick, thought she had felt all of the feelings acted out and crooned over in song, but she hadn't, she had never felt anything like what she felt with Grady. Buttoning up her jacket, Kate was certain she never would again. She suddenly wanted the warmth of her home, her couch, where she would heal this time, not fall apart, and move on. Life was good. She had done good work and her city was richer for it. Kate got in her car and went home.

Chapter Thirty-Seven

*K*ate woke up on Wednesday, November 5th, with a headache that promised to only get worse as the day went on. She lay in bed staring up at the ceiling and wondering how long it would take, how many weeks, months, after today it would be before the pain eased. She knew it would never completely go away, but relief... when would that come? She already missed him, terribly, everything about him. It had only been two days—forty-eight hours—but her heart knew he wasn't coming back. Not from this. Her phone buzzed on her nightstand and she snatched it up. Hoping, maybe. Nope, it was an email from Mark outlining today's schedule. Technically she didn't need to be there, Grady had certainly moved on and grown up. He no longer needed a babysitter, so Kate should be free to skip, but she would be there anyway to help Mark out, finish the job they'd started.

Kate swung her feet around and slid her feet into her slippers. It was time to get up, democracy had worked its magic last night, and her company was successful. They had been instrumental in re-electing a United States senator. That was huge, an accomplishment, Kate told herself. She turned the shower on and hoped by the time she was at her front door, leaving for the office, she would actually believe the bullshit she was feeding herself.

After she dressed, still thrilled to see all of her shoes in a closet instead of boxes, Kate watered her two plants, ate her oatmeal on the couch, and watched the early morning coverage. The same political talking heads groaning on about what happened on election night and how things would be different now that . . . blah, blah, blah. She'd never liked politics, the spectacle of it all, which was ironic, she knew, considering her job, but politics was different because, unlike celebrity, it pretended to be human, standing tall in expensive suits and promising things it knew it would never be able to deliver. Kate didn't like the dishonesty, but she was good at her job. And once again as she grabbed her keys, she realized she needed to be good at something.

Later that same day, Senator Malendar stepped out of the back seat of a black sedan and asked his driver to wait. If Grady even agreed to speak with him, he wouldn't be long, and chances were pretty high the newly re-elected senator would never even get the chance to say two words. He knocked. No answer. He knocked again. Still, no answer. The senator took a deep breath and went around the back of Grady's house. He found his only son reclined on a wooden chaise with a cream-colored cushion. He had a coffee cup in one hand and a book in the other.

For a moment, the senator's pride actually stopped him in his tracks. Grady had grown into a wonderful man. The frenzy of the election, the last-minute reveal, and the re-election win had all been a spin, but now things had settled. The senator was standing on the deck of a beautiful home, and for maybe the first time he saw his son as separate from himself. The man in front of him was solitary, of his own making, and his heart hurt, the pride was so strong. This wasn't going to be easy.

He took the chaise next to Grady and looked out over the green rocky shore at a winter ocean, raging with nearly as much anger as his son. Grady didn't look up. He set his coffee down and turned the page of his book.

"Do you have any more of that?" his father asked. Grady opened the small cabinet next to him and handed his father a cup. He pushed the French press across the round table between them, and both men sat in silence. The only sound was the occasional page turning.

"What are you reading?"

Grady looked at his father, no expression, and held up the cover.

"All right, that's enough. Christ, it's like you're seventeen again and I took your phone."

Grady raised an eyebrow, still saying nothing.

"We need to talk," his father said, loosening the tie around his neck and unbuttoning his collar. Grady closed his book and set it on the table.

"There's not much to say, Dad."

"Well, I think there is."

Silence again as both men looked ahead.

"We won."

They both sipped their coffee.

"The election. We won," the senator reiterated.

"I knew you would," Grady said in a calm steady voice. "You always do," followed no louder than a whisper.

The senator ignored it and tried to move forward. "I couldn't have done it without you. You're a huge part of this win, and you have my sincere gratitude, Grady."

Grady laughed. "I don't want it."

"You don't want what?"

"Your gratitude."

"Oh come on."

"What's this about, Dad? You've won the election. I'm happy for you. Are you here because you feel guilty that you won that election on the back of my foundation?"

There was a pause as both men looked at each other.

"No, actually I'm fine with that. The discovery of your foundation did help, and I'm grateful, even if you don't want it. Why would I feel guilty?"

"Because you have to take, touch, everything that is mine. Put it under your big bad senator umbrella until it's yours."

"That's probably true."

Grady was taken aback by his candor. "It is?"

"Yeah, your mother is forever telling me that I'm overpowering. I'm a—what the hell did she call me again? Oh, yeah, an eclipser. I shut people down. Kill their light." The senator took a sip of his coffee. "I'm not sure I know how to be any other way." He looked at Grady.

"Bullshit, you know exactly what you do, but oh boo hoo, you can't help yourself? I'm not buying it. My whole life—it's been this way for thirty damn years. Hell, even my girlfriends loved you. Shit, everyone loves you. Dad, it's your thing."

"You used to like that about me. Follow me around, remember when you went to school for career day as your dad?" The senator smiled waiting for a look from his son that might ease the lump in his throat. He stood and moved toward the edge of the patio.

"Oh, yeah," Grady mocked, "was that before or after you screwed my favorite math teacher?"

The senator turned to face him. This conversation had been a long time coming, buried deep in the wall that had divided them since Grady was fifteen years old. "Well, hell, it must have been after," Grady continued. "I was in high school when I came home and . . . do you remember that day, Dad?"

The senator said nothing.

"Probably the first and last time you were ever caught with your pants down, am I right?" Grady's laugh was laced with such anger, so much disgust, that his father physically felt the squeeze of it. He poured some more coffee, hands a bit shaky, and sat back down next to Grady.

Silence hung between them for a beat.

"That was a mistake. I told you back then, but you didn't want to hear me. You shut me out after that. I'm a human being, son. I fuck up just like everyone else. Did I not tell you that when you were growing up? Did I give you the impression that I was—"

"A good man? A committed husband? Yeah, you kind of did, Dad. At the very least, we all had the impression you were an honest and decent father that would never risk his son walking in on—"

"You were ditching class. You should have been at school."

"Yeah, and I sure as hell never ditched again."

"And I *am* a good man, committed husband and an honest father. I messed up. Made a mistake at a time in my life when mistakes happen. I was figuring things out and I took a wrong turn."

"Pfft . . . you think? I mean on the desk and everything, Dad. I suppose now that I'm older, I should say, 'Well done!'"

The senator turned on him so quickly, Grady started. His father held his arm and despite the years, Grady's accomplishments, his own physical strength, he was a child again. Preparing to receive his punishment.

"Don't you dare. I am still your father. I don't owe you a damn man-to-man explanation. I messed up and I have apologized."

Grady looked right into his face. "Did you ever tell Mom?"

His father returned his glare. "No."

"Don't you think that's the honest thing to do?"

"No."

"Too much of a scandal for the political career? Afraid she'll leave you?"

"No."

"No? Then why not clear the air, let her know you screwed a twenty-four-year-old teacher on your desk in the middle of the damn day. A teacher that you knew your son had a crush on. I mean shit, let's get it out there if you're such a decent guy."

His father released his grip on Grady's arm and sat back in the chaise.

"This has nothing to do with politics. Telling your mother, bringing her into my mess, serves no purpose. It was a long time ago, it was one time."

Grady snickered and his father turned to look at him.

"It was one time," he said slowly. "One lapse in judgment. She doesn't need to know. It serves no purpose. I love your mother deeply. She is my best friend and I owe it to her to live with the guilt and prove myself deserving of her love."

Grady's head dropped.

"Which I have done. I am not a scumbag. It has taken me a very long time to get here, but I rest easy, Grady. I've forgiven myself and I'm wondering why you can't do the same."

Grady laughed. "Do you have any idea what it was like walking in on that, on you?" Grady stood up, suddenly restless and boiling with so many things he realized were not as simple as anger. He turned to his father. "I worshiped you. You were everything, and then you were just some cheating bastard, like the rest of them, with your pants around your ankles."

The senator stood and walked toward him.

"Grady, we are not defined by one act in our lives. You can't—"

"Oh Jesus, please don't quote some inspirational poster from your campaign headquarters. You were, defined as you put it, in that moment for me. I was fifteen, Dad. Confused, awkward, and trying to figure out what the hell I was doing. That time wasn't, shouldn't have been, about you. I wanted you to be, needed you to be, a father. My father." Grady looked at the man in front of him and despite all his best efforts, his eyes watered and the senator reached for him. Grady pushed his hand away. "Shit, I don't know. It was just a blow."

"But you know what, it's over. You're right, it was a long time ago. I'm a grown man now. I'm sure I've done things you don't understand," Grady said.

"Not really. I mean you're all kinds of stupid sometimes, but for the most part you're an incredible son," his father said.

Grady laughed. "Easy to say now that you've won the election."

"Grady, this has nothing to do with the election. Contrary to what Stanley says, I would have won that election without your big reveal."

"*I* didn't reveal anything, remember?"

"Right. Something else for you to be pissed off about. Poor Grady was a closet do-gooder and now he has to be a man. You see,

Grade, it's easy to hide behind the mask. Sure you don't get any recognition, which is why everyone thinks what you've done is so commendable, but you also don't have to deal with any of the mistakes. Kind of weak, don't you think?"

"Are you for real? You came to my home after you completely used me and my work to win your dog and pony show to tell me that I'm weak? Wow, well thanks for coming down, Dad."

"I didn't say you were weak. I'm just saying that it's harder being out in front, under the always-scrutinizing eyes of the public. There's pressure to not screw up. Maybe when your father let you down, embarrassed you and himself, you decided my public life, politics was to blame. Maybe to keep your heart from splitting open, you figured it was business, the pressure of my job, that turned me into something you hated."

A tear escaped Grady's eye and he quickly wiped it away. "I never hated you."

"Oh, I'm not so sure about that—"

"I was scared, alone. I felt on my own that day. If I told mom, I'd lose you both. I had to grow up that day and it was too early for me to be on my own. I needed you, and after that, I just couldn't count on you anymore. I didn't know you anymore, but I've never hated you."

His father took a deep breath as the pain of his mistake surfaced yet again. He faced him. "I'm sorry. If I could go back, if I could have gotten my head on straight back then, not turned down that path, I would, but I can't. It had nothing to do with you or your mother. I messed up and I'm sorry, so sorry, that something so stupid came between us."

His father hugged him and Grady felt years of angst, anger, and pain wash away into the crashing tide below his house. The sun was setting. Grady was older now, knew a bit more about being an adult, a man. Maybe that was why, or maybe he was just tired of being angry, so he let it go. His father wanted to be his father again, and Grady could sure use one.

"I love you, Grade." The senator held his shoulders. "And I'm so damn proud of you."

Grady smiled, wiped his eyes. "Thanks. I love you too."

The senator hugged him again. "Christ, I miss the sound of that. It's been a long time."

"Yeah, well Miss Kramer was totally into me before you came along," Grady laughed.

"Not funny," the senator said.

"Too soon? Okay, maybe later," Grady said, feeling such relief that he could finally make light. His chest opened up for the first time in nearly fifteen years.

The senator shook his head. "You always were a smart ass. So, can we move on now and discuss how you're going to step up and run your multi-million dollar foundation?"

Grady's smile dropped. "You mean now that your merry band of circus performers have exposed my private business?"

"Yeah, that," the senator said, topping off Grady's coffee. "Best thing that ever happened to you."

"Oh, really. How's that?" Grady said, taking a sip.

"Because look at you. It's been a few days and you're already starting your next project." Grady searched his face for how he knew that. "Bryce and I played tennis last week."

"Christ. You are everywhere, aren't you?"

"I suppose I am, but this is exciting, and it's time for you to put all this 'oh poor senator's son' crap behind you. You're a man, a damn smart and extremely accomplished man. You won't screw up. I promise."

Grady looked at him and didn't know what to say. His father's one sentence had explained what several months of therapy hadn't been able to touch. Grady was scared to death of screwing up and making a mistake—in his real life, where it mattered. Sure he had no problem making stupid surface mistakes, but not something real. Not like the confusing, jumbled mess he'd seen in his father's office all those years ago. He wouldn't be able to bear that, couldn't live with himself if he somehow turned into that.

"You have no way of knowing what I'll do," Grady said, leaning back on the chaise.

His father joined him. Both men looked out to the crashing sea as the sun dipped into the water, and daylight passed to the softer glow of evening.

"I do. I know, Grade. You have too much of your mother in you." The senator smiled, still looking ahead. "You've got her in you, remember that. And if, and probably when, you stumble, misstep, you've got me in you too. Your mother and I, that's a brilliant combination. You'll be just fine, son." He looked at Grady and then back out to the sunset.

Both men finished their coffee.

"Now, it's time for you to kick some ass and do the work you were meant to do. Quit being such a damn baby."

Grady laughed and felt less alone.

Chapter Thirty-Eight

Grady met one of his best friends, Samantha, at Neptune's Net in Malibu. They had fried clams, sat on the wood-planked patio, and watched the view of Highway 1 and the ocean.

"So, how are things?" Sam asked.

Grady smiled as he chewed some fries.

"Things, things are . . . pretty shitty, thanks for asking."

"I heard from the guys and Peter that you are now out of the shadows. About time, don't you think?"

"I'm not so sure. My all-important life will probably find some way to screw it up."

"Grady, you *are* it. You've been running the thing for over twelve years now and doing a great job. Just think of the time you'll save not playing Batman."

He shook his head and looked out at a car of surfers packing up for the day.

"It's a great thing you've done." She touched his hand.

"We've done. We all have a part, that's why it works. One of us isn't the odd under-the-microscope leper."

"You're not a leper. You're brilliant, thoughtful, and humble. Those are all you too, Grady. You're not one thing, you know?

What's wrong with being it all, showing all of your sides? There's no way you're going to get Kate back without the whole package."

"Great, this is great. She rats me out, exposes things I specifically asked her not to, and I need to work on getting her back? I don't think so. I should have known better. This crap, being a Malendar, poisons everything."

"Oh come on, you know she didn't spill that information. She wouldn't do that to you and you know it. You're angry. Pissed that you can't be the Dark Knight anymore—that you have to grow up and take responsibility for the great work you do. Accept praise and learn to deal."

"I was doing fine before."

"Really? Before Kate? You were what? Acting like an idiot and hoping no one caught on? Sorry, too late, she knows you now and in spite of it all, she loves you."

Grady's heart ached. "Have you seen her?"

"No, but Peter mentioned she was on the video conference when the board was discussing the PR for the new Police Resource Center. Said she looked awful."

Grady knew that was not possible, but appreciated that his friends were trying to help.

"By the way, I saw the finished sculpture of dad, Peter's dad." Sam choked on her words. "It's an incredible tribute, meant the world to Peter. What you do, how you use what you've been given, you give things soul, Grady. Something as cold as money or publicity and you make it human. It's really beautiful. You should be proud. Step into the damn sunlight and take a bow, be with the woman you love. You deserve her, you deserve all of this."

Grady wondered why the thought of deserving anything felt strange to him. When had that happened? He sighed.

"I'm glad you like it. I thought it was too much for him to design, so your future mother-in-law helped."

"I know. She loved doing it. She loves you even more now than she already did. It's pretty nauseating."

He bumped Sam and they both kept eating.

"I never wanted to love her, you know?"

"Peter's mom, oh that's just nasty," Sam said with a straight face.

Grady shook his head.

"I know. I'm pretty sure Kate's plan was to stay hidden too, but it's too late for both of you now. Election's over. Remember when you told me to go get Peter, to jump?"

"Yeah, that was one of my better speeches, but you two were a wreck without me."

Sam rolled her eyes. "Sure, whatever you need to tell yourself. Anyway, it's your turn to take the risk. It's time for you to get a life."

"I could always just become a biker," Grady joked, looking out over the parking lot filled with dozens of Harleys. Sam laughed and put her arm around him. Looking out at the vast ocean, Grady was grateful for her, grateful for his friends.

"So, I love her," he said, going for as casual as he could muster.

"I know."

"It's bad. Up at night, doodling on shit, can't-focus-on-a-damn-thing love. How does anyone survive this?"

"You do. You become better for it." Samantha smiled.

"She thinks I'm mad at her, that I blame her for all of this, and I did, I was, but now I just want her back. I want her in my home, I want to walk the dog with her and eat cereal." Grady looked up because Sam hadn't said anything and he was feeling stupid.

Sam's eyes welled and her smile stretched until the tears streamed her cheeks.

"Oh Christ, Sam! Keep it together. I'm trying to tell you that I want Kate back, I want to marry her. I need your help. What am I supposed to say? How do I ask her?"

Sam wiped her eyes, took her oldest friend's hands, and said, "Just like that."

Grady was confused at first and then he saw what she was trying to tell him. He kissed Sam on the cheek, they finished their lunch, and he walked her to her car. He took Highway 1 home, and by the time Bo licked him silly and they had gone on their walk, Grady had a plan.

Chapter Thirty-Nine

Kate rang in the new year with Reagan and Ben at their new house. It was part open house, part New Year's celebration. Kate had slept over in their guest bedroom, which would soon be a nursery. Kate smiled remembering their big announcement after the ball dropped. She should have known, she thought as she brushed her teeth, when Reagan didn't have any champagne. Reagan was going to be a mommy. She pictured clay and markers everywhere. Ben would officially be the happiest man alive.

Kate walked down the stairs toward the kitchen. It was quiet. A sure sign Reagan and Ben were sleeping in because they were never quiet. Kate walked across the wood floor of the dining room and into the kitchen. She would just grab something quick and head home.

She stopped short when she saw Reagan and Ben both sitting at the large yellow enameled kitchen table, both of their faces in the newspaper. Kate rubbed her eyes and went to the coffee.

"Morning guys. Rough night, I didn't even hear you in here," Kate said, grabbing a mug and pouring some coffee.

"Morning," said a third voice.

Kate spun around. She knew that voice. Sitting next to Ben was another man, in pajama bottoms, bare feet, with his face in the newspaper too. Kate knew that chest, knew those shoulders and the hands holding the LA Times. She couldn't breathe. She set her coffee down and leaned against the counter.

Ben lowered his paper. "Hey Kate, can you hand me a bowl?"

"Oh yeah, me too," Reagan said, lowering her paper.

Kate nodded and turned toward the whitewashed cabinets.

As she reached for the bowls, the third voice said, "If you don't mind, Kate. I'll have one too."

She looked over her shoulder, still touching the bowls, and there he was. Paper down, morning hair and stubble, in all his glory, Grady Malendar was sitting having coffee and reading the paper at her best friend's house. Kate had no idea what was going on, but she was afraid to speak. She didn't want to ruin it, just in case she was still dreaming. She wanted to spend a few more minutes looking at Grady.

Ben stood up and got the milk out of the refrigerator. Kate put the bowls on the table and stood there, staring at them.

"Kate, sit honey. Let's have breakfast," Reagan said, pushing a chair out for her with her foot.

Kate sat, still saying nothing, and noticed the boxes of cereal in the center of the table. Fruit Loops and Lucky Charms. Kate felt her throat tighten.

Grady had his face back in the paper. They all did. It was like she had stepped onto the set of some sitcom.

"Ben, did you read that article about the new exhibit at the Getty? We should take Reagan and Kate next week," Grady said.

"I did see that. Looks great. I'll look online for tickets," Ben replied, folded his paper, and set it aside. "Kate, can you hand me the Lucky Charms?" Ben asked, as Reagan also folded her paper.

Kate tried to make eye contact, but Reagan was pouring herself a bowl of Lucky Charms. *Since when did she eat Lucky Charms?*

When she was done she handed the box to Grady, who did the same thing—folded his paper and poured a bowl of Lucky Charms. Kate couldn't take it anymore.

"Okay, what's going on? What is this?" She looked at Reagan. "You don't eat Lucky Charms."

"I do now, honey. Must be the baby. Are you going to eat?"

Kate looked at Grady, who was across from her eating Lucky Charms. "Grady, what's going on? Why are you—"

Grady picked up the box of Fruit Loops and handed it to her. The look on his face was so comfortable. Kate bit her bottom lip to keep from crying, to keep from babbling that she was so sorry, but she was so proud of him too. That she understood, but she missed him. She wanted to tell him that she just bought this great new mirror and hung it in the entryway to her apartment. She wanted to say so many things, but nothing came out.

"Pour some cereal, Kate," he said, smiling at her as if they had just woken up together and were sitting around the kitchen table. As if it were just the most natural thing in the world.

Kate looked at Reagan, who looked like she was about to cry, and Ben, who had his face buried in his cereal.

Kate opened the flap of the Fruit Loops and poured some into her bowl. Something hit the bowl with a thud, and when Kate looked down, there among the rainbow rings was a red and gold box sitting in her cereal bowl. A red and gold ring box. She touched the box, and by the time she looked up, Grady was on his knee next to her, Reagan was crying, and Ben was trying to calm Reagan down.

Kate was now certain this was a dream. It played like one. People she recognized from her life, but all mixed up and in different places. Most of her dreams were that way. In what real world was Grady Malendar kneeling on a kitchen floor in his pajama bottoms?

He reached into her cereal bowl, took out the box, and opened it.

Kate was pretty sure that's when she stopped breathing. The ring looked antique. A thin band with tiny diamonds and a large square diamond in the center that looked like a royal pin cushion.

"Katherine Galloway."

Kate looked at him and he took her hand.

"I need you in my life, real and completely unreal. I'm sorry that I blamed you. I didn't know how to have a real life, didn't know I was allowed, until I met you. You're my protector and I want to be yours. We sort of rescue each other."

Kate started to cry as Grady continued.

"I love you so much and I want to spend the rest of my life eating Fruit Loops with you and doing laundry on Friday nights."

Kate laughed through her tears and mouthed that she loved him too.

"Please, forgive me for being stupid and marry me."

Kate nodded her head, and when she could finally take a breath, she said, "Yes!"

Grady slipped the ring on her finger, stood up, and pulled Kate into his arms. Kate turned to see if Reagan and Ben were still there, but they had gone. Grady put a finger under her chin and turned her to face him. He wiped some of the tears from her cheeks.

"No one is watching us, Kate. Just you and me."

She started to cry again, and just before it seemed like he might too, he said, "That's Nana's ring. She would have loved you."

"Because I'm such a straight shooter?" Kate asked through watery eyes.

"Eh, you're a bit of a fox in the hen house, but she would have loved that too."

Kate rolled her eyes and laughed. "Honestly, how many of these phrases did she have?"

Grady looked into her eyes and she saw everything she would ever need, as he said, "You will have a lifetime to find out."

Neither of them was the most likely candidate for love. But standing in her friend's kitchen, with Fruit Loops, wearing his Nana's ring, and kissing the man she loved, Kate knew Grady was her person. He made her feel. They had opened the window, pulled each other into the light, and it didn't get any better than that.

Thank you for reading *Candidate – A Love Story*! I hope you enjoyed Grady and Kate's story as much as I enjoyed writing it. If you liked the book, please consider leaving a review at the book retailer of your choice, as well as Goodreads, to help other readers find this story.

Please make sure you're on my newsletter mailing list at: tracy-ewens.com to keep up with the latest news about my books.

Thank you, wonderful readers, for making this amazing journey possible. I appreciate each and every one of you! Keep reading for a look at *Taste – A Love Story*, which is Kara and Logan's story.

All the best,
Tracy

Chapter One

Kara Malendar was a bitch. She hadn't planned on being one and hadn't always been one, but as she stopped during her mid-Saturday morning run, it was clear she must be the very worst kind of person. Catching her breath and taking a sip from the little water bottle fastened around her waist, Kara fixed her eyes across the street at Marco Polo. Men in blue jumpsuits were emptying the local Italian restaurant. Boxes, tables, and chairs were being loaded onto a large moving van with a cartoon kangaroo painted on the side. Tony and Pam Forte, the owners, were a husband-and-wife team. He was the business part and she was the chef. Pam was classically trained, or so Kara had read in the *About Us* portion of their website. She had always hated the term "classically trained" because it was assumed that was synonymous with great chef. Trained and great were two very different things in Kara's book.

She pulled her UCLA cap down low and sat on the bench just up the road from where the Fortes were saying good-bye to their dream. They'd been open a little over two years. Seventy percent of all restaurants collapsed after a year, so they were luckier than most. And who really knew why they finally decided to call it quits? There could have been several reasons Kara was not privy to, but as she took an even larger sip of water, she felt certain it was the scathing review she'd submitted six months ago to her employer, the *Los Angeles Times*. That had probably finished them off for good. "The last nail in the coffin," as her Nana would have said. Granted, Pam's linguini was overcooked and the wine pairing their sommelier had suggested was awful, but the atmosphere was wonderful, with old exposed brick and fantastic Venice-like lighting. Their bruschetta was on point. It wasn't clumsy or overblown. Very few restaurants could pull off bruschetta. Kara had been to Marco Polo a couple of times, but the night she went for her review, things were clearly not working in the kitchen and the critic in her pounced. She could have remembered their bruschetta and come back another day, but she hadn't. She'd listened to the nasty beastie that whispered in her ear. *The best survive*, it growled. *You're doing the California dining population a service. It's your job. No mercy*, the beastie had insisted. Her review was front page of the Food Section with the headline, "One Word Every Italian Chef Should Know—Al Dente."

Six months later, as Kara stood across the street sweating, her stomach knotted with something she didn't often let in: sympathy. She felt bad. They were human beings after all—the sleeves-rolled-up, worried-about-paying-their-bills type. She could have walked away, given them a break, but she didn't and that made her a bitch. Her reviews had power. That was something she'd loved, wielded even, over the years, but lately she wondered if instead of powerful she'd simply become detached.

As she watched the still-new-looking Viking range top being carried into the moving van, Kara tried to remember the last time she had even enjoyed a meal. Was it at a restaurant? Which one? It couldn't have been at home because she barely cooked anymore. The next question that popped into her mind could have been easily dismissed, but the knot in her stomach tightened, telling her she was onto something: did she even like food anymore? Sure, she knew all the check boxes: what made a perfect cassoulet or which microbrew went best with Wiener schnitzel, but that was just semantics. She used to love food:

the sizzling pop of cooking, the blending flavors, the dance of a meal. Kara used to feel passionate about a lot of things, but now, as she slowly let out a breath, she realized she felt very little at all these days.

Oh, boo hoo, she thought, quoting her father as she stood and prepared to finish the last leg of her five-mile run.

"Boo hoo, you'll survive," was one of Senator Patrick Malendar's favorite pieces of parenting advice for her and her brother, Grady, whenever either of them complained. Turned out he was right—she and her brother had survived.

Kara took one more look at Marco Polo, shook herself back to indifferent, and put her headphones on. In the time it would take to finish her run, she would have forgotten all about the sad, failed Fortes. *They should have done better, worked harder*, she told herself as sweat soaked the brim of her cap. Kara started up the hill that would twist two more times before delivering her home. She wondered, not for the first time in the past few months, if who she'd become was who she was meant to be.

Logan Rye wasn't superstitious, but he did believe in good and bad energy or karma. People got back what they put out. For that reason, he was a little reluctant when Tony Forte called to tell him Marco Polo was going under and he would give Logan a great deal on anything he wanted. It felt like benefitting from someone else's misfortune, but Logan went anyway. He'd given the Fortes a more-than-fair price for the food processor and a few copper core pans. Logan was a sucker for copper. He hugged Pam, wished them both the very best, and left through the side door leading into the alley.

Apparently the universe didn't care about his more-than-fair price or his best wishes, because right before he stepped out of the alley, karma punched him in the face. Kara Malendar was sitting on a bench across the street, right in front of his truck.

Shit! He should have just wished Tony good luck over the phone and stayed home, but no, here he was taking a couple of steps back into an alley and hoping the only woman to have put his heart through a meat grinder hadn't seen him. Not that she would run over and throw her arms around him even if she did happen to notice him. Yeah, that fantasy died a long time ago.

She still had legs for miles and he was sure those same hazel eyes that used to crawl right into his soul were tucked somewhere beneath the cap she was clearly hiding under. Logan knew he would bump into Kara Malendar eventually. After all, he was a newbie restaurant owner; didn't her kind prey on his? No one wanted an enemy at the *LA Times*. He'd have to find his way to cordial, but that wasn't going to happen today. He wasn't in the mood and definitely wasn't ready.

He did allow himself one more look. She was too thin, too pensive, and even from a distance, a little sad. That part he hadn't expected. In the few short months they had spent together his senior year of college, she had never seemed sad—the opposite actually. Kara Malendar, or Winnie Parker as she'd been known to everyone in their cultural food exchange program, was a little shy at first, but then she simply exploded with color.

At the memory, Logan suddenly became aware of his heart in his chest. Her hair was pulled back now, but he remembered Paris and the gold streaks of curly blonde hair. Winnie wore bright peasant tops and no makeup. She was spectacular. He couldn't keep his eyes off her back then, and eventually they couldn't keep their hands off each other. Logan looked out from the alley as Kara stood and turned to leave. How could all of that breath-stealing, uninhibited sunshine turn into Kara Malendar, cynical food critic? It seemed a shame, but it wasn't like she cared what he thought anyway. Whatever game she had been playing in Paris was over a long time ago. He would admit it took him a while to forget the depths of her eyes and the silky curve of her body, but he had. Most women in his experience were game players, and Kara Malendar had proven herself a master.

Once he was sure she was gone, Logan crossed the street, loaded the box in the back of his truck, and by the time he arrived at his new restaurant his heart had settled down.

Entering his kitchen through the back door, he found Travis finishing up the pizza dough and mushrooms for the lunch crowd that would hopefully arrive in about four hours.

"Whatcha got there?" Travis asked as he floured, balled, and placed his morning's work in the dough boxes lined with parchment.

"Fire sale at Marco Polo." Logan put the box down in his office, which acted more like a storage room than anything else.

"Aw, man! Really?"

"Afraid so." Logan stepped over to the utility sink to wash his hands.

"Their bruschetta was the best. Shit, I had my last decent date there. Another one bites the dust. Make you nervous?"

"I'm not sure nervous is the right word." Logan dried his hands. "Gets me up earlier, puts me to bed later. I mean that's all we can do right?"

"And cook kick-ass food."

Logan laughed. "That too."

"So what do you think it was? I mean, I like to analyze this stuff. Figure out what they did wrong, so I can make myself feel better." Travis stacked the finished dough boxes.

"I don't know." Logan shook his head. "Who knows why anyone succeeds or fails? I mean shit, Applebee's is still in business. Nothing makes sense." He put pieces of the food processor into one of the dishwasher bins.

"True, but if you needed to make your favorite sous chef feel better . . ." Travis gave him a pleading look. "Help a man rest easy."

Logan shrugged because there was nothing he could say that would ease the constant uncertainty of the restaurant business.

"Oh come on, we both know you've thought about it." Travis turned, leaning on the counter now.

Logan sighed. "They never found their groove, I guess." As soon as the words came out of his mouth, he felt like he was jinxing himself, speaking ill of the unlucky. Because it was luck, wasn't it? He considered Marco Polo's demise as he broke down the box he'd brought in and the three others up against the wall from last night's wine delivery. No, he didn't believe in luck. Hard work—

that's what he was raised on and he had to believe it's what separated his from the hundreds of other restaurants trying to succeed. Hard work, good energy, and great people who knew more than he did—those were the keys.

Travis was still looking to him for comfort.

Logan let out a steady breath. "Their parking lot was too small and the valet company they used kept screwing up. They lost customers because it was a bitch to even get in there. Their bartenders were inconsistent, and they had almost fifty percent turnover with their wait staff. I don't think their clientele ever felt like they knew the place."

Travis smiled, so Logan finished strong.

"And Pam's sauce was too sweet, too many carrots."

"There he is! I knew you had a list, my fearless leader. I feel better already." Travis wiped his brow with his forearm.

Logan smiled, walked into his office, and returned with two pages torn from a yellow pad.

"That being said, here's my punch list for this place."

He handed the pages to Travis and watched his ego deflate.

"The top ten are ongoing overall issues. Makenna is taking the lead on most of those, but I need you to deal with the last one. The left walk-in is a mess. I'm not sure what system you've got going on in there, but it needs to be redone."

Travis glanced toward the huge refrigerator taking up most of the wall behind them and nodded.

"The other fourteen items at the bottom are things I observed last night. When we all meet later, I'll go over those, but I wanted to give you a heads up. Most glaring, the eggplant on our bruschetta was overcooked, and I'm not sure what's going on with the grater, but the shreds of white cheddar on the spinach salad are too big. It's overpowering. We need to figure that out and tone it down by lunch today."

Travis read the list with wide eyes that traveled to Logan and then back to the list. He didn't say a word and Logan laughed at the look on his face.

"Okay, so back to work." He patted Travis on the back. "We don't want to be next." Logan left to turn the floor lights on. He'd cut some new flowers for the giant vase standing among the round tables. It was a tall copper pot really, and they tried to change out the flowers every few days. The last ones were all wrong, so Logan replaced them and noted which windows needed to be recleaned once Summer, their hostess, arrived in a few hours. He heard bins being dragged around and the opening and closing of cabinets back in the kitchen, along with Travis cursing. That was always a good sign that work was getting done.

Acknowledgements

I would like to thank:

Barb Froman and Barb Vitelli for reading, sharing, and supporting my work.

Katie McCoach for reining in my manic points of view and for being a joyful positive force.

Phyllis Stern for helping me with my "drinking problem" and making sure we had a campaign and not champagne.

My family for putting up with my closed door, imaginary friends, and often absent mind.

Tracy Ewens is a recovered theatre major who writes smart contemporary romance from a beautiful piece of Arizona desert. When not working on her next book, she drinks copious amounts of tea, prefers an exit row seat, and reads well past her bedtime.

www.tracyewens.com